Michele Giuttari was born in 1950 in the province of Messina. He was head of the Florence Police Force from 1995 to 2003, where he was responsible for reopening the Monster of Florence case and jailing several key Mafia figures. He is now a special adviser to the interior minister in Rome, with a remit to monitor Mafia activity.

THE
DARK HEART
OF
FLORENCE

MICHELE GIUTTARI

Translated by Howard Curtis
and Isabelle Kaufeler

ABACUS

First published in Italy in 2012 by Biblioteca Universale Rizzoli
First published in Great Britain in 2013 by Little, Brown
This paperback edition published in 2014 by Abacus
Reprinted 2014 (twice)

A CIP catalogue record for this book
is available from the British Library.

ISBN 978-0-349-13933-3

Typeset in Horley by M Rules
Printed and bound in Great Britain by
Clays Ltd, St Ives plc

Papers used by Abacus are from well-managed forests
and other responsible sources.

MIX
Paper from
responsible sources
FSC
www.fsc.org FSC® C104740

Abacus
An imprint of
Little, Brown Book Group
100 Victoria Embankment
London EC4Y 0DY

An Hachette UK Company
www.hachette.co.uk

www.littlebrown.co.uk

To Christa

The measure of love is to love without measure.

Saint Augustine

PROLOGUE

The Last Hours

July 2004

These days even the bed annoyed her.

It seemed narrower and narrower. And she hated the mattress: misshapen, worn flat, covered in stains. It was filthy. She couldn't stand it any more. Just as she couldn't stand the food. She hated that, too. It was so awful, and it often made her feel sick.

She hated everything.

She lay on her back, wearing nothing but white knickers, her hands down by her sides, her eyes closed. Every now and then she would open them and glance distractedly at the small TV screen on the wall, her mind filled with fantasies about the coming hours.

Not much longer, she kept telling herself, and then she'd never have to see this shithole ever again.

Suddenly a voice from the TV caught her attention and her big dark eyes focused on the face of a blonde presenter, a face that had probably undergone countless rounds of plastic surgery.

Shit, were they going over all that again?

The programme was reconstructing the crime that had

brought her to this damned prison fourteen years earlier, when she was only sixteen. A teenager full of life and dreams, like any other girl her age. She was a grown woman now, and she was going to make up for lost time.

Why didn't they mind their own fucking business? Why didn't they talk about the deaths in Iraq? The torture of civilians? World hunger? Dying children? Rape and violence against women? No, they had nothing better to do than rehash these old stories.

She watched the programme through to the end, and the final question they asked sent a wave of anger through her: 'Can we really be sure that she's no longer dangerous?'

Furiously, she pressed the OFF button on the remote. If she could have, she'd have thrown the TV set out of the window. She closed her eyes, covered her face with her hands and took a series of deep breaths. Then she got up and put on the usual bright red cotton overalls. She brushed her jet-black hair and tied it in a ponytail.

'It's time for your phone call,' the guard said, stopping outside the door and looking in at her through the spyhole. 'Are you ready?'

'Yes.'

'Come on, then.' The guard put the key in the lock and turned it several times, then motioned to her to follow her along the corridor. As they walked, they were hit by a strong whiff of garlic: someone must be cooking. It was always the same in this wing, at any hour of the day.

'So, my girl, off tomorrow, are you?' came a woman's voice she recognised, shouting raucously. 'What are you going to do next?'

The woman sounded as if she'd only just woken up: the same woman who usually stuck her nose into other people's business, who hadn't taken kindly to the news that, thanks to advantages not available to the other inmates, *she* was being released.

'Bet you're counting the hours, eh?' the woman continued.

'Mind your own fucking business,' she replied, irritably, and walked faster, though not fast enough to avoid hearing the last few words: 'You're going to have it hard outside, sweetheart, take it from someone who knows life better than you do.'

She spun round and stared at the woman; the face, trapped behind the iron bars, seemed deformed. 'Fuck off, you bitter old witch – don't you dare pass judgement on me and smile with the few rotten teeth you have left!'

'That's enough!' the guard yelled, grabbing her by the arm and pulling her away. 'Let's get a move on! As for you,' she added, turning back to the woman in the cell, 'just shut it. You're always poking your nose in where it's not wanted.'

The corridor fell silent except for the echo of their footsteps.

They finally reached the telephone attached to the wall. She dialled the number while the guard moved about six feet away, although still keeping her in view. She knew the number off by heart. She had been given it during their last session the previous week.

The phone was answered on the first ring. 'It's me,' she said, and felt an immediate sense of wellbeing. The anger had suddenly disappeared. She looked up at the ceiling. The paintwork, peeling in places, reminded her of the old villa where she had spent her childhood. A whole lot of images and sounds flashed through her mind, things she had never forgotten: the city's chaotic traffic, the deafening noise of the discos, the excited voices of young people in the squares.

'I've been waiting for your phone call, darling,' the voice at the other end said.

'I'll be out of here tomorrow. You hadn't forgotten, had you?'

'Of course not! Call me as soon as you get out.'

'OK. I can't wait to see you. Until tomorrow, then. Love you.'

'Me too.'

She hung up and walked back to her cell, barely aware of the guard, who never took her eyes off her for a moment. Her heart was beating ever faster with the thrill of freedom. She could almost smell it. She had dreamed of it and wanted it for so long, it no longer scared her. In the morning a new life would be waiting for her. In the morning she would leave the past behind, a past she wanted to erase completely, to bury.

And then you can all fuck off! she said in her mind to the short, plump guard, to that inmate who couldn't mind her own bloody business, to the others who had either shunned her or tormented her, to the smell of garlic in her nostrils, and to the boredom, which only someone who had been in prison could understand.

Tomorrow, tomorrow I'll be a free woman!

PART ONE

A LONG NIGHT

1

Dead silence.

A man dressed completely in black was sitting behind the big, solid desk.

In the last few hours, he had gone over and over his carefully worked-out plan until it was burnt into his mind. He couldn't afford to make a mistake. The fateful moment was drawing near. Only a few minutes now, at most a few hours. He didn't want to leave anything to chance, which was why he was weighing up all the things that could possibly go wrong.

All at once he took his hands away from his temples and rubbed his eyes. Maybe it was the light from the candelabra bothering him. He took a deep breath.

Abruptly, he turned his armchair towards the wall behind him and looked at the brocade curtains covering the windows, on which the light in the room seemed to throw unsettling shadows, then at the big oil painting hanging just behind the desk.

It was a portrait of a man with a thick grey beard, wearing a severe uniform and a long dark cloak over his shoulders. It had struck him immediately as soon as he had entered the room: the man seemed to be staring at the spectator, the eyes so piercing that they seemed alive. The longer he looked at the painting, the more the hate boiled up in him. He wanted to tear the man's heart from his chest, erase all trace of him from the face of the earth for ever.

After a moment or two, he looked again at the curtains then turned and folded his hands on the desk.

Just then, the silence was broken by the creaking of the front door, a sound that was like heavenly music to his ears. He turned to the half-closed door of the room and listened. Now he could hear footsteps in the corridor. Someone was coming closer. He quickly glanced at his watch: the fluorescent hands showed 11.47.

He was really close now.

How he despised him!

After a few moments the door opened and an old man, impeccably dressed in a dark blue lightweight suit with a carefully knotted matching tie and shiny black shoes, appeared in the doorway. He was extremely thin, with a pale face and a slim moustache. When he saw the stranger, he froze, and a shudder went through him.

How could it be? he wondered. How could it possibly be *him*? But those hard, ice-cold eyes were unmistakable.

Calmly, the man in black raised his right arm. The old man saw the barrel of the gun pointing straight at him, and understood.

At last! the man in black said to himself.

The hour had come: his journey was about to begin. His adventure. The real thing, just as he had imagined it.

The first piece of the jigsaw.

It was the night of Saturday 28 August 2004. A night that would be long remembered. The Florence police would come to call it a night of horror, the start of a new nightmare.

A sudden cry rang out.

Just one.

'Go to hell!' the man in black whispered.

His finger squeezed the trigger.

2

That was just the beginning.

The man in black was outside now, beneath a starry sky, lit by a weak crescent moon. Around him, quiet and calm. All he could hear were the sounds of the night, the hum of insects, that buzz that disappeared during the day. The hill was deserted. There was nobody and nothing in sight, not even the headlights of a car.

It was so peaceful here.

He knew the place very well. Here and there he could see a few weak lights outside sleeping villas and cottages. Cautiously, keeping a safe distance, he passed a few of them, breathing in the scent of wild herbs. At the end of a narrow path he came to a security fence. It was about eight feet high, but there was no barbed wire at the top. He stretched his arms up as high as they would go and grasped the netting, at the same time bracing his feet against one of the posts. He put his left arm over, then the right, then one foot after the other, and in the blink of an eye he was on the other side. He landed on a lawn.

Then, camouflaged by the darkness, he walked along the edge of the road. For a while he was accompanied by the song of an owl. From time to time he paused amid the undergrowth to catch his breath. He calculated that the first glimmer of dawn would soon appear on the horizon; the outlines of the hills would become ever sharper, the countryside ever greener.

Coming to a small clearing among the trees, he stopped for longer.

He had planned this, too.

He took off the black tracksuit, from which he had removed the label. It was splattered with fresh blood in several places. From his backpack, he took a change of clothes and shoes and put them on. He dug a hole in the ground with a small stick and hid the clothes he had been wearing, and then, in a separate hole a short distance away, the shoes and the gun. He was not the least bit concerned that the police might find them, assuming they were capable of doing so. He took another gun from his backpack, a Beretta 7.65 semi-automatic, which, like the first gun, had had its serial number filed off, and tucked it into the back of his jeans. Then he tied his long fair hair into a ponytail and set off again. The only sound was the noise of his steps on the little cobbled road.

His one aim was to get away from here as quickly as possible. That was all that mattered. He was sure he had left no clues behind: no prints, no traces of DNA. Nothing at all. The police would be driven crazy. Their investigations would lead them nowhere, he was sure of that. The most dangerous part was behind him.

And as he continued walking at a steady pace, he had to hold back a laugh. He had really enjoyed himself, more than he had done for a long time.

He had watched the bastard die!

He went over the whole sequence of events in his mind, from the beginning, as if it were a horror film. Down to the smallest detail, the slightest gesture. It hadn't been a fleeting, elusive dream. It hadn't been the death scene he'd imagined every time he'd closed his eyes to sleep over the last few days. No, this time, it had all been real. No longer a fantasy, but pure reality, the realisation of his evil dreams.

One of many.

He would remember tonight as one of the most beautiful of his life. He was as sure of this as he was that nobody would stand in the way of his plans.

The man had collapsed at his feet, arms dangling like a puppet's, imploring him with his eyes, moving his lips once or twice, but to no avail. He knew why, he knew what had been going through the man's mind. Then the final touch: the blood spurting from his head like water from a fountain.

He had been patient, and he had been rewarded for his patience.

He suddenly heard a noise and turned. It was only a night bird. He watched it as it disappeared into the woods.

He felt free. Incredibly free.

3

7.35 a.m. Chief Superintendent Michele Ferrara's roof terrace

Ferrara was enjoying the slight coolness of the morning. It wouldn't last long: in a few hours the summer heat would descend on Florence, as it had in the past few days. Even though summer was coming to an end, this infernal heat seemed to be holding on for as long as possible. And today, as every day, time would move as slowly as the people in the streets.

He had been back in Florence for a couple of weeks. While he was away, he had really missed this view – from the Ponte Vecchio to San Miniato al Monte and beyond, as far as the wonderful hills – which he enjoyed from the roof terrace of his apartment on the Lungarno degli Acciaioli. He had bought the apartment ten years earlier, when the property market in the city, as in the rest of the country, was in crisis, and the prices were affordable. Both he and his wife Petra considered this one of the most beautiful spots in the historic centre.

The city would soon come to life. In Florence, Sunday was a day like any other. You could already see the first street vendors pushing their stalls towards the nearby Uffizi Gallery, where in just a few hours' time the usual queue, made up of visitors from every corner of the earth, would form, drawn by the museum's outstanding collection of Tuscan and European art.

The street artists and performers would also be showing up soon: painters, portrait artists, mimes. The bars had already started to serve their first coffees and the few shops that opened on Sundays would shortly be ready to welcome tourists, mostly Japanese and American, devoted customers of those fashion brands that could boast the prestige of a branch in Florence.

Ferrara glanced at the hills, where the morning mist was evaporating in the sunshine.

As he waited for the usual hearty breakfast that Petra was lovingly preparing in the kitchen, he opened the newspaper. The front page headline announced twenty-one deaths on the Italian roads the previous day. Another bloody Saturday: all too common at this time of year, he thought, shaking his head. The most serious accident had occurred on the autostrada between Salerno and Reggio Calabria, the notorious A3 with its endless roadworks. A family of four, husband, wife and two teenage children, had burned to death after a terrible collision with a speeding four-by-four. There had also been tailbacks and long delays on the roads to the major northern cities and around the border areas.

So staying at home at this time of year wasn't such a bad idea after all, he thought.

'My parents send their love,' Petra said with a smile, putting the tray down on the Caltagirone tiled table.

'Did they ring again?' he said, his voice tinged with gentle sarcasm, as he folded the newspaper. His parents-in-law had phoned the night before and talked to him for nearly half an hour, as well as to Petra.

'*Ja, die Mutti rief an,*' Petra replied: the odd sentence in her native German slipped out from time to time in spite of the many years she had spent in Italy.

'Your mother again? Has something happened?'

'No, Michele. She wanted to know how you'd slept. That's all.'

'That's nice of her.'

Ferrara had just returned from a period of convalescence after receiving a bullet wound to his left shoulder during a shootout in Germany, which was why his parents-in-law, who saw him as a son, were so worried about him.

They started eating. On the table were slices of locally produced cured ham, fresh cheese, butter, blackcurrant jam, and sliced Tuscan bread, one of those baguette-style loaves, in their opinion the best thing their local baker sold, the only kind that kept its flavour right through to the evening.

Just five minutes later, as Ferrara was buttering a slice of bread, the telephone rang.

It was the inspector from the Operations Room at Headquarters, calling to tell him that a body had been found.

It looked like a homicide.

'I have to go,' he told his wife once he had hung up.

Same as usual, Petra thought, nothing ever changed. She looked at her husband anxiously. These days, she didn't make any attempt to conceal how worried his work made her, especially since he had been wounded in a shootout with Leonardo Berghoff, the crazed killer who had terrorised Florence earlier in the summer.

Ferrara had already gone back inside, carrying in his nostrils the scent of the rambling roses and jasmine that Petra grew in the greenhouse which occupied a small area of the terrace. It was her favourite hobby and kept her busy for a good part of each day.

He got dressed, gave his wife a goodbye kiss on the lips, and went out. He never left home in the morning without that loving gesture.

Never a moment's peace, he thought to himself as he hurried down the stairs.

4

'Well?' Ferrara asked. 'Did he say anything else? The victim's name?'

They were crossing the city, the blue light rotating slowly on the car roof. The driver, Giancarlo Perrotta, had just summarised what he had learnt from the Operations Room.

A man had phoned 113 to report, his voice shaking with emotion, that he had just found his employer dead.

'No, he didn't say anything else. He hung up straight after giving the address and directions how to get there.'

The driver spoke with a noticeable Neapolitan accent. He had joined the force a couple of years ago and had only recently been transferred to the *Squadra Mobile* here in Florence, one of the most sought-after postings for young police officers eager to experience the glamour of detective work.

They drove along the Via San Domenico towards Fiesole and its surrounding hills. Having left the built-up area they drove in silence for a few miles. Then the radio began to crackle.

'Car One calling Central,' they heard.

'Come in, Car One!'

It was the team that patrolled south of the city. They had been the first on the scene.

An officer communicated the victim's particulars, gathered from his identity card.

As soon as Ferrara heard the name, he swore and instinctively grabbed the microphone to tell the team to make sure they didn't specify their location in case anyone was listening in. It was now common knowledge that journalists, criminals and even curious members of the public tuned into the frequencies used by the State Police and the Carabinieri.

Then he put the microphone back and started thinking, eyes fixed on the strip of asphalt stretching ahead of him. Apart from the sound of the air-conditioning, which wasn't working very well, it was quiet in the car.

Coming to the turning they had been told to take, the driver steered left off the main road onto a narrow but paved private road. They drove along it for about half a mile until they came to a heavy iron gate. For a moment, Ferrara's gaze lingered on the rectangular slab of Tuscan sandstone on which the owner's name was carved in capital letters. They drove through and found themselves on a tree-lined avenue surrounded by flowerbeds and manicured lawns. At the end of it, they could see a large, austere classical villa, like some Medici residence from the Renaissance. The driver stopped the grey Alfa Romeo 156 in the space set aside for parking. The crunch of gravel could be heard beneath the tyres.

There were already a few police cars there, some white and blue, some unmarked, together with an ambulance. Next to the ambulance, two paramedics stood talking. They both looked nauseous and were inhaling great lungfuls of smoke from their cigarettes. There was a stretcher on the ground by the back door, but it was too late for them to do anything. They were only waiting for someone to give them the green light to leave.

At least there weren't any journalists, Ferrara thought.

'Good morning, Chief Superintendent!'

A uniformed police officer had seen Ferrara arrive and had rushed up to greet him, pausing first to grab his regulation cap from the dashboard of one of the cars and put it on. He had a boyish face, which was perhaps why he had grown the beginnings of a beard. He must have been twenty-one or twenty-two at the most.

A short distance from him stood his female colleague. She too was quite young. She wore her long blonde hair in a plait and her face was as white as a sheet. Ferrara thought about the feelings the young policewoman must be experiencing. Fear? Anxiety? Horror? Something she had probably never thought about before, at least not seriously. When she saw Ferrara she tried to pull herself together, quickly checking her uniform to make sure it was neat and tidy, and assuming an alert stance. She didn't want Ferrara to think she was just a woman who got scared easily: you needed strength and determination to work in the presence of death.

As he returned his greeting, Ferrara realised the young male officer was looking just as nauseous as the two paramedics and the young policewoman. Maybe they're just tired, he thought as he walked towards the solid wooden door, his footsteps crunching on the gravel.

At that moment, Teresa Micalizi, the senior officer on duty, appeared in the doorway. She was wearing a cotton jacket over a crumpled T-shirt, a worn pair of jeans and a pair of plimsolls. Her face, too, bore unmistakable signs of disgust. After a moment's hesitation, Teresa approached the young policewoman, who was holding a tissue pressed to her mouth, and tried to reassure her, glancing from time to time at Ferrara, then at Superintendent Rizzo, the deputy head of the *Squadra Mobile*, who had come out of the villa just after her and was now conferring with Ferrara in a corner of the parking area. Teresa wondered why Ferrara had not gone straight in to look at the crime scene.

There was, in fact, a good reason.

'All right, Francesco, give me your first impressions.'

Ferrara knew his deputy well: down to earth, a man of few

words, in many people's opinion the perfect embodiment of what a detective should be. He was of average height and solid build, but over the past few months he seemed to have aged rapidly. His greying hair bore testimony to that. He had been working at Ferrara's side for several years now and their understanding was so great that they each knew what the other was thinking with a mere exchange of glances.

That was why Ferrara had decided to trust in his colleague's intuition rather than immediately ascertain the facts, which he would learn soon enough anyway. To him, intuition – the first impression – was the most reliable interpretation of what was observed at a crime scene, and he had almost always found that indulging that intuition had set him on the right path.

'Definitely the work of a professional, I'd say, chief. It has all the characteristics. We could be looking at a revenge killing.'

Ferrara nodded.

'He may well have got rid of anything that could connect him to the murder,' Rizzo went on. 'We'll have to check every dustbin in the area.'

'Let's get every available man on it,' Ferrara said. 'And we'll need to go over the lawns carefully with a metal detector. I think we should also interview the staff at the restaurant near here and the residents of the neighbouring villas – in fact, any potential witnesses we can track down.'

It was highly likely that, before committing his crime, the killer would have reconnoitred the area, presumably at the same time of day that he intended to strike. It must indeed have been a professional, with such careful planning, but they could not rule out the possibility that someone might have noticed him.

'I'll get right on it, chief. We'll speak to the owner and staff of the restaurant as soon as it opens, and the neighbours as soon as we can.'

They both knew that most of the residents in the area were doctors, lawyers, engineers and well-known businessmen. In other words, the upper–middle class and nouveaux riches who had abandoned the centre of Florence, where they no longer felt safe, and taken refuge in the hills around Fiesole, protected by high walls and hedges, convinced they could live a more peaceful life there. They were bound to feel a lot more vulnerable now.

'Have the pathologist and the deputy prosecutor arrived yet?' Ferrara asked Rizzo.

'Only the pathologist. He's already checked the temperature of the corpse and how far rigor mortis has progressed. He's just finishing the external examination now. The victim was shot in the forehead, that's one thing we can be sure of. It looks like a genuine execution.'

'Which deputy prosecutor is on call?'

'Luigi Vinci, theoretically. I spoke to him on the phone and he said to go ahead with the crime scene investigations and he'll join us later. He's at his holiday home by the sea, at Follonica.'

So, Ferrara thought, Vinci was 'on call' more than a hundred miles away!

'Any witnesses?'

'Not at the moment.'

Ferrara took a few steps forward, then turned and gave Rizzo a long look. Rizzo nodded. 'Francesco,' Ferrara said, 'we need to handle this very carefully. We don't want to get into any trouble over this. Leave the official stuff to me. When I'm back at Headquarters, I'll contact the Commissioner and the Prosecutor's Department and deal with the media ... the usual crap. I want you to stay here and coordinate the investigation.'

'Of course, chief. I'll call you if anything turns up.'

They moved back to the villa and Ferrara, glancing up and to his right, noticed a surveillance camera trained directly on the front door. He had not spotted it when he arrived. They might be in luck after all!

'Have you checked that?' he asked Rizzo, indicating the camera.

'Yes, chief. It was the first thing I did. Unfortunately, it wasn't working, so there's no footage.'

Ferrara put on the plastic overshoes and latex gloves that the driver had brought him in the meantime. There was always at least one box of them in every car from the Headquarters pool. He ordered Teresa Micalizi to take some officers and start a search of the garden, the secondary crime scene, and at last walked up the two sandstone steps and crossed the threshold after Rizzo, who was a few steps ahead of him.

He was prepared for the worst.

5

There was nothing unusual just inside the front door, nor at the beginning of the corridor. The floor, covered in terracotta tiles arranged in a herringbone pattern, was spotless, as were the white walls. The pictures hung straight. The only thing out of place was the telephone handset lying on a nineteenth-century side table. All was calm. Even the pendulum of the old wall clock seemed to move in total silence.

They came to the doorway of a large room. The door was wide open and Rizzo stopped for a moment. 'Everything's in order in here, chief,' he said.

Ferrara glanced in and saw an enormous sandstone fireplace and two separate living areas with various items of genuine antique furniture. The cushions were perfectly arranged, as were the rugs. The valuable paintings on the walls were untouched. Everything gave the impression of good taste and evident wealth.

'Let's carry on, Francesco.'

They continued down the corridor, and as they walked red marks on the floor seemed to announce the slaughter. The bottom of a section of wall was spattered with blood. Carefully avoiding it, they entered the nearest room: a spacious study with a high coffered ceiling, two of its walls lined with well-filled bookshelves. There were further bloodstains on the floor near the door.

'Where's the body?' Ferrara asked.

'In the bathroom.'

'Let's go, then.'

Ferrara noticed more drops of dark blood on the floor along the way. And other marks of the same colour clearly left by something being dragged. In front of the bathroom door lay several items of men's clothing: a jacket, a pair of trousers, and a shirt that had once been white.

They had arrived.

The Carrara marble floor reflected the glow of the numerous spotlights shining down from the ceiling. In the middle of the room was a Jacuzzi. The taps were dripping and the slow patter made the atmosphere even grimmer. Two men stood by the Jacuzzi: Francesco Leone, the pathologist, and a technician from Forensics. They were both wearing overshoes and sterile gloves, and the technician had a single-use cap on his head. He was writing down everything Leone told him in a notebook.

'Typical burn marks are visible round the entrance wound . . .'

On seeing Ferrara, Leone broke off. 'Good morning, Chief Superintendent,' he greeted him, emphasising the word 'good'.

Ferrara returned the greeting formally. Although they had worked together on many cases and established a good understanding, he preferred to keep things businesslike when they were on the job.

Leone, who was of stocky build and completely bald, with an egg-shaped head, was wearing rumpled trousers and had his shirtsleeves rolled up. His forearms were completely hairless. He gave the impression that he had only just got out of bed and come running straight to the crime scene. He wiped the sweat from his gleaming forehead with a tissue.

At first glance, he might have seemed a man of little account. But when he was at work, he exuded power. He admired only a few detectives, Ferrara being one. He couldn't stand the vast majority of them, with their endless requests: they wanted first one thing then another, the results of the post-mortem, the results of the toxicology report. And they wanted everything straight away, almost before he had had a chance to consider the evidence. They seemed ignorant of the fact that science had its own rhythms that had to be respected.

'Come closer, Chief Superintendent,' Leone said, shifting a bit. 'He was shot at very close range, most probably with the weapon pressed to his forehead. The bullet exited through the back of the neck.' Leaning forward, he used his hands to turn the head.

Ferrara stared at the corpse.

There was a sudden glint in his eyes, a momentary disturbance, that the others recognised. At that instant, he had realised that this was not just another crime scene.

There was something special about the body in front of him, something he had never witnessed before. He had seen so many corpses, both in person and in photographs, that he had lost count. Corpses of men, women, children . . . This scene, though, was the most gruesome of all.

It was like something from a horror film.

On second thoughts, it was even worse.

6

The victim was an elderly man. He was sitting in the Jacuzzi, completely naked, his head against the backboard, his face turned towards those now observing him. His skin was the colour of alabaster and his legs were as spindly as sticks. A thin line of blood was trickling down his left cheek. His mouth was wide open, as if he had been saying something just before he was shot. His hair was caked with blood.

Ferrara's gaze moved to the victim's face and he abruptly felt his stomach heave. He leant slightly forward to confirm his first impression.

The eye-sockets were empty.

The eyes were gone.

The killer had gouged them out, preventing the investigators from catching the expression, whether of terror or disbelief, that might have made it possible to understand the last moments of this man's life.

Why the eyes?

For now, he could not even imagine the answer.

He turned to Leone and looked at him questioningly.

'The killer must have taken them with him,' Leone said, as if reading his thoughts. 'We're dealing with a serious case here, Chief Superintendent,' he added in a grave tone, wiping his forehead again. 'A really nasty business.'

Ferrara shook his head and shrugged. He opened his mouth to speak, but no words came. He sighed, gave Leone a piercing look, and moved away a few steps.

He needed to think.

Leone went back to his work. 'No external indication that the victim tried to defend himself,' he dictated to the technician, who was still by his side. 'I'm now going to check the nails for any possible fragments of skin or organic matter . . .'

A few minutes later, Teresa Micalizi appeared. 'Chief,' she said, out of breath, her voice betraying her agitation, 'there's another body.'

'What?'

'We've found another victim.'

'Where?'

'In a small building in the garden.'

'All right, Teresa, let's go!'

As they hurried back towards the front door, Leone's words echoed in Ferrara's mind. *A serious case, a really nasty business.* Why should Leone, an experienced pathologist, have to emphasise that this was a nasty business? Did the old fox know more than he was letting on?

At that moment, they heard the roar of a police helicopter approaching.

The investigative machine was now in full operation.

The corpse lay on the almost completely blackened floor of what had once been a small chapel and was now reduced to a storage shed for garden tools and building materials. He was on his back with his arms by his sides, and his jet-black hair was caked with blood. His eyes were wide open in an expression of terror, staring into space. He must have been about thirty, thirty-five at the most, and wore what looked like a butler's uniform.

Kneeling, Ferrara noticed a bullet hole in his left temple.

Another full-blown execution, he thought.

A trickle of blood from the wound had run down the victim's cheek. It was no longer fresh.

Why had he been killed? Had he seen something he wasn't supposed to? And which of the two had been killed first? Most likely the man in front of him, Ferrara decided.

There was no bullet casing on the floor. They would have to look carefully under the body and in every corner.

He left the chapel, his head buzzing with thoughts. Probably too many at this point.

One, though, predominated: this was likely to be a long and difficult investigation.

7

'How did you get in?'

For more than half an hour, Inspector Riccardo Venturi had been questioning Rolando Russo, the man who had called 113, at the villa.

He had been working for the villa's owner as a driver for a couple of years. Of average height, with short dark hair, he was twenty-two and lived with his parents in the nearby town of Borgo San Lorenzo.

He had told Venturi that he had driven his employer to Milan the previous day for what he presumed was a routine appointment at the National Tumour Institute. It wasn't the first time they had gone there. Back in Florence, he had dropped him off at the Hotel Villa Medici in the Via Il Prato, from where he had collected him at 11.15 to take him home.

'As I already explained to your colleague,' he said, 'I found the front door half open this morning and when nobody came, I got out of the car. I went to the doorway and called. As there was no answer, I guessed something must have happened.'

'And so you went into the rooms?'

'That's right. I saw the bloodstains and then the body—' He broke off, his eyes brimming with tears, and took a deep breath.

'Did you touch anything?'

'No, only the phone. I was shaking all over and felt as if I was going to faint. I couldn't wait for the police to get here. While I was waiting I sat on the steps outside the front door.'

'When you went in, did you happen to notice anything suspicious?'

'Suspicious? What do you mean?'

'Was there anyone in the area? Did you hear any noises, notice any particular smell?'

'No, nothing like that.' He seemed very certain.

'And why was the door half open?'

'They leave it like that sometimes.'

'Did you notice anything strange yesterday, or the day before yesterday, let's say in the last week?'

'What do you call strange?'

'Someone following you? A car? A new face in the area?'

For a while, the young man was silent, as if looking for the right words. 'Let me think about it,' he said at last.

'Take all the time you need.'

8

9.15 a.m. *The countryside between Dicomano and*
San Godenzo

A hand shook her gently. She opened her eyes and saw that it was
already day.

'You slept more than twelve hours,' her companion said, smiling.

'I haven't had such a deep sleep for years,' she replied, sitting
up in bed and stretching.

'I'll make you breakfast,' the other woman said. 'What would
you like?'

'Toast, butter, jam and a soft-boiled egg.'

'Great. I'll put the egg on at the last minute.'

Rubbing her eyes to rid them of the last traces of sleep, she got
up, staggered to the bathroom, stripped off and got into the
shower. As soon as the water was nice and hot, she let it flow over
her head. She stood for a good ten minutes with her eyes closed
and her hands on the ceramic tiles. When she got out she
wrapped herself in a bath towel and dried herself. Then she let it
fall to the floor and stood in front of the mirror to examine her
body.

She no longer saw the young girl with small breasts and an
undeveloped body whose dark eyes had looked back at her from

the dressing-table mirror in her mother's room. She no longer felt ridiculous and uncomfortable, the way she had whenever she and her basketball teammates showered in the changing rooms after training or a match. She was no longer jealous of anyone else. She had grown into an attractive woman, with a good, firm pair of breasts and a perfect physique.

The transformation had taken place, almost without her realising it, in that depressing ten-by-six-foot cell which she wanted to erase from her mind as quickly as possible.

I need to start living! she said to herself, examining her own profile. She pulled a flirtatious face at herself, then turned and went back to the bedroom. She stretched out on the small double bed with its leather headboard. Facing her was a reproduction of Klimt's beautiful, intense *The Kiss*.

'Breakfast is almost ready!' came the call. 'You can come now!'

She turned her eyes away from the picture, dismissing the thoughts that had sprung into her mind. But she did not get up. She did not want to, even though she was starting to feel hunger pangs.

'You come here, Angelica, please!' she called out, her voice imploring, her eyes gleaming with a special light.

Angelica came running. 'What's up?'

'Will you give me a massage? Just for five minutes. I'm aching all over, as if someone had given me a beating.'

'But your egg's almost ready . . . '

Do you think I give a fuck about an egg right now? It's you I want.

'OK, Guendi, five minutes. How could I refuse you? You crashed out straight after dinner last night. I helped you to bed. Don't you remember?'

'No, I don't remember a thing.'

'Turn over then.'

Angelica let her silk dressing gown fall to the floor. Then she sat astride Guendalina, gently placed her hands on her back and began to move them with great skill.

Guendalina's body started to tingle.

Soon, though, Angelica's hands went lower and her fingers started to move between her thighs. Guendalina turned abruptly, pulling her companion to her, and kissed her. It was a long, deep, passionate kiss. Their bodies started to move in unison, at an ever-accelerating rhythm.

Angelica, who had only discovered her own bisexuality as she grew to adulthood, had felt a strong physical attraction to Guendalina since their first meetings in Sollicciano Prison.

She kissed her now, with ever-increasing intensity, all over her body, and soon the air was filled with sighs, gasps and moans.

The room was empty of everything else – objects, thoughts, worries – and they alone were left, with the love that had thrown them into each other's arms and the unstoppable desire to embrace and caress and melt into each other until they became a single body and a single soul.

When they both felt fully satisfied, they moved apart and lay side by side, exhausted. Only their fingers remained locked together, an afterglow of the desire they had just experienced. The deep silence of the room was disturbed only by their breathing.

An hour later, Angelica brought in the breakfast on a tray. Guendalina, who was still lying on top of the sheets, sat up and propped herself against the headboard. And when her friend turned to go, she watched her as she walked back to the kitchen. With her enviable physique, tall and slim with small breasts and a flat, firm stomach, she was truly beautiful and sensual, enough to take your breath away.

Angelica had been her social worker for two years. But actually she was more than that: she was her confidante, her safety valve. It was Angelica who had arranged for her to be assigned a single cell, following the first attempt by another lesbian inmate to take advantage of her.

Guendalina had told her about her sad childhood, the suffering experienced by her mother, who had died of stomach cancer while she was in prison. Her grandmother had had the same disease, and she was scared that one day she too might be struck down by that terrible monster.

Angelica was the only person she had told her true motive for killing her stepfather. He was a brute who would return home in a drunken rage and beat her mother, who, either out of fear or to avoid a scandal, had never called the police. One day, shortly after her sixteenth birthday, unable to stand yet another act of violence, she had steeled herself, taken a long, sharp knife from the kitchen, gone to his bed while he was asleep and cut his throat. The memory of his hot blood spattering her hand and face had stayed with her for years, haunting her dreams.

But she had never felt any remorse. Why should she? The man had also tried to abuse her. And it was that attempted assault that had reinforced her lack of interest in men.

Angelica was also the only person to whom she had dared reveal what had become her obsession: to live in such a way as to make up for lost time.

And it had been Angelica, in her role as social worker, who had written a report assessing her character that had contributed in no small measure to her sentence being reduced: ... *the detainee seems genuinely repentant for the act she committed and does not demonstrate any criminal impulses. On this basis, the possibility that she would commit further criminal acts once released can be ruled out. Her reintegration into society seems a foregone conclusion.*

Now, at last, Guendalina felt happy.

For the first time she felt comfortable in the world, the real world. And comfortable with love too, perhaps. She closed her eyes, and was unaware that Angelica had come back into the bedroom until she felt her lean over the bed and received her passionate kiss and heard her sweet, languid voice: 'I want to make love to you again.' She felt Angelica's lips at her ear and the warmth of her tanned body as she embraced her.

'You're so damn sexy, Angi, with these little hearts and flowers tattooed on your back. In prison I always looked forward to our meetings. Every time you left it seemed like an endless wait until I saw you again. I was always really sad.'

'And I couldn't wait to have you here with me. Just the two of us, alone.'

They took up just where they had left off, with an urgency even greater than last time, if such a thing were possible. It wasn't just desire, it was also anticipation, the hope that Guendalina's world could be rebuilt – with all the things she thought she had lost for ever, but which she now wanted more than ever.

They consummated their passion voraciously, but this time, rather than moving apart, they clung together, bathed in sweat, and for a good hour not just the room but the entire world seemed to disappear. The first to regain consciousness was Angelica, who got up, went to the bathroom, then outside to breathe in the fresh country air.

She lived in a charming, lovingly renovated stone cottage between Dicomano and San Godenzo. She had inherited it from her parents, who had died several years earlier: her father had killed his seriously ill wife and then killed himself, unable to live without her. Angelica had been their only child.

Lounging in a deckchair under a chestnut tree, she stretched out a hand and took an apple from a basket. She ate it in big bites then threw the core into the grass.

Next, she typed a text message on her mobile and sent it.

Just a few words:

Let's meet in that place. Time as agreed.

Shortly after midday, the corpses were put in body bags, ready to be transferred to the Institute of Forensic Medicine.

The Forensics team had only just left, as had Francesco Leone and Deputy Prosecutor Vinci, who had arrived late as usual.

They had done their job, photographed the victims, examined every square inch of the house. The residue of the reagents used to detect organic liquids and prints were scattered all over the place, but especially in the study, the bathroom and the former chapel.

The Luminol and the Mini Crimescope 400 had been no help. The former was capable of showing bloodstains even after some time had passed, thanks to a characteristic electric-blue luminescence observable in complete darkness. It could also show up marks or smears that the killer had tried to wash away or remove.

The Mini Crimescope 400, perhaps less well known, indicated the presence of possible latent traces invisible to the naked eye, like fingerprints, fibres, strands of hair, or fingernails. Thanks to its ultraviolet light source, it could work on various wavelengths.

So they would have to wait now for the detailed technical report to learn the likely position of the killer in relation to the victims, the distance at which the shots had been fired, and any prints that might be of significance.

For Ferrara, the moment had come to give his men their orders. And to perform the thankless task of informing the victims' relatives before the media arrived. The latter he decided to leave to Rizzo. He had things to do.

9

1.50 p.m. Piazzale Michelangelo

He really loved Florence.

To him, it was the most beautiful city in the world. The only one apart from Paris that really stirred him. He had lived in Florence until he came of age and had many memories of those years, both pleasant and unpleasant. Every time he came back, he felt welcomed by these streets, so human in their scale, however anonymous.

He had lived the past week to the full. He had eaten lunch in the best restaurants, visited museums, and gone for long strolls in the evenings, especially around the Piazza Santa Maria Novella, one of his favourite spots. There, his gaze had lingered for a long time on the façade of the basilica until, his attention drawn by their voices, he had turned and looked at the large number of young people sitting on the grass and the benches, many of them drug addicts.

It was almost two in the afternoon. The city lay beneath a cloudless blue sky, and the roofs of the buildings glittered in the sun.

He was in the Piazzale Michelangelo, from where you could see the whole heart of Florence, from the Belvedere fortress to Santa Croce and beyond, by way of the riverbanks and bridges, the

Ponte Vecchio in particular, as far as the outlines of the hills on the horizon. It was a wonderful view, reproduced on countless postcards.

Florence reminded him of Titian's *Venus* in the Uffizi Gallery. A young woman, lying naked on a sofa, her two small but proud breasts like rosebuds, her languid gaze seeming to invite the observer to enjoy her, silently conveying a feeling of sensual anticipation.

He moved to the middle of the square to photograph the bronze copies of *David* and the four allegories, the originals of which were in the Medici Chapels at San Lorenzo. *How wonderful it would be to see the originals here*, he said to himself as he walked around the statues.

He was dressed anonymously in a pair of ripped jeans, a white T-shirt with an incomprehensible logo, and well-worn tennis shoes. A pair of dark glasses, not designer ones, hid the green of his eyes: a new colour, part of his collection of contact lenses. On his head was a scruffy baseball cap, from beneath which flowed a black ponytail. He had chosen the colour black specially for the occasion. He looked like a down-and-out, someone no one would pay any attention to. He knew how indifferent people were in a tourist city, and he was taking full advantage of that.

Having left his four-by-four in the pay and display car park near the Ponte Vecchio, he had walked through the medieval Porta San Nicolò then up the monumental steps, proceeding at a normal, relaxed pace. What did he have to be worried about, anyway? Hadn't he taken great care to disguise himself?

He could surely have fooled anyone.

Along the way he had passed a group of French tourists and had eavesdropped on a young couple. She was a beautiful girl in shorts and a tight-fitting white T-shirt and he was tall and fair-haired. They were holding hands. He had heard them exchange words of love.

Poor fools, he had thought. All those illusions!

After taking a few photographs, he glanced at his watch, put his digital camera away in his black nylon backpack, and went down to the terrace below. He sat at one of the free tables, the one closest to the railings. He placed the backpack on a chair and took out *The Lonely Planet Guide to Tuscany and Umbria*, making sure it was clearly visible.

The only people about were tourists, mostly elderly.

The waitress, a blonde girl of about twenty, probably Russian, came slowly towards him. He gave her a knowing look.

'What can I get you, signore?' she asked with a smile.

He ordered an espresso with cream. 'And extra cream on the side,' he added. He felt like something sweet and he absolutely loved cream.

While he was waiting, he pretended to leaf through the guide-book.

'Your coffee and cream, signore.' The young waitress put his order on the table and moved away quickly. Other customers were waiting for her.

The cream was delicious.

He checked his watch again. He needed to make a phone call that he had been putting off for several days, more through inep-titude than anything else. She would already be awake and must have had breakfast by now, he thought. He took his mobile out of his jacket pocket and dialled an international number. He heard two rings, then her voice.

'I can't believe it, Daniel. Where are you calling from?'

'I'm in Rome.'

'How lovely. Rome's wonderful. I haven't been there for years.'

'Why don't you join me? What's stopping you? I'll book a flight for you.'

The woman at the other end did not reply immediately. 'Do you need anything?' she asked. 'Is everything OK?'

'No, I don't need anything, thanks. But what about you? How are you?'

'The usual ailments that come with age. You know. But I need to tell you something.'

'I'm listening.'

'I want to fire the maid, that Romanian slut.'

'Why?'

'I'm missing some jewellery and I think she was the one who took it, but how am I supposed to prove it?'

'You can't prove it. Just fire her!'

Inside, he was overjoyed. He was the one who'd been pilfering the jewellery, little by little, and selling it. He needed money. Lots of it.

'And how's your business going, Daniel?'

'Very well. I'm about to seal a very interesting deal.'

'Will you be in Rome much longer?'

'Just a few weeks.'

'Tell me all about it.'

'Another time. I've got an important meeting this evening, with the director of a big IT company. I'd better say goodbye now.'

His mobile was indicating that he had a call waiting and he had realised who it was.

'All right, but try to phone me more often. You know how anxious I get when you're away. I'm stuck indoors here, and when I hear about all the things that are going on I start worrying.'

'There's no need. I'm not a little boy any more. I'll call you soon. Bye.'

He ended the call abruptly and answered the other call just before it went to voicemail. 'Hello?'

He listened patiently.

'OK,' he replied, and hung up.

There had been a change: it wouldn't hinder his plan, but it was annoying all the same.

He needed to go to the Piazza San Marco.

He got up abruptly, paid the bill, giving the waitress a wicked smile as he did so, and went back down the way he had come.

10

3.20 *p.m. The Commissioner's office*

'The Commissioner's expecting you. Go straight in, Chief Superintendent.'

The secretary, no longer young but well groomed, was standing in the corridor, apparently waiting anxiously for him. As soon as she saw him, her face seemed to relax. She went back to her desk, pressed a button and announced Ferrara's arrival.

The Commissioner had called him a couple of times in the course of the morning for updates. He had sounded quite tense, which was understandable given the seriousness of the double murder.

Filippo Adinolfi had only been in Florence for a short time, following a career largely spent in the offices of the Ministry of the Interior in Rome. Like many officials, he had built his career behind a desk, writing reports, notes and proposals. He had absolutely no experience in the field, and had no idea what it meant to risk your life. He had progressed as far as he had by sucking up to each of his superiors as they came and went. How could he understand what real police officers faced on a daily basis? He wasn't someone Ferrara found easy to talk to about detective work.

Adinolfi, who was even redder in the face than usual, motioned him to the visitor's armchair as soon as he saw him come in. As Ferrara took his seat, Adinolfi put the folder he had been holding down on the desk, folded his arms, and assumed a serious expression. Ferrara wondered what his blood pressure level must be right now.

Adinolfi went straight on the attack: 'Chief Superintendent, you and your men need to make this case your top priority. The phone's ringing off the hook here. Radio stations, television channels, newspapers. As if that weren't enough, the Ministry's press office keeps hassling me for constant updates, as if we're supposed to provide some kind of minute-by-minute sports commentary. Now they're asking for a detailed official report. You can speak to the press, I'll say a few words to the TV people later if they insist. But I warn you, none of your men should talk to the media, do you understand? If there are any leaks, I'll hold you personally responsible.'

He grabbed the telephone receiver and put it down on the desk.

It was clear he had no intention of answering lots of questions from journalists. In fact, the powers that be preferred to avoid that: before making any kind of public statement, a commissioner was expected to ask permission from the Head of the State Police, through his own press officer – another official who had forged his career in the shadow of Rome.

Ferrara agreed.

'All right,' Adinolfi said, in a calmer voice. 'What can you tell me?'

Ferrara began a detailed summary but was soon interrupted.

'Chief Superintendent, is there any chance that this was a robbery that went wrong?'

'No, I've already ruled that out. We've found a wallet with cash and credit cards, and an expensive watch, a Rolex Daytona. Plus . . .'

'Yes?'

'There's something else you need to know.'

'What is it?'

'His eyes were gouged out.'

The Commissioner looked at him, stunned, and a grimace of disgust crossed his face. He shuffled some random papers on his desk, perhaps to hide his horror. 'His eyes?' he echoed, almost as if wanting confirmation.

'Yes, that's right. The murder was carried out in a highly professional manner. At the moment that's the only thing we're sure about.'

'If that's the case,' Adinolfi said, leaning back in his chair, 'you're right to rule out robbery.'

His expression was a mixture of disappointment and anxiety. It couldn't be doing his ulcer any good, Ferrara thought.

Adinolfi leant forward slightly, placed both his hands on the desk, and spoke in a low voice, as if afraid of being overheard. 'But don't rule out anything else. Follow every possible lead. This thing with the eyes might be a red herring.'

Ferrara merely nodded.

At that moment, there was a knock on the door and the secretary peered round it nervously.

'I told you I didn't want to be disturbed!' Adinolfi cried. 'What is it?'

'But, Commissioner,' the woman said, her voice trembling, 'it's the Ministry on the line and I haven't been able to put the call through. The Head of the State Police wants to speak to you in person.'

Adinolfi put the receiver straight back on its cradle and assumed an air of perfect composure, adjusting the knot of his tie, almost as if wanting to make himself more presentable to the person on the other end of the phone.

'Are you still here? Put him through straight away!'

'We're very worried here in Rome.' These were the first words spoken by the Head of the State Police. 'The minister and myself are both quite unhappy with the way public order and security are being handled in Florence.'

Adinolfi flushed. He leant forward abruptly, as if about to reply, but a moment later he sat back in his original position. There was nothing he could do but submit in silence, which was what he was accustomed to doing. There was no doubt that not contradicting his superiors was a stance that had served him well as he'd climbed the professional ladder. It was not for nothing that he now found himself in charge of Police Headquarters in Florence, one of the most important and sought-after postings for a man in his position.

'It's obvious you aren't in control of things up there,' the Head of the State Police ranted.

'As you know, sir, I haven't been in Florence long—' Adinolfi began in self-justification, but he was immediately interrupted.

'I expect you in my office at eight o'clock tomorrow morning, on the dot. Bring me a detailed report on the latest incidents, in particular what happened last night. Have I made myself clear?'

'But . . .'

The sentence was left hanging in the air. There was no longer anyone at the other end of the line.

The bastard! Adinolfi thought. The man didn't have the faintest idea of the kind of state he'd found this fucking Headquarters in. Catastrophic didn't even begin to describe it.

That was the way it had always been. Each new commissioner criticised his predecessor, more or less vehemently, for doing little or nothing to solve the problems of public order or improve the working conditions of the staff.

Complete silence had fallen in the room. Trying to conceal his anger, Adinolfi resumed his conversation with Ferrara, asking him if anything useful had been found during the search of the villa.

The officers were still hard at work, Ferrara replied, but he had been told that they had found about two hundred grams of cocaine, too much for purely personal use.

Silence fell once more.

The Commissioner started to fidget in his chair and his gaze wandered, as if he were searching for something. When he looked again at Ferrara, there was genuine dismay in the Commissioner's eyes. The thought of a scandal that might destroy the city's upper classes terrified Adinolfi. Not drugs: that was all he needed. It would open a whole new can of worms, especially as it was already rumoured that illegal narcotics were in circulation in certain circles.

'Let's keep that discovery quiet,' he said. 'Make sure your men are aware. I don't want this place leaking like a sieve. We must avoid journalists creating their own unfounded hypotheses, spicing up the murders with sordid details. Have I made myself clear? I repeat: have I made myself clear?'

On this point, Ferrara was in total agreement with the Commissioner: if the media got wind of these details, they would make their reports even more salacious, and hide behind the constitutional right to information if any complaints were brought against them. Just as they had recently done in defending themselves from accusations of having revealed the contents of intercepted telephone calls – conversations about the private lives of politicians and celebrities – which had been recorded in the context of police investigations.

'Absolutely, Commissioner,' Ferrara assured him. 'I'll make sure nothing gets out.'

'Proceed with caution, then. I don't think I need to remind you that Senator Enrico Costanza was a very important figure here in Florence. I don't want this case blowing up in our faces.'

Adinolfi picked up the sheaf of papers on the desk in front of him and started writing, as if Ferrara had already left the office. On raising his eyes after a few moments, he was surprised to see him still sitting on the other side of the desk, watching him quietly.

'Do you have something else to say to me?' he asked.

'No.'

'In that case you can go, and try not to exceed the overtime budget.'

Ferrara got up and went out, these last words echoing in his head. They had to investigate a double murder while being careful not to exceed the monthly limit of thirty-five hours overtime to which each of his detectives was entitled. How on earth anyone was supposed to work with that sword of Damocles hanging over them, Ferrara did not know.

Before he continued writing the report for the following morning, Ferrara extracted two painkillers from a blister pack, held them in his left hand for a moment, then swallowed them down with a glass of water.

Getting away from his office, leaving all this behind him, were just dreams to him now. He had another thirteen months to go before he was eligible for a pension. Thirteen damn months before he might at last be a free man.

11

The murders were the kind that caused a big stir, especially with the series of horrendous events that had taken place in the two-week period starting on the night of the festival of San Giovanni, 24 June, still fresh in everyone's memory.

The first victim had been Giovanna Innocenti, the daughter of an internationally renowned Florentine wine producer.

Then the charred body of Madalena, the owner of a private club, had been found in a small deconsecrated church in the hills of Sesto Fiorentino, a few miles outside Florence.

Silvia De Luca – expert on the occult and friend and confidante of Inspector Riccardo Venturi – had been the third victim, her only crime having been to provide the police with some useful tips. But that had not been the end of it. Because the killer had yet to strike his true targets: Alvise Innocenti and his wife, Giovanna's parents.

The fear engendered in the populace by this escalating violence seemed to have faded with the death of the culprit: Leonardo Berghoff. Now, with the killing of Costanza, that fear would return.

It was only natural, then, that the media should try to gather as much information as they could – not only from the Commissioner, but also from the *Squadra Mobile*, where, unusually for the time of day, a number of young reporters were prowling the corridors, hoping to catch someone out in an indiscretion that might provide them with a scoop. They may be only small vultures, but they were no less dangerous for that, and it was best to keep them at a greater distance than usual. Ferrara knew them well and did what he could to avoid them.

The owner of the villa, Enrico Costanza, seventy-five years old, had been a senator under several governments. He had also been a Freemason. That much everyone knew, at least in Florence, so no one had been surprised when his name had featured on the membership list of a secret lodge that had been discovered at the start of the eighties in a well-known Tuscan villa by some Milanese prosecutors. A powerful lodge, whose members also included other highly influential political figures. A lodge that had used its power without ever exposing itself to the gaze of publicity.

Holed up in his office, Ferrara was writing a press release containing just the basic information. Only the victims' names and the briefest description of how they had been killed. No details of the search of the villa, which was still ongoing, or the results of the initial tests, which in any case were covered by confidentiality rules. He was sure the journalists would be disappointed, but he was trying to buy a bit of time. He could always fob them off with a few new details without compromising the investigation. It was a tactic that had proved useful in the past.

When he had finished, he called in his secretary, Nestore Fanti, who was working in the adjoining office and to whom he had diverted his phone calls. The dividing door between their offices was almost always open.

As always, Sergeant Fanti, tall, disconcertingly thin, with wiry blond hair, materialised immediately. He had been born in Trento, but had been assigned to Florence immediately after joining the police and had never moved on. An IT fanatic, he distinguished himself by his precision and discretion and by his accurate research, both in police records and online. It was these qualities that had prompted Ferrara to choose him as his personal secretary.

'You called, Chief Superintendent?'

Ferrara gave him the sheet of paper, a few lines printed out from the computer. 'Fax this to the press agencies, the local television channels and the newspapers.'

'Right away, chief,' Fanti said, heading straight back to his own office.

It was now almost five in the afternoon and the crime scene was starting to empty.

Some officers set off back to Headquarters with material gathered from the scene. Others stayed in the area to help with the search for evidence and useful information. Others still would check the places where drug dealers hung out to see what they could dig up. Soon the only things left in the parking area were paper napkins, cigarette ends and empty polystyrene cups stained with coffee.

The last to leave were Francesco Rizzo and Teresa Micalizi.

It was still very hot, and as soon as they left the villa they were hit by a wave of heat. Their car had spent the whole day in the boiling sun and when they got in they felt as if they were in an oven. The air-conditioning was not working. They lowered the windows, but the air that came in was even hotter.

As they drove through the gates, they were filmed by a couple of cameramen from Tuscan television. The crews had been there for several hours, waiting patiently to grab a few images for the evening news.

After a mile or two, they both noticed a terrible country smell.

'What a stench!' Teresa exclaimed. Her cotton T-shirt clung to her body and she could feel the sweat trickling down her chest. She took a tissue out of her bag and dabbed her neck. She ordered the driver to go faster, and he obeyed without a thought for the thirty-mile-an-hour speed limit or the watching speed cameras, which, according to the rumours doing the rounds of the piazzas and cafés, had been installed so that the fines could help bring the local municipalities' budgets back into the black. These cameras had been springing up like fungus all over the place, not just in Tuscany, and some had been confiscated by court order because they had not been correctly calibrated.

'It's just bullshit,' Rizzo said. Just like the shit he and Ferrara were knee-deep in, he thought. They had to solve this thing as quickly as they could.

Teresa recognised her straight away: the blonde policewoman who had been at Costanza's villa. She was waiting for Teresa in front of her office door, holding several sheets of paper in her right hand.

'I've brought you my chief's duty reports on the operation this morning, but there's something else I'd like to ask you. Can I talk to you for a minute, Superintendent? I'll only take a moment of your time.'

'Please come in.'

The policewoman followed her in and stopped in front of the desk.

'Don't just stand there, sit down.'

'Thank you.'

'So, what did you want?'

The young woman hesitated for a moment, then said, 'I'd like to work with the *Squadra Mobile*, if possible with you. I was actually wondering if you needed reinforcements after what's happened.'

'You mean the double murder?'

'Yes. It would be a chance for me to learn. This morning was the first time I'd been present at a murder scene, so I'd like to know what happens next, how the investigation develops, how you track down the culprit, how—'

'What happens next,' Teresa interrupted her, 'is that you have to work like a donkey, give up your private life, your friends, your family, and sometimes you don't get anywhere in the end. Sometimes it's all for nothing.'

But these words did nothing to discourage the young officer. 'I'd guessed that much, Superintendent, but I joined the police because I believe in this job and I'm prepared to make sacrifices.'

'But you don't have any experience,' Teresa replied. 'You still need to learn the ropes. You need to know the area really well, the places, the people.'

'I know that, but I'm good at collating reports, classifying papers, doing research online and in records. I'd like to help out and learn more about investigative methods first-hand. I'm in my second year studying law, and after I graduate I want to take the exam to become either a superintendent or a prosecutor.'

Teresa shifted some papers on her desk as she thought about it. 'All right,' she said, 'I'll talk to Ferrara about it. But tell me, why did you ask me instead of going directly to him?'

'The Chief Superintendent is always really busy and I didn't want to disturb him. Plus, I thought you might understand me better.'

The girl didn't know how helpful the Chief Superintendent could be, Teresa thought.

'I'll let you know,' she said, holding out her hand.

'Thank you for whatever you're able to do,' the young officer said. She was about to leave when Teresa called her back.

'You haven't told me your name.'

'Alessandra Belli, member of the Auto Unit since the first of March 2004.'

Teresa made a note of her details on a sheet of paper.

12

They knocked at the door.

'Come in!'

Francesco Rizzo and Teresa Micalizi entered.

Ferrara motioned to them to sit down. 'Any developments?'

'A few,' Rizzo replied, settling himself in one of the two black chairs in front of the desk. Teresa had already taken her seat in the other, visibly tired. Her beautiful face, which usually turned heads, looked drawn, and her eyes had lost their normal sparkle.

After attending the Police Academy in Rome, she had been assigned to Headquarters in Florence, and on her first introduction to real investigative work had immediately distinguished herself by her insight and intelligence. She had soon realised that the *Squadra Mobile* was not actually what some of her female colleagues had told her it was: *an old boys' club where we're seen as intruders.*

No, she had been made welcome and had gone straight into Ferrara's good books. He recognised that she had the potential to become an excellent detective, and he wasn't usually wrong about things like that. *Keep doing what you're doing, you've got what it takes,* he had told her on more than one occasion, making her break out in goose pimples.

'So, Francesco, what's new?'

Consulting his notes, Rizzo summarised the outcome of the forensic examination and the search of the property. Only two bullet casings – from a 7.65 calibre pistol – had been found in the villa, one on the floor of the study, to the right of whoever had been sitting at the desk, the other in the corridor near the study door.

'Have they found any bullets?' Ferrara asked.

'Only one, in the corridor. Forensics suspect it's too twisted to be any use for making comparisons. It was crushed when it hit the wall.'

'What about the time of death?'

'Leone thinks it was the early hours of this morning, but he said he'd give us a more definite answer after the post-mortem, which he'll do tomorrow. He'll also let you know his hypothesis about the bullet's trajectory—'

At that moment, someone knocked twice, sharply, at the door. It was the sentry from the guardhouse downstairs.

'The butler's wife is here, Chief Superintendent,' he announced.

'So, she's turned up at last. Put her in the waiting room. We'll call her in a few minutes.'

'What have you found apart from the cocaine?' Ferrara asked Rizzo once the door had closed again. Rizzo explained that they had searched everywhere and taken away a great deal of paperwork – bank and financial documents – as well as correspondence, diaries, CDs, DVDs, videotapes and a computer.

'Have you checked the computer?' Ferrara asked.

'Not yet. We'll do it as soon as we can.'

'Anything else?'

'We found the key to a safe-deposit box at the Florentine Savings Bank,' Rizzo replied, then corrected himself, 'Actually, Micalizi found it.'

'It was in the desk drawer in the study,' Teresa said, 'along with a copy of the contract.'

'And what about the person who called 113? What did he say?'

'Nothing useful, chief,' Rizzo said. 'He was the victim's driver. He told us he'd gone to pick him up at seven on the dot, because that was the time Costanza had specified the previous day. He made it clear, though, that he didn't know where he was supposed to be taking him. He didn't notice anything strange when he arrived. He hadn't noticed anything in the previous few days either. He has absolutely no idea what the motive for the crime might be.'

'Who questioned him?'

'Inspector Venturi.'

'Good.'

Ferrara had great respect for the scrupulous, patient Riccardo Venturi, a walking encyclopedia of the unit's history as well as an IT wizard. Like his other colleagues, he spent more time at work than with his family.

Ferrara was ready to give his instructions.

Rizzo would check out the safe-deposit box and coordinate the investigation, especially the interviews with the immediate families, relatives and friends of the victims, who would have to be grilled thoroughly if they were going to get at the truth.

Teresa would work alongside Venturi, going through the material removed from the villa.

For his part, Ferrara would go to the prison the next morning for an interview.

'I'm sure I don't need to remind you to keep me updated,' he said as he got up from his chair. 'Francesco, you take care of the butler's wife. We'll need to get her to identify the body too.'

Rizzo nodded, and was about to leave the room when Ferrara called him back.

'What's up, chief?'

'A team from the SCO are coming from Rome along with an inspector. I want you to deal with them tomorrow. Take them to Costanza's villa, then give them any jobs that need doing, working alongside some of our men. Do you understand?'

The involvement of the SCO, the Central Operational Service, the pride of the State Police, consisting of investigators of proven experience – in theory, the best there were – was a clear sign that the case was making waves in the upper echelons in Rome.

Rizzo merely said, 'OK,' a smile playing on his lips.

Ferrara glanced at his watch. It was time to go home.

He put the papers on his desk in order and closed up the office. At last he was ready to leave Headquarters, mentally exhausted. As soon as he crossed the threshold of his apartment, he would put all thoughts of work aside. He wanted to devote himself to Petra alone.

It was a special occasion; one he would not miss for the world.

What a thankless job awaited Rizzo!

As a police officer, it fell to him to inform the butler's wife of her husband's death.

It was a task that, as with many of his colleagues, he was still not accustomed to. And having to accompany a victim's relative when he or she identified the body was just as bad.

Luis Rodriguez's wife had rushed back to Florence from the village in the Veneto where she had been visiting her sister. When the officer from Headquarters in Venice had gone to find her, he had told her only that she needed to present herself to the Florence police as a matter of urgency on a family matter.

'What's happened to my husband?' was the first question the woman asked after sitting down opposite Rizzo. 'Where's Luis? I haven't been able to contact him all day!' She stared at Rizzo with frightened eyes. He looked down, searching for the right words, then looked up again and said in a thin voice, 'Signora, I'm afraid your husband was killed last night, along with Enrico Costanza.'

The woman did not move at first, did not react. It was only after a moment or two that she cried, 'Tell me it's a joke!' and started pinching her arms, rocking backwards and forwards in her chair, and sniffing noisily. She looked bewildered, like a boxer stunned by a blow from his opponent.

Rizzo let her unburden herself. He just had to wait for her to calm down a bit before carrying on with the interview. Nervously, she took a tissue from her handbag. As she did so, her purse fell on the floor, and she picked it up with a trembling hand.

'No, it can't be true,' she said in a choked voice. 'Luis didn't have any enemies, nobody wished him any harm. All he wanted was to support his family.'

She took a sip of water from the glass that Rizzo passed her.

When at last she was calmer, Rizzo told her it was important for their investigations that she answer some questions.

Had her husband happened to mention noticing anything suspicious in the last few days?

Had he told her anything about Enrico Costanza's private life? Did she know whether he had any enemies?

Had he been in any kind of trouble?

The answer to all these questions was a blunt no.

'My husband is a wonderful man,' she said in conclusion, her voice shaking with emotion.

Rizzo noticed that she had used the present tense, a very common reaction: no one could get their head around the death of a loved one, not even when faced with the evidence.

He realised he had reached a dead end and, more importantly, that now was not the time to insist.

'We've had to search your home, signora,' he said, 'but you

won't find anything out of place. We got in using the key your husband was carrying.'

He then told her that she would have to go to the morgue to officially identify the body. A patrol car would take her there. It was a distressing task, but a vital one.

13

9.10 p.m. Fiesole

An attractive young woman approached the table. She was wearing jeans and a T-shirt with the restaurant's logo. 'What would you like?' she asked, handing them a couple of menus with the dishes written in black marker on yellow paper.

'Do you have porcini mushrooms?' Venturi asked.

'Yes.'

'Are they local?'

'No, they're imported.'

'Forget it, we'll have two margherita pizzas.'

'And to drink?'

'Draught beer.'

A barely visible grimace of disappointment appeared on Inspector Carlo Rossi's pockmarked face. Once the waitress had moved away, he said, 'What a pity! They're supposed to have really good starters and meat dishes here.'

Given that they had skipped lunch, he had hoped for a decent dinner at least.

'We'll come back another time, Carlo. Right now we're here to work and we can't waste time.'

Venturi looked down at the yellow sheet of paper in front of him. It was an imitation of the famous 'straw paper' that used to be made from wheat or corn, an excellent material much favoured by grocers and greengrocers for wrapping food.

He smiled a touch sadly, remembering when he was little and his grandmother would wet a small piece of the paper and put it on the sore spot after he fell off his bike, convinced that it would prevent swelling.

He shook his head to dismiss these thoughts and looked around at the other customers.

The restaurant was near the road to Enrico Costanza's villa, no more than five hundred yards as the crow flies. It was small, some ten tables altogether, and had a handsome ceiling with beams, from which hung legs of Tuscan cured ham. There were few customers at this hour, but those few were busy talking away happily, with not a care in the world.

In the background, songs from the seventies were playing, livening up the atmosphere.

Venturi had been sent here by Rizzo, who was convinced that people were more likely to speak freely on their own territory than in an office at Police Headquarters.

When the beers arrived, Venturi asked the waitress if he could talk to the owner.

'Who do you mean? The father or the son?'

'Whichever. Just tell him we want to ask him a few questions.'

The girl looked at him, slightly bewildered, then said, 'I'll go and call the father.' She walked away, wondering who these two customers could possibly be. She had never seen them before.

They had barely finished taking their first sips of beer and putting their tankards back on the table when they heard heavy steps on the wooden stairs. They turned and saw a tall, sturdy, giant of a man with barely a hair on his head, wiping his two huge hands on a cloth.

'Good evening,' he said, somewhat suspiciously, pulling out a chair and sitting down opposite them.

'Are you the owner, signore?' Venturi asked.

'Yes, I am, but my son Alessandro manages the place. He's not here at the moment, though. Can I help you?'

Venturi took out his badge. '*Squadra Mobile*,' he said.

'Ask away,' the man said, with a sigh of relief: these two were police officers who wanted to ask him a few questions, not crooks come to demand money which, according to them, would go to help prisoners' families. That had happened before.

Venturi got straight to the point. 'You've heard about the murder of Senator Costanza, I assume?'

The man grimaced. 'Yes, but I don't think I can help you. I don't know anything. The Senator wasn't a customer here. This isn't a restaurant for VIPs. It's very basic. As you see, we use paper tablecloths, the kind they used to use in wayside inns.'

'So you don't know anything, even though the Senator was killed just down the road?'

'It's terrible. It's the first murder that's taken place in the area since I opened this place around twenty years ago. I realised something serious had happened when I saw lots of police cars go by as I was opening up this afternoon.'

'You're not from around here, are you?' Venturi asked, aware that the man did not have a Tuscan accent.

'I'm from Puglia. From Altamura, a town near Bari.'

At this point the waitress came back with two plates, which she put down on the table.

'Here are your pizzas,' the owner said. 'Eat them before they get cold.'

He waved the waitress away, gesturing to the couple sitting by the entrance who were ready to order. The way she had been looking at the two police officers annoyed him. Was it just curiosity or was there something else? He meant to find out as soon as he could.

Neither of the police officers touched their knives and forks.

'What time did you close the restaurant last night?' Venturi asked.

'Same time as usual.'

'What time is that?'

'Around midnight, half past, something like that.'

'Were there any customers?'

'The regulars. They come from the city, or some of the nearby hamlets.'

At that moment the waitress came back to their table. 'Your son is on the phone and wants to speak to you,' she said to the owner. 'He says it's urgent.'

He frowned and looked at the waitress as if he wished he could strike her down with the force of his gaze. 'Tell him I'll call him in a bit.'

'But he said it was urgent.'

'Didn't you hear me? I said I'll call him in a bit.'

The young woman moved away and they resumed their conversation.

'Did you notice anything unusual?' Venturi asked. 'Any new customers you'd never seen before?'

The man hesitated, and Venturi thought he saw a twitch in the corner of his eye.

'No. Nothing to arouse my suspicions. I normally work in the kitchen, anyway.'

'And did your staff mention anything to you?'

'No.'

'What about your son?'

'No, he didn't either.'

'Did you hear any strange noises?'

'What kind of noises?'

'Gunshots, for instance.'

'No. If that had happened I'd have been worried and would have called you or the Carabinieri.'

'Now I'd like to talk to the waitresses. Were they both working yesterday?'

'Yes,' the man said. He got up and went to call them.

Both girls assured Venturi that they hadn't noticed anything either.

Venturi thanked the owner and took a business card from his wallet. 'Please get your son to call me.'

'OK,' the man said and walked away.

In the kitchen, he reprimanded the waitress.

'Listen, when I'm busy you mustn't disturb me. You could have told me my son was on the phone afterwards. And what were all those looks for? Do you happen to know those two? Or do you know something about what happened? I don't want any trouble from you, or you can walk right out that door.'

Stammering, she told him she wanted to keep her job and he had nothing to worry about.

The two police officers were at last able to enjoy their pizzas, cooked in a wood oven and delicious.

'A shame it's not hot any more,' Officer Rossi said.

Venturi signalled to the waitress for the bill. They went halves.

They had found out nothing useful. Apparently, it had all been a waste of time. But the twitch in the corner of the owner's eye, the phone call from his son, and the way he had glared at the waitress had roused Venturi's suspicions. As they walked to the car, he said to Rossi, 'I think we ought to question the big man at Headquarters, and perhaps the son too.'

'Why?'

'It's possible that one or both of them know something.'

The wizard has spoken! Rossi said to himself with a small smile on his lips as he started the engine and put it into first gear.

14

What a smell! Ferrara could feel his stomach rumbling. He hadn't eaten a thing all day and had drunk nothing but a couple of cups of coffee.

As soon as he got home, he noticed the linen tablecloth, a gift from his mother-in-law, and the plates and cutlery that only came out on special occasions. Petra was just adding the finishing touches. He went to her and kissed her on the lips.

'You've had a lot going on today, haven't you?' she said. 'You didn't even phone me.'

'You're right, darling. That's exactly how it was.'

These were the only references to his work they allowed themselves. End of subject. The details were his business only. And Petra was used to not asking questions. She didn't want to know. She had heard about the double murder on the radio and could imagine how busy he must be. She looked him in the eyes as if trying to understand his problems.

He took a small sealed package with a silvery bow from his jacket pocket and handed it to her with a little smile. 'As you can see,' he said, 'I didn't forget.'

It was the anniversary of their first meeting. They had met on Lampedusa, a dream island where they had set the seal on their love under a canvas tent. Their matchmaker had been Massimo

Verga, Ferrara's oldest and most trusted friend, now the owner of a bookshop in the Via Tornabuoni.

'I was sure you hadn't,' Petra said, unwrapping the package.

She held the small shell-shaped leather box in her hands for a moment, then lifted the lid. Her eyes lit up at the sight of a red ruby necklace with matching earrings. They took her breath away.

They came from a jeweller's on the Ponte Vecchio, the true heart of Florence.

Petra took out the earrings and immediately put them in her ears, then asked her husband to help her with the necklace. He moved her hair out of the way and closed the clasp at the end of the fine chain.

'They're stunning, Michele. What a wonderful present! Thank you.'

'They look perfect on you.'

'Thank you again, darling. But you're mad to get me a present like this – God knows how much they must have cost you!'

He shrugged.

'The best present, though,' she went on, with that smile he loved so much, 'is that you remembered in spite of all you had to do on a busy day.'

'Actually I bought them a few days ago. The jeweller was very helpful. He ordered exactly what I asked for. But if you don't like them, you can always change them.'

'No. They're just what I wanted.'

He went to the bathroom to wash his hands then came back and sat at the table. Petra had been admiring herself in the mirror while she waited for him.

They enjoyed a meal of roast lamb with potato and aubergine gratin, accompanied by a truly delicious classic Chianti, Rocca di Montegrossi 1997 reserve from the San Marcellino vineyard. They had first drunk it while having dinner at their favourite restaurant, Giovanni's in the Via del Moro.

As they ate, she told him about her day: how she had started writing a fashion article for the magazine she had been working for since the previous year when Michele had been in Rome.

He actually had seconds. His exhaustion had done nothing to diminish his appetite. And the lamb really was delicious.

15

He had seen the item on a local channel.

Stock footage of the city had been followed by shots of the villa where the crime had taken place, filmed from a distance. Then Police Headquarters, with a few officers outside. Their exhaustion was clearly visible on their pale faces, along with suspicion and confusion.

The camera had lingered on the face of Teresa Micalizi.

The reporter for the item was the one who usually handled crime stories, and he embroidered his presentation with a few unconfirmed rumours. 'The police are looking for a professional killer who may have come from another city. They are keeping a watch on airports and railway stations and at tollbooths along the main roads. Roadblocks are in place at strategic points.'

In the end he had pressed the button on the remote to switch the TV off.

What idiots they were, looking for a professional killer! They were only capable of seeing what was in front of their eyes and jumping to the most obvious conclusions.

The first twenty-four hours had passed. That was good, very good. They'd be hearing from him soon. He'd give anything to see the face of that 'legendary' Chief Superintendent when he ...

In just a few hours, he was going to make him look a complete fool, and the rest of the Florentine police force with him!

He knew a lot about that legendary Chief Superintendent. He had read about him in the newspapers, had seen him on television, speaking at press conferences or making brief public statements at crime scenes.

He was very familiar with the case of the Monster of Florence, on which the legendary Chief Superintendent had led the investigation. In his opinion, the fame he had gained thanks to that case was undeserved. What was there to be proud of? He had pinned it all on an unskilled labourer, but had let the people behind the murders go, the people who ruled the city behind the scenes.

He, on the other hand, knew who they were. He could go straight to the target. He understood certain areas of human behaviour, and was able to go beyond appearances.

He would soon show that Chief Superintendent which of them was the clever one. He knew so much about him, while the Chief Superintendent knew nothing about *him* and would never find him. He'd merely be fumbling about in the dark.

Soon he would concentrate on the next piece of the jigsaw.

There was no way that he could ever be tracked down.

He burst out laughing.

He took off his shoes and curled up on the sofa, which was a bit short for him. From the small side table he took one of his favourite CDs: *Deep Purple in Rock*. For a while he stared at the faces of the five band members on the cover, carved like Mount Rushmore, then put the CD in the player, pressed the play button on the remote and turned up the volume. He closed his eyes, feeling he could fall asleep like that. Ian Gillan's voice flooded the room, singing 'Child in Time'.

Hard rock was his favourite kind of music. Hard music, as hard as he was. Before long, though, he became aware of the usual pain and lifted his hands to his head. Ritchie Blackmore's guitar seemed to be trying to burst his eardrums.

'Damn!' he whispered, opening his eyes. The beast he could

not tame, no matter how he tried, was attacking him. He took some Rohypnol, a powerful drug he had recently discovered, from the side table and swallowed it with a little water. It would take effect within fifteen minutes, and then he would be fine for at least six hours. He would relax and fall into a deep sleep.

16

Yorkshire, England

Sir George Holley had called an urgent meeting in the private study of his castle near Fountains Abbey. There were important issues that needed to be discussed, issues that could not wait.

After a long pause, the white-haired, impeccably dressed Sir George, the owner of this fairy-tale building, resumed speaking. The eyes of his guests, who were sitting in comfortable green leather armchairs, were all on him.

'Things haven't gone according to plan,' he said, 'and we need to understand why before we take any further steps.'

The youngest person present, who was tall, with chiselled features, asked for the floor. From his appearance, most people would have assumed him to be of aristocratic stock. But although everyone knew him as a wealthy investor in the world's financial markets, he was actually a major drugs trafficker who resided officially in the United States; a true gangster, whose main business was laundering dirty money with the support of people who were above suspicion. When Sir George nodded his permission for him to speak, he said, 'Well, in any case, he got what he deserved. He's paid for his mistakes. We should soon know exactly what happened.'

The others nodded.

'I know that Enrico had a Swiss bank account,' Sir George said. 'In Lugano, to be precise. We need to get there before the police do, assuming they even find out about it. We'll have to get in touch with his informer to see what they're up to.'

The others agreed again.

'Will you take care of it, Richard?' Sir George asked the young man who had spoken.

'It'd be an honour. I'll get on to it right away. I'll take the first plane. And I'll make Enrico's informer an offer he can't refuse.'

He sounded absolutely sure of himself. What he was really thinking was that Costanza's murder suggested they should be looking for other, more reliable sources of information.

'Excellent, you take care of it then. But be careful. We can't afford to make any mistakes. I'm leaving for Tuscany on Tuesday. We'll meet again there.'

'Of course, Sir George,' Richard said. He already had a very clear idea of what needed to be done.

Sir George handed him an envelope. 'You'll find all the details in here.'

Richard took it and slipped it into the inside jacket pocket of the hand-tailored linen suit that he wore with total nonchalance. He would destroy it later, once he had read it.

He got up, said goodbye to everyone and left without staying for the rest of the meeting: he was sure it would continue late into the night.

He needed to get down to work immediately.

17

It was impossible for Ferrara to get to sleep that night. He was unable to shake off the terrible images that had shocked Florence over the past three months.

He looked at the digital clock on the bedside table. It was 1.46 a.m. and there was no chance he would fall asleep now.

The bedside lamp was still on. He looked tenderly at Petra, who was fast asleep, her blonde hair spread across the pillow and her mouth slightly open. He switched off the lamp, got up and went into the living room, a fairly large room split into two. On one side were the sofas, the armchairs and a desk, at which he sometimes spent entire nights working. On the other, a long, narrow eighteenth-century table, which served as a surface for his work when necessary.

He sat down at the desk, opened the drawer and took out a file. The first document in it was the letter Leonardo Berghoff had written to him shortly before his death.

In the past few days he had re-read it several times in search of some meaning hidden between the lines. Now, though, he realised this letter was a problem in itself. The fact that he had kept it to himself, without informing the Prosecutor's Department, could cost him dearly.

How could he justify his conduct to his superiors? How could he explain that he had not followed up on the letter? Would they hold him morally responsible for the double murder as a consequence?

No, he reassured himself. But he was far from certain, given how little he trusted certain people in the Prosecutor's Department.

Leonardo Berghoff had met his end the previous month, on 5 July at Marienbrücke in Bavaria. On the same wooden suspension bridge over the river where Ludwig II had often gone at night to gaze at the castle of Neuschwanstein illuminated by hundreds and hundreds of candles. At the same spot, Ferrara had been wounded in the left shoulder from a shot Berghoff had fired at him before being killed. A sniper, hidden in the vegetation on the other side of the bridge, had killed Berghoff before he could fire at Ferrara again, and had then disappeared into the darkness of the mountains without leaving a single trace.

He re-read the letter.

In it, Berghoff explained the reason for the vendetta he had planned against the man who had wronged him: Alvise Innocenti, his natural father, who had abandoned him immediately after his birth. A plan so diabolical, he had had to wait many years to carry it out.

Ferrara lingered over the last part:

A group which has been hindering your every move from behind the scenes, and which could take drastic action against you if its secrecy were to be endangered. I don't know the leaders, but I know for certain that they represent the blackest evil.

But I will give you two names connected to them, though in different ways. One is that officer of yours they call Serpico. The other is former senator Enrico Costanza, who has the rank of prince and who has now reached the end of the line because of the cancer that's killing him. He's my godfather. It was he who introduced me into the secret world of the hooded men and the black rose. It was also he who ordered the murder of Madalena

*after she had seen him with his face uncovered during a
ceremony. But it's all too complex to explain in detail. I'll only
tell you that they intend to destroy the Bartolotti family, which
is why the killing was carried out on their property. A word of
advice: look into the past of that family and leave the Black
Rose alone. It will never die.*

Farewell!

Leonardo Berghoff

It will never die.

Had the lodge been hindering him from behind the scenes? If
so, why?

Having killed Leonardo Berghoff, had the Black Rose really
decided to eliminate his godfather, Enrico Costanza, to punish
him for allowing his face to be seen by Madalena and putting
them all in danger?

Suddenly he remembered the words of Angelo Duranti, who
had been the Commissioner when he first came to Florence, and
with whom he had struck up a close friendship: *Be careful, Chief
Superintendent. In this city, if you put your finger in shit, you'll usually end up with your hands full of it.*

And he had not been mistaken. ·

Florence was a city with two faces, as he had discovered to his
cost. A city where hidden powers, deviant lodges, worked secretly.
As this letter seemed to prove.

As he sat at his desk, the question that had been nagging away
at him for several hours came back: Could he and his men have
prevented this double murder? His answer was a decisive one:
No!

Recovering from his wound far from Florence, in Germany,
had prevented him from carrying out the necessary investigations
in person. But Rizzo had done so in his place. They had talked
about it that very morning in front of Costanza's villa.

He knew he would have to inform the Prosecutor about the

letter, although he wasn't sure how. For the moment, he told himself, he had to concentrate on its contents. Somewhere in those lines, he might be able to find a motive for the murder of Enrico Costanza. Then, and only then, would he decide how to inform the Prosecutor's Department.

The letter, written by Berghoff shortly before he died, could be a genuine piece of evidence, the key to everything. It was of primary importance to look into the victim's life to discover its secrets, its hidden aspects.

They would also need to clarify the exact role of Inspector Sergi, known as Serpico, who was one of Ferrara's best men, a man who had even saved his life.

He remembered the raid a few years earlier on a small house in Montecatini Alto used by a dangerous gang of Albanian drug traffickers. With a shove in the back, Sergi had thrown him to the floor and the shot fired by the leader of the gang had grazed the officer behind him. The criminal had then been killed by a perfectly timed burst of submachine gunfire by Serpico.

Could he really be a mole in the service of the Black Rose? A traitor? A corrupt cop? Could he, Ferrara, who prided himself on knowing his colleagues, have been wrong about him all these years?

It suddenly occurred to him that Sergi hadn't called him once during the day. That was strange, not like him at all.

Where had he gone for his leave?

He got up from the desk and went back to bed, taking care not to disturb Petra's sleep.

It was now 3.32 a.m. by the clock on the bedside table.

He couldn't move.

He was defenceless, watching the figure approach him from the distance. Gradually, as the figure came closer, its features became more and more distinct. It was wearing men's clothes and towered above him. When it was just a few steps away, he was able to make out its face. It was anonymous. No distinguishing features. Nothing. Suddenly it burst into loud laughter.

Then the figure came even closer and opened one of its hands, revealing a long, sharp knife. Terrified, he watched the knife glimmer in the light of the lamp on the bedside table. Then he saw it come down towards him and into his eyes . . .

His cry woke Petra.

'*Schatzi*, darling . . . ' she said, shaking him gently.

Tossing and turning in the bed, he struggled to return to reality. At last, still terrified, he opened his eyes.

Petra's voice had inserted itself into a lake of blood.

He saw her.

'What happened?' he asked her.

'Nothing, Michele,' she replied, stroking his clammy cheek with her hand. 'You were delirious, that's all. You were flailing around. I'd hoped the nightmares were over . . . ' She held him tight in her arms, whispering, 'It's time to let go, you can't carry on like this.' It was not the first time recently that she had asked him to make that decision. 'You were also talking in your sleep, *Schatzi*.'

'What was I saying?'

'I didn't understand any of it, it was just disjointed words. But your voice was sad.'

They got out of bed, and he went straight to the bathroom – a hot shower would do him the world of good – while Petra headed to the kitchen to prepare breakfast.

A new day had started.

PART TWO

IN THE DARK

18

Monday 30 August

She opened her eyes and looked towards the window.

Pitch black.

The luminous figures on the face of the digital clock on the bedside table said 5:46. She passed her hand over her forehead. It was damp with sweat, as was the pillow. She had been delirious all night, tormented by recurrent nightmares, recalling the words her parents exchanged after a kiss on the lips as her father left home each morning, always at the same time.

Be careful, darling!

Don't worry!

As a teenager, she had watched them tenderly, clutching her school satchel in her hand. She had already realised that her father's work was quite risky, and a bit more complicated than the way they had described it to her: 'Daddy makes sure the bad people stop doing bad things.'

She remembered the day she had got home from school – unusually, a family friend had come to collect her – and heard the news. In the living room she had found a man in uniform with lots of stripes on the jacket and her mother in tears. She had thrown herself into her mother's arms and hugged her tight and cried. She had cried a lot. Her father had been killed by some of those 'bad people' in a shootout near the Galleria Vittorio Emanuele in Milan, the city where they lived. Later, she had seen her father's photograph on television, the one from his ID, which she had sometimes held in her hand. In an emotional voice, the newsreader had announced his name, his age and his rank: police marshal, one of the old ranks from before the shake-up. That day she had sworn to herself that her father would be her model. That was why she had chosen to join the police.

Now Teresa lay in the dark, waiting for the dawn.

When a faint light started to filter through the curtains, she decided to get up. She walked wearily to the bathroom and looked at herself in the mirror. She wasn't at all happy with her appearance. Her eyes seemed to have shrunk, and there were circles round them. She turned her head sideways and saw the marks from the pillow on her face. She sighed, climbed into the shower and turned on the tap. She shivered at the first jet of cold water, but that only lasted a couple of seconds.

When she came out and saw her reflection again, it seemed to her that she was looking better already.

She wrapped herself in her bathrobe and went into the kitchen, furnished unremarkably, like the rest of her two-room apartment. In the corridor, Mimì, her black and grey tabby cat with eyes as big as coins, jumped down from a chair and followed her, meowing. She had brought the cat with her from her mother's house just a few days earlier, when she had found this apartment in the Piazza del Mercato Centrale and moved out of her room at the police barracks. Ten years earlier, Teresa had saved Mimì's life, pulling her out of a dustbin in the neighbourhood where she lived. And the cat had immediately become attached to her, like a faithful friend.

She put her Neapolitan coffee pot on the gas, all the while thinking of the image of Enrico Costanza's body in the bathtub. She poured some kibble into a plastic bowl. 'Look how thin you are, eat up!' she said to Mimì, stroking her little head.

She leant against the sink while she waited for her coffee to be ready. It seemed to be taking for ever to come to the boil. She needed to drink at least two cups straight away in order to feel ready to face the day. She was sure it was going to be a tough one.

Eventually she heard the coffee bubbling. She inhaled the pleasant aroma as it spread through the air. She looked at the wall clock. It was seven on the dot: still early. She decided she'd do a bit of shopping. The fridge was half empty.

She put on jeans and a white T-shirt and went out.

The only thing on her mind now was that she had to tell Ferrara what she had discovered working on the material taken from the villa.

She crossed the Piazza del Mercato Centrale, walked up the few steps, and went in through the door on the right-hand side.

Almost all the stall-holders were finishing arranging their wares on their stalls. You could buy meat, fish, fruit and vegetables at more reasonable prices here than in the shops. And everything was top quality, sourced not just from Tuscany but in other Italian regions too.

The hustle and bustle was constant. Most of the people who shopped here refused to patronise the new supermarkets or big shopping centres. Many had grown fond of this nineteenth-century covered market. Although, to tell the truth, some of the produce that had been appearing on the stalls recently was anything but local.

This morning Teresa made a quick round of the stalls. She was early, but she wanted to get to the office as soon as possible. She bought the absolute minimum: milk, Tuscan ham, turkey breast and some fresh fruit. She left with her hands full of plastic bags.

She was only just outside when she heard shouting and saw a tall, solid-looking man running after a young girl. From her clothes – a long, loose skirt, a multicoloured low-cut top, sandals on her feet and a shawl around her waist – Teresa guessed she was a gypsy. She couldn't have been more than thirteen or fourteen. After a hundred yards or so, the man gave up the chase, and when he turned back Teresa recognised him. He was a fruiterer whose stall she had often frequented. A good person, always friendly, smiling, and well turned-out. Now, with his check shirt hanging out of his trousers, sweating profusely, and especially with that angry look in his eyes, he seemed like a different person.

'What happened?' Teresa asked, going up to him.

'I'd only just opened up when that girl came and stole a bunch of bananas,' he replied, and even his voice sounded different. 'It happens all the time. I can't take it any more. Should I be running after people at my age? What are things coming to in this city? I can't stand it any more, and I'm not the only one. If it carries on like this, we'll have to shut down!'

'Please calm down,' Teresa said. 'I'll call 113 for a patrol car.'

'No, don't bother, it's no use. They couldn't do anything, even if they caught her. The law is on the criminals' side now. And the police have more important things to do at the moment. You just have to read *La Nazione*, don't you?'

Teresa preferred not to reply.

She headed back to her apartment building, thinking that the man had a point.

19

7.30 a.m. Police Headquarters

Ferrara was already in his office.

At Petra's insistence, he had put a few drops in his reddened eyes before leaving the house.

Enjoying the morning hush, he read the newspapers, the reports by the various patrols, the details of responses to 113 calls, the telexes received from the Ministry and from other Headquarters.

It had been a quiet night.

There were only two detainees in the cells, two Albanians without the right residence permits, who had been caught in the act stealing petrol from a self-service garage in the Via Pisana. They would be taken to court later to be fast-tracked through the system.

This morning, he and his men would be concentrating on the double murder in Fiesole.

The name Enrico Costanza and the savagery of his killer were all over the front pages of the papers, along with photographs of the villa and of the victim when younger, and a brief biography. There were further articles and commentary on the inside pages. Ferrara noted with relief that they had avoided any particularly awkward details.

Basically, they all reported that the crimes had been commit-ted in the dead of night, that the victims had been shot, and that nothing was yet known about the killer, except that he had acted with unusual barbarity.

Each journalist then set out his own theory. *If only one of them was reliable*, Ferrara thought. *What wouldn't they come up with to sell a single extra copy?*

Costanza was described variously as a 'highly respectable figure' and as 'a man always eager to help'. They all agreed that his death was 'a great loss' to the city.

Ferrara lingered in particular over the articles in *La Nazione*. The headline here was EX-SENATOR ENRICO COSTANZA EXECUTED IN HIS VILLA.

Beneath a photograph of the victim was the caption *Enrico Costanza, the prince who will be missed by Florence.*

The prince? Ferrara thought. *Did that mean there was a king above him?*

Even here, though, there were no awkward details, just a great deal of discretion.

Ferrara wondered why the journalists were still maintaining a low profile. Surely the regulars would soon be hanging around the corridors, peering into offices whose doors had been left open, even if only to catch a glimpse of the expressions on the detec-tives' faces.

Bloodhounds on the hunt for a scoop.

He was particularly struck by the comment by the news editor, a bright young man who was making a name for himself. So far this year, he pointed out, there had been twelve murders in Florence. It was a lot, more than the nine that had occurred in the whole of the previous year. All were unsolved, except those com-mitted by Leonardo Berghoff.

There was no reference to murders involving non-EU immi-grants. These cases were particularly hard to solve. The victims were found in back alleys, on the pavements of streets on the outskirts of the city, sometimes even in squares in the historic centre. They were either completely unknown and unidentified, or at best were known drug dealers who lived their lives in the shadows.

Murders committed by the Mafia were a whole other story. Here, once the victim had been identified, it was possible to follow the trail back to the killer.

These were all different worlds, very distinct one from the other, and they required different methods of investigation.

As Ferrara was staring at the papers, Teresa came to his door. 'Sorry to disturb you, chief.'

'You're not disturbing me at all. Come in, sit down.'

Ferrara noticed that she was carrying a diary and a notebook in one hand and a videocassette in the other. It was this on which his eyes came to rest as she approached. 'Anything new, Teresa?'

'Yes.'

A glimmer of light, he hoped.

At first all that could be seen were black and white dots.

Then the screen filled with colour.

A man's dark suit, lying on a floor.

It was the scene of the crime, beyond a shadow of a doubt.

Then a shirt, then a tie. And at last, the victim. He had been filmed sitting in the Jacuzzi with his head to one side: the exact same position in which he had been found.

Ferrara felt his stomach contract into a knot.

More black and white dots followed.

'Is that it?' Ferrara asked impatiently. In his head, he was already formulating a number of hypotheses.

'No, chief. Wait a bit longer and you'll see.'

After a couple of moments, the black and white dots were replaced by a figure, filmed from the waist up, sitting behind the huge desk in Costanza's study. The face was hidden behind a dark-coloured balaclava. His top, perhaps part of a tracksuit, was also dark.

Ferrara threw a questioning glance at Teresa, who said, 'Get ready . . . '

And then they heard the voice.

'This was just the beginning. You won't stop me, you should know that. Today, 24 August 2004, I have put just one piece of the jigsaw in place. The first. You will hear from me again soon. And when you think of me, just call me Genius. So long.'

The whole message had taken thirty-two seconds. The tone was artificial, the words articulated slowly and clearly as if to hide the sound of a sneer.

Ferrara tried to imagine that figure at the scene of the crime, after the killings. The killer was so sure of himself, he was making fun of them. More than that, he was challenging them, telling them that he was cleverer than they were and that there would be further murders.

You will hear from me again soon.

When?

You won't stop me.

Why was he so sure he would get away with it?

Genius!

Why choose that name?

The black and white spots had now reappeared on the screen, but Ferrara paid no attention to them.

'Do you want to see it again, chief?' Teresa asked, interrupting the flow of his thoughts.

'I want to hear the words again.'

Teresa rewound the tape, then pressed PLAY. This time, Ferrara noted the words down on a piece of A4 paper from the printer.

They were dealing with a madman, he thought, when Teresa pressed the STOP button. A madman who thought he was unbeatable. Just like a serial killer. In this case, a serial killer who had planned everything and was ready to strike again in accordance with a specific programme.

One serial killer? Or two?

Ferrara re-read the words and considered the possibility of a serial killer with a split personality: normal on the outside, but basically violent and destructive.

But which of the five categories of split-personality serial killers did he fit?

The Visionary? Had he carried out the murders after hearing voices or having a vision? It didn't seem so.

The Missionary? Had he felt compelled to accomplish a mission to cleanse the world of people he considered the dregs of society, like prostitutes and tramps? Maybe. If that was the case, he must consider deviant Masonic activity the 'dregs'.

The Thrill Killer? Had he killed for the pleasure that the act gave him? Was it a kind of emotional orgasm, the way gamblers got turned on waiting for the hand to be revealed? Maybe.

The Control Freak? Had he killed to exercise his own power over the lives and deaths of his victims? Possibly.

The Lust Killer? Had he killed to obtain a purely sexual satisfaction? No, that was one they could rule out.

And what role did the Black Rose play in all this? From what he knew so far, maybe none at all. It could just be a coincidence.

The thought that the murders of Costanza and his butler were unconnected to the Black Rose almost revived his spirits.

But the room was like ice, and the voice of 'Genius' seemed to echo endlessly between the walls.

A few minutes had passed. Ferrara's instinct, which he trusted implicitly, told him he had to get back in control of the situation.

'Did you find anything else, Teresa?'

'I think so, chief.'

'Go on.'

She summarised what she had ascertained so far in examining the material that had been taken. In particular, the entry in

Costanza's diary for 20 August 2004, which she handed to Ferrara.

> 11.15 p.m. I met him today and he told me everything
> was under control. But he doesn't want to expose himself
> any further. Idiot!!!

The last word was underlined.

Ferrara made a note of these sentences too. They might constitute a clue.

There was a brief pause, during which he could not help linking this diary entry to Serpico, then he immediately hoped he was wrong.

'Anything else?' he asked Teresa Micalizi.

She opened the notebook she had put down in front of her – the kind typically sold by Florentine stationers, with a leather cover and gold lettering – and leafed through it. 'I've transcribed the names and telephone numbers from the diary, and also those from various scraps of paper and on business cards. There are several foreign ones, mostly English.'

'Good. Do some more research on the people named, and put in a request to Interpol for information on the foreign nationals. After that, we'll decide how to proceed.'

'OK, chief.'

'Thanks, Teresa. Carry on with your work. We might find the motive somewhere in Costanza's papers.'

Teresa left the office, determined to watch the video again, alone this time. She had a hunch, and she wanted to follow it up.

20

9.07 a.m. Ministry of the Interior, Viminale Palace, Rome

Sitting in a small armchair in the second-floor waiting room, Adinolfi re-read his memo for the umpteenth time. The result of meticulous work, it ran to seven pages. He had tried to find the most appropriate words, the style most befitting of the recipient. It had kept him busy all week and had forced him to resort to further painkillers.

His usual headache had kicked in as soon as he had woken up.

Dressed in a dark blue suit, a white shirt, a blue tie with light polka dots and black shoes, he had left Florence at five in the morning in order to be punctual. He had told the driver they absolutely had to reach Rome by eight, and that he would have him transferred if they didn't. It hadn't been a genuine threat, but the possibility had been enough for the young driver to put his foot down more than he might have done otherwise.

During the journey, Adinolfi had read the copy of *La Nazione* he had picked up at the news stand near Santa Maria Novella station, the only place where you could get the city's daily paper at that hour of the morning. What he had read had made him more than a little nervous.

The fact was, he wasn't worried about criminals in general. He didn't really care about fraudsters or corrupt politicians, or even tax evaders. He understood how people got involved in that kind of thing. He was even fairly indifferent to organised crime: after all, they settled their scores among themselves. The ones who really made him angry were the violent ones: the rapists and the muggers. And the small-time crooks, the pickpockets and bag snatchers who bothered tourists in the historic centre. That was the kind of thing that left the victims traumatised, especially if they were elderly, that spoilt the city, turned its streets into a jungle and its homes into prisons, aroused feelings of insecurity and damaged Florence's image. He was convinced that sentences had to be tougher and, most of all, that they should be fixed.

For now, though, there was a high profile victim and a truly horrible crime, and his men didn't have much time to shed light on it.

Having finished the newspaper, he had sat back in his seat with his eyes half closed, trying to hold back the anger eating away at him.

Even though he had arrived on time, it was now after nine and the Head of the State Police still seemed in no hurry to receive him.

'He's busy on the phone to the Minister,' his personal secretary had explained on his arrival, motioning him into this waiting room, where the smell of furniture polish was overpowering. To make matters worse, the only window was closed.

At last, at 9.45, he was given the green light.

The Big Chief's door opened wide.

'Have you brought the memo I asked for?'

Armando Guaschelli, the Head of the State Police, did not even give him time to come in. Nor had he got up to shake his hand, just looked up distractedly from his paperwork.

'Yes, sir,' Adinolfi replied. Still standing, he opened his folder, took out the memo and handed it to him.

Guaschelli began reading it immediately, his gaunt, pallid face – a chain-smoker's face, as his nicotine-stained yellow fingers confirmed – betraying no hint of emotion. When he had finished, he put the pages to one side. 'I need to be kept up to date with all the latest developments. I don't want to be left exposed, not when the Minister is so worried. And, above all, a word to the wise: I think what we need is a crackdown. There are people in positions of power who ought to be transferred.'

Adinolfi nodded several times, hoping that this last comment did not refer to him.

'Don't worry, sir,' he reassured him. 'You'll be informed of everything immediately.'

'Good. Now, go back to Florence and don't breathe a word to anyone, not even your prefect, about the crackdown. Do you understand?'

'Absolutely, sir. You can count on me. I'll be as silent as the grave.'

Guaschelli stood up and offered Adinolfi his hand. As so often before, Adinolfi wondered how on earth they'd let him join the police. The man was a dwarf!

But he was perfectly well aware of the rumours circulating about Guaschelli, and not just in the corridors of the Ministry. Right from the start, he had been thought to have friends in high places and to be destined for a successful career, which was exactly what had come to pass.

His path had been smoothed even more by the way he had personally handled criminals who turned State's evidence, of whom there had been an increasing number since the beginning of the nineties.

On the one hand, their testimonies had provided certain police officers with major successes; on the other, it had caused the fall from grace of a number of important political figures, but nobody had ever questioned what these criminals' true motives were. Was it just a tactic to avoid prison or were they settling accounts with their enemies? Clearly, their intentions were not entirely honourable.

Guaschelli could not have cared less. He was only concerned with making arrests, capturing fugitives and, above all, getting his name into the papers.

What he craved was success at any cost. And now, as Head of the State Police, he enjoyed a salary of over five hundred thousand euros a year, in addition to the use of a service apartment and other benefits. He was the best paid major police official in the world, earning more than the director of the FBI and the head of Scotland Yard! A slap in the face to all those public servants who struggled to make it to the end of the month on their salaries. And to those police officers who had not been paid the overtime due to them.

21

The last images from the dream vanished.

It had been a lovely dream, much nicer than those she had had in the past few days.

Those nightmare days, when she had woken up between those four walls and told herself yet again that she would never know true affection, were over.

She opened her eyes, turned onto her side, and in the half-light saw someone watching her from the doorway.

'Good morning, darling.'

'Angelica, you scared me.'

'I didn't want to disturb you. You were sleeping like an angel.'

'How long have you been watching me?'

'A couple of minutes.'

Guendalina stretched. 'What time did you get back last night? I didn't hear you.'

'I was trying not to wake you.'

'What time was that?'

'Maybe about one, quarter past one.'

'Where were you?'

'At dinner with the friends I'm organising a charity art exhibition with.'

The suspicion that Angelica was not telling the truth, as they had promised each other they would, suddenly crossed

Guendalina's mind. Friends? Charity? Why wouldn't she say more than that? She knew little enough about her anyway: only that, apart from her job as a social worker, her main interest was painting, especially landscapes and still lifes.

She looked at Angelica for a while, trying to conceal her disappointment, then asked, 'So where are you going to hold this exhibition?'

'We haven't made up our minds yet whether to do it in an art gallery or in the main hall of a bank. But don't worry, I'll take you along.'

Guendalina merely said, 'Thanks,' got up from the bed, turned and went into the bathroom.

The only thing to break the strained silence that followed that 'Thanks' was the noise of running water.

Outside, the sun shone down on the countryside, illuminating the chestnut, oak and ash trees and the green lawns.

It was still hot and close. And there were irritating swarms of insects everywhere.

Nice and snug in the corner of the house where he spent his best hours, he had just checked the main news on teletext.

TERRIBLE DOUBLE MURDER IN FLORENCE. What a pleasure it was to read such headlines!

He switched off the TV and fired up his laptop. He wanted to do some research. He typed *Enrico Costanza* into Google News and found lots of links to newspapers' websites. He read everything carefully, realising that all the articles featured the same photograph, a portrait of a much younger Enrico Costanza, looking in good shape with a dazzling smile.

After a while, a certain name caught his attention.

Teresa Micalizi.

First female superintendent in Florence involved in brutal murder case, a sub-heading read.

Google came up with only two items relating to Teresa

Micalizi. Both had a picture and referred to a narcotics operation which had taken place some months before she joined the *Squadra Mobile*, as a result of which a ring of drug dealers had been broken up.

Interesting, he thought. This policewoman must play an important role.

Then he clicked on *Images* and found two hits. It was the same photograph, a close-up featured in two local newspapers.

He frowned. He would have liked to see all of her.

He continued with his research but didn't find anything else.

'You'll be getting a surprise very soon, beautiful,' he murmured.

He abruptly shut down the computer, picked up a bottle of whisky, filled a glass, took a long swig, and before long slid into a black hole.

At the bottom of it was his whole damn life. Year by year. Each one carved into his memory and still intact.

He saw that same dark, icy room, felt a fat man's sweaty hand slip inside his trousers and fondle his genitalia.

Again and again.

He heard the threats: Don't say anything, don't tell anyone.

He felt the pain on his back as the leather belt kept striking him.

That feeling of inferiority that day by day had isolated him from his peers.

He saw himself in the bathroom, masturbating in front of a pornographic magazine.

His eyes had turned flame-red. There was so much anger in him, so much hatred, so much evil!

He abruptly poured himself another half-glass of Scotch and downed it in one.

This was a part of his secret past, his violated childhood, a knife-blade lodged permanently in his heart. This was his life blood.

This was what had long ago turned him into a killer.

The evil had penetrated his flesh, so deeply as to become part of his essence.

When he came back to the present, he squeezed his temples between his hands, rubbed his eyes, switched off the lamp and went out into the daylight.

It had once been a convent.

Situated between Dicomano and San Godenzo, it stood in the midst of the Mugello countryside, a broad belt of hills and mountains sloping down to the plain across which the river Sieve flowed.

It was a stone building with more than three thousand square feet of floor space on two levels. There was an artificial lake a short distance away, which was used to irrigate the spacious garden.

He had spent his childhood and adolescence in this magical but cursed place. Then, at eighteen, he had moved to France.

Letting his gaze wander about, he took a series of breaths, each deeper than the last.

It was so peaceful! Whenever he came here, he would forget the pleasure of losing himself in the hustle and bustle of city streets. He would even forget the elegant apartment buildings of Paris, the majestic Eiffel Tower, which guided him as he walked along the streets of the City of Lights.

Just hills and mountains.

He took a path that led to a wooden stall with a broad lean-to roof. He had once kept a horse here, a faithful companion with which he had spent a lot of time.

For a while, he pictured it as it ate its fodder and he stroked its long black mane and whispered in its ear, 'We'll go for a nice gallop later, you wait and see.'

Then he took out his phone and wrote a text message.

Just two words:

I'm waiting.

22

What was that?

Teresa thought she had seen a slight flicker among the black and white dots on the screen.

She was in the room reserved for hearing and viewing audio and visual recordings. In the centre was a rectangular table with a couple of workstations, personal computers, monitors, video and DVD players and other apparatus whose function she was not yet sure of. On one wall was a large screen.

She wanted to watch the video again, several times if necessary, with the utmost concentration and in complete silence.

And now, even before the images had appeared, something had caught her attention, a detail that had escaped her before, perhaps because she had only been concentrating on the figures. For a few moments, she stopped to think. Then she turned the video player off, took out the cassette, and got to her feet. She had to go and see Ferrara again.

He was with Rizzo, who had just got back from the Prosecutor's Department, where he had received the warrant to search and empty Costanza's safe-deposit box at the Florentine Savings Bank.

Ferrara and Rizzo had just decided to give priority to Costanza's bank details, and were debating the best way to get hold of them quickly, that same day if possible.

'Francesco,' Ferrara was telling Rizzo, 'make sure you check the deposits and withdrawals for the last few months, and make a note of any irregularities. It's best you go now. The sooner, the better.'

When he saw Teresa with the video in her hand and obvious excitement on her face, he gave her a questioning look, as if he had guessed that there was something new.

'Sorry to interrupt, chief,' she said. 'You've got to watch this again.'

And, without waiting for a reply, she switched on the television, picked up the remote and pressed the PLAY button.

Ferrara folded his arms and concentrated on the screen.

'What does that look like to you?' Teresa asked, after playing the video forwards and backwards a few times.

'We need to talk to Gianni Fuschi,' Ferrara said. 'He might be able to give us an explanation.' He picked up the phone and dialled Fuschi's number at the Tuscan Regional Forensics Centre.

He briefly explained to him the strange effect on the video, imagining Fuschi in his white coat, hard at work on the samples they had taken from Costanza's villa.

'You're splitting hairs as usual, Michele.'

Ferrara wanted to tell him that this time it was Teresa who was splitting hairs, but he restrained himself. Instead, he said in a grave voice, 'Forget about that now, Gianni, I need you to give me a hand. Can you ring your Rome office? It's urgent.'

'If you want a quick answer, there's another way to get it.'

'What's that?'

'Rome can be pretty slow, as you know, with all the work they have, all the requests they get from different parts of Italy, and you're telling me this is really urgent.'

'So what do you suggest?'

'Consult one of the external experts the Prosecutor's Department uses. They're serious and they're discreet.'

'Can you give me a name?'

'You need to talk to your colleague in Special Ops. He'll be sure to know a reliable person. Actually, I know for a fact that he does, but don't tell him it was me who suggested it.'

'Thanks a lot, Gianni – I'll talk to you later.'

Having hung up, Ferrara told Teresa to go straight to Special Ops. In his heart of hearts, he had little hope of a positive outcome. He knew that Special Ops were tight-lipped at the best of times, reluctant to share their information with others. And when they had to collaborate, they were more than a little suspicious. In other words, they had their own way of working, rather like the Secret Service.

Teresa was just leaving the room when she remembered Officer Alessandra Belli's request. She told Ferrara about it.

His reaction was one of puzzlement. 'You want to involve an officer who's still wet behind the ears in a double murder case? Are you sure she can be of any help? I think she still needs to put in some time on the beat.'

'She has the enthusiasm of the young,' Teresa replied. 'She can help me out in the office and do research in records. I asked the head of the Auto Unit about her and they say she's very meticulous and always willing to help.'

Just like you, Ferrara thought.

'Teresa,' he said, 'enthusiasm isn't enough in our job, but I'll ask the Commissioner to second her to us for a month. Is that long enough to try her out?'

'Yes.'

'Fine, I'll let you know. For now, good luck.'

Teresa smiled. She was going to need it.

23

The Special Ops team occupied a separate wing on the third floor. They mainly dealt with terrorism and cases of a politically sensitive nature.

Teresa was sceptical. But she was wrong.

She was received by Giuseppe Barba, the director, a massive man, his physique even more impressive when you heard his delicate, almost girlish voice. He did not even ask her why she needed a reliable expert, but he could tell from her anxious look that it was urgent. He took a pen and a piece of paper and wrote down the name and address of the person he normally used.

'He's young and extremely discreet. He wanted to be a police officer, but failed the medical. He was about an inch short of the required height.'

'Only an inch?' Teresa said, amazed.

'That's all. Obviously the examining board was very strict that year.'

'Or perhaps he just didn't know the right people.'

Barba nodded. 'That's a possibility.'

'Can you phone him to let him know I'm coming?'

'I'll do that right away.' He found the number in his diary, picked up the phone and rang the young expert. When he hung up, he smiled at Teresa. 'You can go right now, he's expecting you. You owe me a coffee.'

'I owe you more than that,' she said, returning the smile. She was just about to leave the room when Barba called her back.

'Yes?'

'I'd advise you not to turn up empty-handed.'

'What do you mean?'

'Take him something police-related. A gadget, a crest, something he might be interested in for his collection. He'll become your friend for life. He might even be more helpful.'

'I'll find something. Thanks for the tip.'

Teresa said goodbye and left, the piece of paper with the address clutched in her hand.

In her office, she memorised the address, rolled it into a ball and threw it at the waste paper basket. It hit its target perfectly.

Was it a good omen?

Ferrara picked up the piece of paper and re-read it, slowly, word by word.

The more he re-read it, the more convinced he became that the message did not just announce further crimes, but also contained a secret. They just had to find the key. Only by doing that would they be able to move the investigation forward.

Genius.

It wasn't just a challenge. What secret was he hiding behind that cryptic language? Was there or wasn't there a link with the Black Rose?

The ringing of the telephone interrupted his thoughts. It was the Operations Room, telling him that a bank had been robbed in Coverciano. Two criminals armed with large knives had threatened the staff and customers and emptied the safe.

'Anyone hurt?'

'No. Just an old lady who fainted, but I've already sent an ambulance to the scene.'

'What did they take?'

'The bank's carrying out an inventory, but it may only be a few thousand euros or so.'

'Were they in disguise?'

'Just cloth caps pulled low over their foreheads and dark glasses.'

After he had hung up, Ferrara turned up the volume on the radio that he kept next to the telephone, and followed the communications between the patrol cars pursuing the two robbers, who had apparently left the scene on a motorbike with false number plates. The cold-voiced officer in the Operations Room acted as go-between and continued to issue orders.

He could also hear the police helicopter preparing to go up.

'Poli 46 is ready for take-off,' the pilot informed the Operations Room.

Ferrara took his cigar case out of the inside pocket of his jacket. He put an antico toscano in his mouth and lit it. He took a long drag, then let the smoke spiral up towards the ceiling. He took a second drag before setting it down on the ash tray.

He took a piece of paper from the printer. The time had come to put his thoughts down in black and white. Just a few notes, but they might be useful to him subsequently. When he had finished, he turned his attention back to Costanza's diary.

11.15 p.m. I met him today and he told me everything was under control. But he doesn't want to expose himself any further. Idiot!!!

Unfortunately, he thought, time was a hard master. And he might not have much left.

Perhaps they had underestimated the importance of what Berghoff had said in his letter about Sergi's involvement.

But now the moment to take action had arrived.

First of all, he would have to check whether the inspector had been on duty on 20 August and, if so, what he had been doing.

Then he would instruct Rizzo how to proceed.

24

The main branch of the Florentine Savings Bank was in the city centre, right next to the Santa Maria Nuova Hospital.

At five minutes past eleven in the morning, after taking a moment to admire its beautiful sixteenth-century façade, Rizzo went in through the main door. There were two customers at the counters. At the first window, a young woman rocking a pushchair to send her child to sleep was waiting for the cashier to finish counting out her money. At the next one along, an old man leaning on a stick was complaining to an official about the ridiculous interest rates, which were barely enough to cover the annual fees he paid for the handling of his account. When this customer had moved away, muttering incomprehensibly to himself, Rizzo approached the official.

He was tall and thin as a rake, with white hair and glasses perched at the end of his pointed nose.

Rizzo introduced himself, showed his police badge, and explained the reason for his visit.

'Do you have a warrant?'

'Of course,' Rizzo replied, taking it from his pocket and handing it over. Deputy Prosecutor Luigi Vinci had not made any fuss about issuing it, but had advised him to tread carefully and let him know what happened immediately.

The official took the warrant and read it carefully. 'Do you really have to do this?' he asked.

'Yes, I do. I've got my orders and I have to follow them. And I don't have time to hang around.'

The official sighed. 'All right, but I'll have to inform my manager first. Please follow me.'

They went up to the first floor. The official asked Rizzo to wait for him outside the manager's office while he went in. After ten minutes or so, he came out again and asked Rizzo to follow him down to the vault. When he opened Costanza's safe-deposit box, Rizzo was baffled.

He had expected to find valuables, important documents, jewellery. Instead, there was nothing but a key. For another safe-deposit box.

'It's not one of ours,' the official immediately clarified.

'I'll have to take it away,' Rizzo said. 'I need to know when this box was accessed recently.'

'Within what kind of time frame?'

'Let's start with the last quarter.'

'All right. I'll check the records.'

From the records, it emerged that the last time Enrico Costanza had opened the box had been the previous week.

'Was anyone else authorised to access it?' Rizzo asked.

'No.'

'Please follow me to the office,' the official said once they had returned to the ground floor.

No sooner had they entered than Rizzo asked him for the statements of Costanza's withdrawals, deposits and transfers during the last quarter. This request also met with a certain resistance. The official explained that a specific search warrant was necessary: the other warrant had only referred to the safe-deposit box.

Unfazed, Rizzo took out a second warrant authorising him to

check all Costanza's accounts. 'Here you go,' he said, putting it on the desk.

The official read it then started typing on the keyboard of his computer.

Costanza had only one current account, with a balance of almost two hundred thousand euros. Rather a lot to keep in a current account, Rizzo thought. But maybe he wasn't all that bothered about not earning interest.

'What about withdrawals?' he asked.

'There are a lot of them. It's going to take a while to put them all together.'

'In that case, can you tell me the most recent ones?'

'The last one was a week ago. He withdrew fifty-five thousand euros.'

The same day the safe-deposit box had been opened. Surely too much of a coincidence.

'In cash or in a banker's draft?'

'In cash.'

'Could I speak to the cashier?'

'Certainly, I'll call her in.'

After a couple of minutes a very pretty and very tanned young woman no older than twenty-five entered the office.

'I've already explained the situation to my colleague,' the official told Rizzo.

Rizzo stood up and introduced himself. 'What can you tell me?' he asked.

'I remember that withdrawal. I knew the Senator, and I was surprised when he asked for such a large sum in cash. He wanted it all in five-hundred-euro notes.'

'Where did he put the money?'

'In a leather briefcase. I remember it well. I was amazed that the Senator would use such a shabby-looking case.' She clearly had a very good memory.

'Was he alone?'

'Yes.'

'Did you see whether anyone was waiting for him outside?'

'I couldn't see outside from where I was sitting.'

'Can you remember what time it was?'

'We'd only just opened.'

'Thank you, signorina.' Rizzo took a business card from his wallet and gave it to her. 'If you should remember any other details, please give me a call.' He turned to the official. 'When will the paperwork be ready?'

'In a couple of days.'

'Either I or someone else from the *Squadra Mobile* will be back the day after tomorrow.'

'All right. It'll be ready for you.'

'I'm sure it's not necessary to say this, but I must ask you to be totally discreet.'

The official and the cashier both nodded.

When Rizzo left the bank, he found himself buffeted by a hot wind: the sirocco. He stopped for a few moments, looked around, then walked in the direction of the Via Cavour. After about a hundred yards, he went into a bar. He ordered a glass of mineral water and a cold coffee, then gave in to the temptation of a chocolate croissant. He needed the energy. He still had a long day ahead of him and he would almost certainly skip lunch.

What safe-deposit box did that key open? he wondered. Above all, why had Costanza withdrawn so much cash on the same day? And where had that worn briefcase and its fifty-five thousand euros ended up?

He had been present throughout the search of the villa, and certainly couldn't remember their finding a case like that. Was it possible the killer had taken it with him?

And had it contained anything else apart from the money?

Immersed in his thoughts, Rizzo went back to his car, which was parked near Headquarters. And he realised that the surprises weren't over yet.

The ticket was for parking in a no-parking zone. Rizzo slid it out from under the windscreen wiper with a grimace of annoyance.

The traffic wardens really had it in for the police. The bastards!

He checked, and he had left the sign with *State Police* in plain view on the windscreen. Clearly the warden hadn't given a damn about that, even though he must have known he was increasing the nervous tension the police had been feeling for some time now.

Why were the wardens picking on them? Why were they so determined to fine private cars and motorbikes in the area around Headquarters?

Rizzo got in the car, started the engine and drove off.

Once in the office, he would write a report to explain that his decision to park there had been motivated by urgent police business. Then he would send it to the traffic wardens' head office along with the parking ticket, asking for it to be cancelled. He was certain the ticket would be quietly shelved.

25

The Isolotto district.

Once it had been all vegetable gardens and fields.

Then it had been taken over by workshops and majolica pottery factories. In the twentieth century, housing for the working classes had started to spring up: anonymous apartment buildings of little commercial value, just like those found on the outskirts of any other city. But they had the advantage of being close to the historic centre of Florence.

Almost all the apartments, even those on the higher floors, had sturdy iron bars over the windows to discourage burglars. But on the streets there were none of the pickpockets who infested the city centre, a constant threat to tourists. In fact, in this district, certain crimes were virtually unknown.

Fabio Biondi, the expert suggested by the head of Special Ops, lived in one of these small apartment buildings.

The driver parked near the left bank of the Arno, opposite the Parco delle Cascine, and Teresa got out.

'Wait for me here,' she said, looking around. The morning rush hour had been over for some time, and the street was half deserted. She immediately found Biondi's bell by the entryphone. When she pressed it a man's voice said, 'Third floor'. After a few moments, she heard the click of the lock turning and the front door opened.

On reaching the third floor, she found that there was only one apartment on the landing. Although the door was ajar, she rang the bell anyway. On the doormat in front of the door, which looked very dusty, as if it had not been beaten for some time, there was a drawing of a dog.

After a few moments, a man appeared in the doorway. He was thin, with closely cropped reddish hair and a freckled face. At first sight, he could have been taken for a teenager but, looking at him more closely, Teresa saw the lines on his face, especially under the eyes, and realised he must be older than he seemed.

'Signor Fabio Biondi?' she asked.

The man smiled. 'Thanks for the "Signor", but Fabio's fine.'

She introduced herself and told him straight away that she was a colleague of Barba's.

'I know Barba well. He told me you'd be coming. I've been expecting you.'

She took a small package from her bag and held it out to him. 'This is for you. I hope you like it.'

He seemed dazed as he took the present, then he looked up and smiled as he opened the package. 'Wow!' he exclaimed when he discovered what was inside.

It was a miniature ceramic model of a policeman in uniform with his white helmet under his left arm, his cap on his head and an eye-catching white belt with a holster at his waist. Teresa had received it as a present from a colleague during her course at the Academy. She had looked after it carefully, keeping it in the display cabinet in her office, but she was prepared to give up her memento to obtain the help they needed.

'I've been missing this one. I've got the models of all the police and the Carabinieri, including the ones with the wooden bases and the logos of the different specialist branches. Thank you so much! I'm really grateful. But don't just stand there, take a seat.'

Teresa followed the man down the hall and into the first room on the right, next to the kitchen. She looked around. The place was in an unutterably chaotic state and everything was covered with a layer of dust. She wondered how long it had been since anyone had cleaned this apartment.

The room, probably intended as a living room, was kitted out like a genuine technical lab. The floor was a tangle of cables. Everywhere there was equipment whose function was a complete mystery to Teresa. On seeing it all, she wondered how much it had cost, what it was for, where he had got it from and, most of all, what money he had used to pay for it. Various screens and laptop computers on a long table were the only things she recognised.

'Welcome to my lair,' the man said. 'What can I do for you, Superintendent?'

Teresa looked around again, then explained why she had come and took the video out of her bag. The man pushed a chair towards her and got straight down to work.

The press conference took place in the large room on the second floor.

They had called all the media together to stop the reporters, who had so far been denied an official statement, from going on a hunt for confidential information, with the risk that they might harm the investigation.

It was just after one when Ferrara and the Deputy Commissioner entered the room. The chatter stopped at once.

Deputy Commissioner Carmelo Zichichi was filling in for Adinolfi, who was away. Zichichi was just a few months from retirement and was not at all unhappy at the prospect. He couldn't wait to devote himself full time to his hobby: photography.

He actually looked more like an artist than a high-ranking police officer. He was proud of his thick head of hair, even though it was now almost completely grey, and his long seventies-style sideburns. He smoked a pipe and often kept it in his mouth unlit, giving him the air of a thinker, even on those Sundays at the stadium when Fiorentina were playing and he was in charge of public order.

No sooner was he seated than he removed the microphone from its stand, cleared his throat and began speaking. He went straight to the point, promising the media and the citizens of Florence that the murders would not go unpunished.

'The investigators will be working non-stop to bring the person or persons responsible to justice,' he said, in a well-mannered if somewhat tense tone. 'Our colleagues from the SCO will soon be arriving from Rome and will work alongside the *Squadra Mobile*. There will be a combined effort to bring about a positive result within a reasonable time.'

Then he invited the journalists to ask Chief Superintendent Ferrara any questions they might have.

After the first fairly straightforward questions, which Ferrara had no difficulty answering, the cheap shot he had been expecting arrived. It came from a freelance newspaperman, a short, shabbily dressed character, getting on in years, who liked to pose as an investigative journalist. In local circles he also had the reputation of being a skinflint and a drunk. Among his colleagues there were also those who, if you spoke to them privately, would go so far as to describe him as a fraud who had passed other people's investigations off as his own.

'Ah, look, it's Presti as usual!' Ferrara said in a low voice when he saw him raise his arm.

'Chief Superintendent, I'd like you to tell me whether Florence can still be considered a safe city after all these horrific murders. The victims are very well-known individuals. Wouldn't you agree that your department is proving unequal to the task of providing the required degree of security to the public?'

Quite unfazed, Ferrara was about to respond when Zichichi put his hand on his arm to stop him.

'The Chief Superintendent is responsible for catching criminals once crimes have been committed,' he said in a firm voice.

'Crime prevention and public security are the responsibility of the Commissioner. In his absence, I can assure you that the city is safe. The crimes to which you refer were uncovered thanks to the activities of the *Squadra Mobile*, and this double murder will also be solved. This conference is now over. Thank you all for your participation.'

He stood up, picked up his pipe from the desk and put it in his mouth.

Voices could be heard from the back rows, and a murmur of protest spread through the room. There was the sound of chairs scraping the floor. Zichichi raised his arm to impose silence. A woman had got up and had to shout to be heard over the noise. 'Is it true that the Commissioner has been summoned to Rome by the Head of the State Police in connection with these murders?'

It struck Presti that it might be a good idea to phone and make an appointment with his old friend Guaschelli.

Without missing a beat, Zichichi removed his pipe from his mouth and said, 'The Commissioner is in Rome for a scheduled meeting.'

His words were met with a general muttering. Clearly it was not the answer they wanted, but nobody responded.

Then it was the turn of another journalist, who asked Ferrara whether the killer had had accomplices.

'We don't know,' Ferrara replied, 'but, should it prove necessary, we will consider the possibility. I have no further comment, as I'm bound by confidentiality. Please, no more questions.'

He stood up and followed Zichichi out of the room. He had things to do.

26

'Chief Superintendent Ferrara!'

Someone had called his name as he walked down the corridor on his way back to his office. He turned and saw a man in his early thirties with a thick black moustache and curly brown hair, about the same height as he was, approaching him and holding out his hand.

He was wearing a pale blue polo shirt with the top two buttons undone. He had a blue cotton jacket over his left arm and a gold earring in his left ear. How times had changed, Ferrara thought. The senior officers didn't take any notice of how their juniors dressed any more.

'I'm Inspector Guido Polito from the SCO. I've been sent here with my team to work with your department.'

Ferrara, who had already guessed who he was, shook his hand. He could see the respect in the younger man's eyes, and was sure he was aware of the importance of the investigation in which he was involved.

'Let's go to my office,' Ferrara said, walking a few steps ahead.

The first thing he did once they arrived was take off his jacket and tie. He couldn't stand them any more. They seemed to be suffocating him.

They stayed shut up in Ferrara's office for almost an hour, during which time Ferrara brought his new colleague up to speed, without lingering over the details. He needed a bit more time to get the measure of the man before he involved him in specific activities. It was not distrust, but a necessary sense of caution.

Before they said goodbye, he asked him if he had ever carried out a complex investigation. Guido Polito was honest enough to admit this was the first time he had had to tackle such a tangled case. Ferrara told him that he would get someone to take him to Costanza's villa the next day to show him the scene of the crime.

'That's where you need to start if you want to carry out a good investigation.'

The younger man nodded. He would have liked to ask Ferrara a few questions, but he realised that now was not the time.

Ferrara seemed to read his mind. 'We'll meet again to discuss any questions you might have. My secretary has reserved rooms for you in the nearby police residence.'

'Thank you very much, Chief Superintendent. I'll see you tomorrow.'

The inspector shook Ferrara's hand and left, convinced he had learned very little.

In fact, he had learned nothing at all.

Teresa had been watching Fabio for almost two hours, getting up from her chair from time to time to stretch her legs.

At last he turned. 'Here we are, come and have a look!'

Teresa went over to him.

'There's something right at the start,' he said, 'maybe traces of an earlier recording. I've extracted some of the images and digitised them.' With the confidence of a true professional, he entered a series of commands on the computer and pointed at one of the monitors. 'You can see something here. Come closer.'

Teresa moved so that her face was just a few inches from the image. It was quite blurry, and she had to stare at it for a long time before she had the impression that she could make something out.

'I can try and improve it,' Fabio said, noting the puzzled expression on Teresa's face, 'but that'll take quite a bit of work. Let me show you something a little clearer.' He rapidly typed in another command.

Her eyes widened. 'Hold on, that's . . .'

There was no doubt about it: it was a crucifix.

It seemed to be hanging on a wall, but upside down, like the one they had found at the scene of the murder of Madalena, the woman killed in the church at Sesto Fiorentino.

'Are there any more images?' Teresa asked after a long pause, aware that her heart was beating faster.

'Quite likely, but that's all I've managed to extract for the moment.'

'It's really urgent, Signor Fabio.'

'I told you to call me Fabio,' he corrected her with a wink.

'OK, Fabio.'

'Leave me the video and I'll let you know what I come up with in a couple of days' time. I hope it'll be something useful.'

'OK, Fabio. But make me a copy to take with me and I'll leave you the original. It's police property right now, but we have to give it to the Prosecutor's Department as soon as possible.'

Fabio immediately made the copy and gave it to her.

'Thanks!' she said. 'You've been very helpful. Try and get whatever you can out of that tape, but please, be as discreet as possible.'

'You needn't worry about my discretion. Didn't your colleague Barba tell you? I consider myself to be a police officer like you. They didn't want me because of one damn inch.'

'I know. And I'm sure they made a big mistake.'

He nodded several times.

'If I won't be disturbing you,' Teresa said, 'can I call you tomorrow for an update?'

'Of course. You police officers never disturb me. Let me give you my mobile number as well.'

Fabio wrote the number on a scrap of paper and gave it to her. Teresa folded it and put it in her wallet, behind her police ID.

Fabio walked her to the door and thanked her again for the amazing gift as they said goodbye. 'I'll take good care of it,' he said before closing the door.

Maybe there was a glimmer of light after all, Teresa thought as she walked downstairs.

27

He was slouched in the pale leather armchair, leafing through a hard-core magazine, looking at scenes of extreme sadism. The only kind that ever aroused him.

'Can I have a puff too?' Angelica asked him as she came into the room, indicating the grass on the glass table with a nod of her head.

'Of course you can, but be careful.'

'Why?'

'It's strong stuff.'

She rolled a bit of it in a cigarette paper, added some tobacco from a broken cigarette, took a match and lit it. She took a moderate drag and felt the smoke spread through her lungs and then fill her head. It was the best marijuana on the market at that time.

The air soon became saturated with its bittersweet aroma.

She stretched out on the sofa. She was starting to feel horny. She unbuttoned her jeans and slipped her right hand inside her knickers. She assumed that everything would be the way it always was: that, instead of leaping on her, he would stay where he was, smoking and flicking through his porn magazines.

'What the fuck are you doing?' he shouted at her after a while in an almost hysterical voice, by now highly aroused. 'Are you planning to make yourself come? Don't you realise how ill that makes me feel?'

He got up from the armchair and stood staring at her for a moment or two, then opened the flies of his trousers. At last, she thought, he's really turned on. It had happened before that smoking grass had made things a bit more relaxed between them.

The first thrusts were slow and controlled, then the pounding became almost angry. But they were still a long way from reaching orgasm, which was nothing new.

It wasn't easy for him.

There were other methods he could use, but not with her.

Never with her.

'What about your gun?'

'I don't have it with me.'

'Good. If you'll just wait a moment, I'll let my commander know.'

'Thank you.'

It was 2.45 in the afternoon and Ferrara was in the gatehouse of Sollicciano Prison, a complex with an unusual layout, inspired by the Florentine fleur-de-lis.

The car from the Headquarters pool had already been given a preliminary going over in the inner courtyard, as dictated by the Ministry's strict rules for all visitors, even police officers.

After a few minutes, a young guard came towards him. Ferrara noticed his massive build: he must spend several hours a day in the gym, he thought.

'If you'll follow me, Chief Superintendent,' the man said in a hoarse voice, 'I'll take you through.'

The driver stayed where he was, chatting with the sentry while he waited.

Ferrara and his escort entered the small block to their left, the women's section. They went through a series of gates and down a number of long corridors and stopped outside the interview room.

The guard's keys jangled as he opened it.

The white-walled room was very small, with a table, a couple of chairs and a small barred window. On the ceiling a fluorescent light, which probably needed replacing, gave out a weak buzzing sound.

They were obviously short of funds here too, Ferrara thought.

'Please take a seat, Chief Superintendent,' the guard, who had not said a single word during their walk, now said. 'I'll go and get the prisoner.'

'Thank you.'

After several minutes the door opened and Leonardo Berghoff's accomplice Beatrice Filangeri, who had been arrested for her role in Madalena's death, came in.

Little more than five feet tall, she seemed even thinner than when he had first met her two months before, and older than her thirty-five years. In that brief time, her physical appearance had been transformed. Perhaps it was just the effect being in prison could have, especially on someone who wasn't a repeat offender, which she wasn't: this was her first time here.

To avoid her getting away, compromising an investigation that was not yet complete, or re-offending, she was being held in preventive custody. It was highly likely she would be given a hefty sentence at her trial, maybe even life, unless her lawyer persuaded her to plead guilty in exchange for a fast-track procedure and a lighter sentence.

There was quite a bit of evidence against her, the most important piece of which was her being in possession of the murder weapon, the knife that had been used to kill Madalena, which had been found in her home during the search coordinated by Rizzo.

The guard who had brought her in left silently and closed the door behind him. Beatrice Filangeri came and sat down on the other side of the desk from Ferrara. Her eyes, which she kept fixed on the barred window, seemed calm and distant.

'Good afternoon, Signora Filangeri,' Ferrara said. 'Do you remember me?'

She merely shook her head.

'Do you want to get out of prison?'

No reply.

She looked down at her knees, where she had placed her folded hands as soon as she sat down. She was in the classic defensive position, typical of suspects during interrogation.

'The one condition is that you tell me about your friend Leonardo Berghoff, about the lodge and about Enrico Costanza, who, as I'm sure you already know, has been murdered. In return, we could put you in our witness protection programme.'

Ferrara had lowered his voice: he was sure the guard must have his ear glued to the door.

'Think about it, signora. If you don't cooperate, this prison will become your home for the next thirty years at least, if not for the rest of your life. Talk to me and I guarantee that anything you say will remain between these four walls.'

He waited, but no reply was forthcoming. From the vague look she gave him when she decided to raise her eyes for a brief moment, it almost seemed as if she had not been listening to him.

After a couple of minutes, Ferrara went on to explain the different levels of protection available, depending on the nature of the witness's cooperation: the highest level involved a new identity and relocation.

He stopped again and waited for her questions. They did not come.

After a while, Beatrice Filangeri shook her head, looked up again and said in a thin voice, 'You can go to hell, the lot of you. I'm not interested in all that crap. And anyway, I don't know any of the people you mentioned, and I don't know about any lodge. Just leave me alone.'

Ferrara tried to insist, but Beatrice Filangeri's mouth remained tightly shut.

Too bad, he thought. She didn't seem to understand that she could be in danger even here.

Abruptly he got to his feet. The interview was over. It had achieved nothing.

But at least he had tried.

28

5.05 p.m. Rome

'Just one night, is that right, sir?'

'Yes, one night,' the man replied.

He was at the reception desk of the Hotel Excelsior in the Via Veneto in Rome.

'Would you like to pay by card or in cash, sir?'

'Cash.'

The receptionist put the registration form and a pen on the counter and asked for an identity document. The man handed her his passport, then filled in the form and gave it back.

What a beautiful voice, he was thinking all the while, and what a gorgeous woman!

She gave him his key and explained how to find the lifts, his floor and the breakfast room.

He took the pink carnation from his buttonhole and gave it to her.

'Thank you!' she said with a smile, then went on to remind him that he would have to vacate his room by noon the next day.

'Of course,' he replied as he walked away.

He was planning to leave a lot earlier than midday.

*

When she woke up, Angelica found him still sitting in the same armchair.

She looked at her watch. It was just after six-thirty. Damn, she'd been asleep for ages.

He had dropped the magazine on the floor by the armchair and was now concentrating on cleaning the various parts of the semi-automatic pistol he had just dismantled, putting the pieces on a light-coloured cloth so as not to soil the heavy wooden coffee table.

Staring at the weapon, she picked up her jeans. 'What are you thinking of doing?' she asked.

He ignored her.

He had always been a man of few words and she knew how difficult it was to get inside his head. But she knew many of his secrets and was perfectly well aware that it wasn't a good idea to pester him with questions. Without another word, she went to the bathroom.

They had spent a lot of time together as teenagers.

They had been neighbours and had attended the same middle school in Vicchio del Mugello. Their classmates had nicknamed him 'the icicle', an epithet that suited him perfectly. He never seemed to feel any emotion, never reacted, either to affection or mockery. He was completely detached.

Then, at eighteen, he had moved to France under the auspices of a beautiful woman who was always elegant and impeccably turned out. From time to time he would come back to Mugello, to what had become his second home.

He was now thirty-six and had come a long way.

In Paris, he had moved in select circles, joined a bridge club and a tennis club, and become a regular at the Lido on the Champs-Elysées. At the bridge club, he had met a wealthy plastic surgeon who was always surrounded by attractive women. The doctor had been captivated by his intelligence and his skill at the game. They had soon become friends and had taken to spending more and more time together.

The surgeon had introduced him to his own circle, which was heavily involved in sadomasochism. He had been fascinated by it. Most of all, he had discovered that such techniques were able to arouse an excitement in him that he had never previously felt.

The very first time, in fact, he had experienced something he had been unable even to imagine until that day: he had had an erection. It was as if his small penis had suddenly awoken from a long sleep. The discovery made him more daring, made him take things to extremes. Made him kill. And the more he killed, the greater the pleasure he felt in it.

And so the times when any encounter with the opposite sex would end in disaster were long gone, the times when he was nicknamed Pansy or Little Dick.

To kill, to rape, to dominate a human being, to torture them for pure pleasure had ended up making him feel like a man.

It had actually made him a monster.

He had put the pistol back together and was now holding it in his hand.

He really enjoyed the feel of it, the weight. It gave him a real sense of power. It always had. And she knew it.

As soon as Angelica came back from the bathroom, he went on the attack. 'Who the fuck was that woman?'

'What are you on about?'

'Don't act dumb! Yesterday, when we met in the Piazza San Marco ... I saw you walking away with her, and people turning to look at you. She was standing there at the bar, in a little white dress with a low neckline.'

'She's a friend of mine,' Angelica said, unfazed.

'A friend of yours? And how long have you had this friend?'

'For a few weeks, though I've known her for several years.'

'How did you meet her? You've never mentioned her before. You've been keeping secrets from me!'

'What the hell's got into you? Why are you giving me the third degree?'

'Leave her!' he retorted, giving her a piercing look.

She stared back at him in silence.

He walked away.

And went downstairs to that big, dark room, the symbol of his tortured childhood. He had decisions to make. One was urgent: what to do about this relationship between the two women? It could pose a danger.

Before going back up, he went over the next steps in his plan. All those long-meditated stages that would eventually lead him to his goal, that goal that now seemed within reach.

Their history had begun down here in the dark.

One day, after lunch, they had come down to this very room. Enveloped by the darkness, he had suddenly found her tongue in his mouth, warm and wet. He had put his hand between her legs and felt the heat through the soft fabric of her underwear.

'Let's get undressed,' she had said to him, unbuttoning her blouse.

'No.'

'Why not?'

'Just no,' he had replied, nervously. In his mind, the memories of his bitter childhood experiences were still vivid.

She had looked at him, not understanding. Then her eyes had clouded over and she had leant her head against his chest and stroked his long fair hair. He wore it like that even then. It had been the fashion.

Everything had started that day, when they were both sixteen.

That first encounter had been followed by others.

And she had always been the one to take the initiative, almost hypnotised by his beauty. The first few times she had tried to persuade him to make love, but her efforts were in vain. She had had to resign herself to touching him and his touching her. They had moved on to mutual masturbation while smoking grass.

One day, they had used a pin to draw blood from their fingers and mingle it. From that moment, their friendship had become something sacred and eternal. They weren't lovers, they were blood siblings. And that link had remained strong. When they could not meet up in Paris or Mugello, they called each other often.

The complicity between them had grown stronger and stronger.

29

It was almost eight in the evening when Fanti came into Ferrara's office with an envelope in his hand.

'It's for you, Chief Superintendent,' he said, putting it on the desk. 'Just delivered.'

Ferrara set aside the document he had been reading and opened the envelope.

'At last!' he said to himself on seeing the sender.

Dr Francesco Leone – University of Florence, Department of Anatomy, Histology and Forensics – Forensics Division

As usual, Leone had been as good as his word.

It was a copy of the report on the post-mortems, which had been carried out that morning and for which he had been waiting anxiously. He started to read the first one. The one on Enrico Costanza.

The introduction made it clear that this was a preliminary technical assessment, but that the results were either certain or very reliable.

Enrico Costanza had been killed by shots fired from a 7.65 calibre pistol – which they already knew, Ferrara thought. The time of death was between midnight on 28 August and two in the morning on the following day. This conclusion was based on a serious of elements, including the cooling of the body and the hypostatic marks present in the lower body, caused by the blood filtering slowly down through the tissues after death, in accordance with the laws of gravity. The temperature of a corpse decreases by half a degree per hour in the first three or four hours after death, then by one degree per hour for the next six to eight hours. Finally, after twelve or more hours, the loss of temperature becomes increasingly marked, until the body reaches the ambient temperature somewhere between eighteen and twenty-four hours after death.

Ferrara read that rigor mortis had not fully set in – during the external examination at the crime scene, it had been possible to manipulate the limbs without any particular difficulty.

There were traces of drugs in the blood, but no alcohol, nor any kind of medication.

In addition, the post-mortem had revealed a cancer of the lungs so advanced that the cancerous cells would soon have completed their life cycle.

So Costanza had been a man with a death sentence hanging over his head.

Of the two shots, one, in the back, had fractured a few ribs but missed both the heart and the principal arteries. The other, though, a shot to the head, had passed through the brain, turning it to pulp, and then exited. It had followed a downward trajectory, so there was no doubt that it had been fired when the victim was already on the ground.

The cause of death had been a diffused internal haemorrhage, which had provoked terminal and irreversible cardio-respiratory failure.

Finally, Leone's report mentioned that the victim's last meal had not been substantial. Rice and vegetables. A sample of the gastric contents had still to be analysed.

To provide further answers, Leone concluded, *I have taken samples of the organs and viscera for later histological and toxicological tests, the results of which the Prosecutor's Department will receive directly from the relevant teams at the Institute of Forensic Medicine.*

Ferrara went on to read about the post-mortem on the butler. The bullet had been fired from close range, with the gun almost in contact with the skin, and had completely destroyed the brain. It had been recovered, and was also of 7.65 calibre.

God alone knew if the bullets would be in a suitable condition to make comparisons, Ferrara thought.

He made a note on a piece of paper: *Ballistics report*, and underlined the two words several times. He would call his colleague Fuschi later to remind him how urgent it was.

In contrast to Enrico Costanza, the butler's organs showed no traces of drugs, and no serious pathologies. In other words, Luis Rodriguez had been in excellent health. Before his death he had enjoyed a hearty meal: spaghetti with tomato sauce and red meat and a green salad.

The time of death had been a couple of hours earlier than the senator's, but the cause of death was identical.

He must have been in the wrong place at the wrong time, Ferrara thought.

He closed the second report as well and opened another, smaller envelope, marked *Strictly Confidential*. It contained Leone's own reconstruction of the murders in the light of what he had determined both during his initial investigation at the scene and during the post-mortems.

Because of the initial bloodstains, Leone hypothesised that everything had started with Costanza in the room used as a study. It was there that the killer had fired the first shot into the victim's back. It had been fired from a certain distance, some eight or nine feet, and the wounds inflicted had not been fatal. Costanza had crumpled to the floor, turning as he fell, most likely landing on his back. The second shot had been fired at close range, right between the eyes. This one was the fatal one. A typical contact wound, as Leone described it.

Next, the body had been moved to the bathroom, as could be deduced from the traces of blood on the floor of the corridor.

There, the killer had completed his task with the removal of the eyes. It had only taken a few moments, and had most probably been done with a sharp knife.

The manner of the killing demonstrates deep hatred or rage on the part of the killer towards the victim was Leone's conclusion. Rizzo had been spot on when he had suggested it could be a revenge crime, Ferrara thought.

The butler, on the other hand, had been killed in the same place that his body had been found. It was evident that the killer had forced him there at gunpoint. A single shot at close range. The bullet's trajectory indicated that both the victim and the killer had been standing. Rodriguez had been nearly six feet tall.

Ferrara underlined this last detail with a pencil. It gave them an idea of the killer's approximate height.

He folded Leone's note, put it back in the envelope and locked everything in his desk drawer. Then he leant back in his chair and started to think. He tried to imagine both scenes. He saw the butler on the threshold after opening the front door.

Had he known the killer?

He saw in his mind a hooded man – the one from the video? – pointing a gun at the butler, and the look of fear on Rodriguez's face.

Had there been one man or more than one? As the calibre of the bullets was the same, did that mean the same weapon had been used?

Then he imagined the walk to the old chapel: Rodriguez moving tentatively, with the gun pointing at his back. He imagined his pleas, his tears. All in vain: his killer would not allow himself to show any pity.

He even seemed to hear the shot . . . But what if the gun had a silencer?

He made a careful note of this.

Then he saw the killer, or killers, going into the villa and murdering Costanza following the sequence described by Leone.

But had the senator been at home when the killer entered the building, or was he surprised on his return? And, if that was the case, when did he go into the study? They knew from the chauffeur that he had been dropped off at the villa just before midnight.

At last, he thought, something definite: the killer had been waiting for Costanza in the house. Because the butler's death had occurred between ten and midnight.

He folded the piece of paper on which he had been making his notes, put that in the drawer as well, lit half a Toscano cigar and slowly inhaled.

He was still lost in thought when the telephone rang and brought him back to the present. He picked up the receiver, wondering if something else serious had happened.

He wasn't even close.

30

'Chief Superintendent Ferrara,' he announced himself.

'Good evening.' The voice was male and unsteady. 'I called this afternoon but they told me you weren't there.'

'No, I was out. Go on, signor . . . '

'Do I really have to tell you my name?'

'I'd prefer it, but carry on. Why are you calling?'

'On the night between Saturday and Sunday . . . '

The voice came to a halt, and Ferrara thought they had been cut off. A moment later, though, he heard the caller's breathing.

' . . . I was driving along the road that goes from Borgo San Lorenzo to Fiesole and then carries on to Florence – the Via Bolognese.'

'What time was this?'

'It must have been about half past two, a quarter to three.'

'Go on.'

'As I'm sure you know, the road winds a lot, and as I came round a bend another car came right at me. The driver was a woman. She was going so fast, I just had time to swerve, or there would have been a collision. My car ended up on the verge, though fortunately there was no damage. I sounded my horn several times but she didn't stop.'

'Where exactly did this happen?'

'Near the turn-off that leads to a restaurant called Il Ferriolo.'

Ferrara knew the place. 'Why do you think this information might be useful?' he asked.

'I drive that way for my work, often at night, and I've never seen a woman driving down that road alone at that time of night, especially not at that speed.'

'What sort of car was it?'

'An A-Class Mercedes.'

'Are you absolutely sure?'

'Yes.'

'What colour was it?'

'Dark, I think. I can't be more specific than that. She was almost on top of me and I was scared.'

'Did you notice anything else about the woman or the car?'

'The woman's head was moving backwards and forwards like a pendulum. I thought she might be drunk or on drugs.'

'You're going to have to come in to Headquarters. This information could be very useful to us.'

'Really?'

'I think—'

Before Ferrara could finish his sentence, he was aware of silence at the other end. He put the receiver down in annoyance. Using the internal phone, he called the Operations Room and asked them to trace the call. A few moments later, the phone rang again. He answered straight away.

'Please don't think I was being rude, Chief Superintendent. I was cut off.'

'I was hoping you'd call back.'

'Do you really think I can be of use?'

Ferrara did not reply at once, because an officer had just come in with a piece of paper which he handed to him.

'You're calling from telephone number 33562 . . .' Ferrara said. 'Making this call from a mobile really must be costing you quite a bit. Come in and see me, or I'll have to send a patrol car out to pick you up from home. What do you say?'

'Give me an hour.'

'I'll be expecting you.'

Ferrara thought of delegating the interview to one of his team, but then dismissed the idea. The man, whoever he was, had trusted him and, if he found himself having to deal with someone else, it was quite likely he'd clam up.

Just over half an hour later, the telephone rang.

It was the gatehouse, telling him that the person he had been waiting for had arrived.

'Bring him to my office,' Ferrara replied.

The man said his name was Sergio D'Amato. He looked to be just over fifty. He was a few inches short of six feet, thin, with light brown hair and an honest-looking face.

'Thank you for coming in,' Ferrara said, motioning D'Amato to the armchair in front of the desk, the one nearest to the window. 'All right, Signor D'Amato, please tell me again what happened to you.'

'I already told you on the phone.'

'Yes, but going over it again may help you remember certain details, even small ones, that you didn't mention before.'

D'Amato nodded, sat back in the chair, and repeated his account, without adding any further details to those he had provided on the phone.

'What kind of work do you do, Signor D'Amato?' Ferrara asked him when he had finished. 'On the phone you told me you often use that road.'

'I'm a mechanic. I own a repair shop in Borgo San Lorenzo.'

'Would you be able to give as detailed a description as possible of the woman who was driving?'

'Chief Superintendent, I was in shock. I was scared, very scared. She suddenly appeared out of nowhere, right on top of me. I only saw her for a few seconds before I swerved to the right to get out of her way.'

The man paused for several moments, as if trying to remember a half-forgotten detail. Then he continued, 'What really struck me was the way she was moving her head. She seemed like a robot, as if she was driving with a veil over her eyes. That's why I thought she must be a drunk or a junkie. At least that's the impression I got in those few seconds.'

'Could you describe her face?'

'A normal kind of face. She had long hair, I'm sure of that.'

'How old?'

'Youngish, I'd say.'

'And was she alone?'

'Yes.'

'There's something I have to ask you to do.'

'Go ahead. I'm here to help.'

'I'd like you to work with an officer from Forensics to put together an identikit. Do you think you can do that?'

'Now?' the man said, glancing at his watch. 'I've got to start work early tomorrow.'

'It's best to do it straight away, while this is all still fresh in your mind. It won't take more than ten minutes and our expert's already here.'

'Ten minutes?'

'I guarantee it.'

Sergio D'Amato nodded his head in agreement.

'In the meantime, let me get you a coffee.'

Ferrara called Fanti on the internal phone and asked him to make two coffees.

31

'We'll be eating in a quarter of an hour or so,' Eleonora said.

Rizzo had been watching her in silence from the doorway for several moments while she cooked. He liked his wife's attention to detail as much now as when they had first met.

This evening she was wearing a striped yellow apron and was cooking spaghetti carbonara, one of his favourites.

'OK, darling,' he said, his mouth already watering.

He went back into the living room and slumped onto the sofa. This was the room he always dreamed about when he was in the office trying to solve a case.

He thought back over the last few hours, and then over everything else that had happened during that hellish summer. He thought about Leonardo Berghoff's letter, about Antonio Sergi, a colleague whose possible collusion with the lodge he found hard to believe, and about the words in Costanza's diary, which might well actually refer to Sergi. And he thought ahead to the inquiries he would have to make the next day, as ordered by the chief.

There were lots of questions and too few answers.

For example, how were they going to tell the Prosecutor's Department that they had hushed up the existence of the letter? Would they be accused of hiding it so as not to wash their dirty linen in public?

Eleonora's voice shook him out of his thoughts.

'Dinner's served, Francesco!' she called him, carrying the saucepan down the hall to the dining room. 'Open a bottle of red wine.'

Yes, he thought, *time to think about eating now. Tomorrow is another day.*

Once they had had their coffee, he got up from the table and went to look in on his little girl. When he had got home, she had been asleep and, not wanting to wake her, he had simply glanced in through the half-open door. She was almost a year old and slept in a cot next to their double bed.

She was just waking up and as soon as she saw him leaning over her, she became agitated, kicked her legs, then started to cry. Eleonora ran into the room and put her dummy in her mouth, stroking her back and murmuring sweet nothings to her. After a while, the girl calmed down.

'It's because you're never here, Francesco,' his wife said, with a touch of reproof. 'She doesn't recognise you. As far as she's concerned, you're a stranger.'

He did not reply. The thing was, it was true. His work kept him away from his loved ones. Feeling dejected, he went back to the sofa and switched on the TV. It was time for the latest local news bulletin.

He recognised the familiar face immediately, that sensation-seeking reporter who was never absent from the scene of a crime. He was standing on the pavement in front of a small apartment block whose front door was blackened by smoke. Next to him were a couple of firefighters who had just finished putting out the flames. In the background were two uniformed carabinieri who had been the first on the scene.

The reporter closed his report with the words: 'Has the Lift Maniac struck again?' This was the nickname the media had given to an arsonist who set fire to the lifts of apartment buildings, leaving quite long intervals between his attacks.

As if Florence didn't have enough problems, they were having to deal with this too. These crazy people just came along one after another.

He picked up the remote, pressed the OFF button and got up. Time to put an end to yet another day it was best to forget.

32

The restaurant, a few streets away from the Via Veneto, was half deserted. It had recently changed hands and the prices had inexplicably gone up.

A couple of confused-looking American tourists were waiting to be served, biding their time by looking with interest at the paintings on the walls, all of which depicted views of the city.

Two men were sitting at another table. 'This is very good, I like it,' the younger man exclaimed, in a marked foreign accent.

'It's *bucatini all'amatriciana*,' his companion explained. His voice left no doubt about his origins: he spoke with a strong Roman accent. He was fifty, fifty-five at most, decidedly well-built, with a bull neck. The nail on the little finger of his left hand was long and pointed. He was wearing a Loro Piana suit.

As they waited for their second course, the foreigner looked at his watch. It was five to ten. The moment had come to discuss the main reason for their meeting, which he himself had urgently requested. A few days previously he had given the bull-necked man a delicate task to perform, in return for which he would get a considerable quantity of cocaine, destined for the Roman market, at a very reasonable price.

Business was business. It brought money, riches and power – all the things that were taking this new Roman group to the top echelons of organised crime, almost on a par with the Magliana gang, which had been headline news in the seventies and eighties. Just like the Magliana gang, it boasted of its connections with the Mafia and with deviant Masonic lodges.

But something had gone wrong. Someone had got there first.

And now they needed to find out who it had been and at the same time handle a new assignment, to be carried out as soon as possible.

The foreign guest put his hand in the inside pocket of his jacket, took out an envelope and gave it to the bull-necked man, who took it and opened it. Inside were two photographs. Both showed the same person but in different poses and locations.

'Let me give you the details,' the foreigner said.

The other man listened to him attentively and, when he had finished, replied with an arrogant smile, 'Rome belongs to us now, and not just Rome.'

'I know that. But we don't want any more mishaps.'

'Don't worry. We'll soon find out what really happened. Whoever got there before us will pay for it dearly.'

'Good. Contact me the usual way.'

'OK.'

At that moment, the waiter approached their table carrying a large tray. The air grew rich with the smell of roast lamb, potatoes and grilled vegetables.

Another Roman speciality the foreigner was tasting for the first time.

Seated at a table by the wall at the far end of the restaurant, two men in dark suits were talking in low voices and glancing towards them from time to time.

These glances did not escape the foreigner's attention. Before they parted, he asked the bull-necked man who they were.

'Friends of ours, regular customers here,' he replied. 'They work for the Ministry of the Interior, although they'd rather this wasn't known.'

'Secret Service?'

The man nodded.

33

At that hour it was completely deserted.

The crowds of tourists who had livened up the area all day until early evening had dwindled away, as had the parked coaches.

It was the middle of the night and still hot. The stars were out, casting a glow over everything. It was a breathtaking sight.

A figure slowly approached the statue of David and walked to the back of the statue so as not to be seen from any passing vehicles.

As usual, he had thought of everything. If any cars belonging to the police or the Carabinieri were sighted in the area, a warning message would be sent to his mobile.

He opened his nylon backpack, took out an envelope and placed it at the foot of the statue.

Then he walked back the way he had come. As he walked, he wrote a text. A single word.

OK.

The back streets were empty and silent, just the way he liked them.

He met just one grizzled old tramp and a lone junkie. The tramp was sitting on a cardboard box, a bottle clutched to his chest, tears running down his cheeks. The alcohol clearly wasn't helping him see the world in a less gloomy light.

The junkie, who had a dog with him, swayed as he walked. He had the empty eyes of someone on the verge of completely destroying his brain.

He looked at these two characters absently.

Florence seemed calm in the dead of night.

But it wouldn't be calm for much longer, not when they saw the great present he had given them.

He was euphoric.

34

Teresa lay on top of the bed, unable to sleep.

When she was little, she used to fall asleep to the sound of her father's voice. He would tell her stories that didn't come from books, stories he made up off the top of his head as he sat on her bed. They were never quite the same, although they were very similar, because the same characters recurred and the beginnings were almost identical. There was just one protagonist, a brave young girl who managed to catch the little thieves who stole her snack, another time her sweets, and another time her doll's house with the miniature dolls.

She jumped when the phone rang.

It was the switchboard operator from Headquarters.

And what she heard sent her leaping out of bed.

On the way there, she mulled over what the operator had told her: that an envelope addressed to her had been picked up in the Piazzale Michelangelo following an anonymous call. The caller had said that it was related to the Costanza case.

When she arrived at Headquarters, she found it all lit up.

In the inner courtyard there was a constant coming and going of officers changing shifts. There were a few lights on in the *Squadra Mobile*'s offices too. Maybe someone was still in there, she thought, or maybe whoever had left last had forgotten to switch them off. That often happened.

She went straight to the top floor, where the Operations Room was located, with its computers and screens and luminous maps of the city on which little red lights indicated the positions of the patrol cars.

She walked through it to the duty inspector's room.

That was where the members of the Auto Unit would have taken the envelope once they had picked it up.

'That's the one,' the inspector told her, gesturing towards a desk. He was an older man, nearing retirement, who had to do night shifts instead of staying at home and spending quality time with his family. The Operations Room was as understaffed as everywhere else.

Teresa went to the desk and read her own name stencilled carefully on a padded brown envelope. She was tempted to touch it, but restrained herself.

'Was the call recorded?' she asked.

'No, the stranger called the switchboard, not 113. But the operator's writing up a transcript.'

'Has Ferrara been informed?'

'Not yet, because we don't know if it's a hoax. We need to check out the contents first.'

'Well, if we're going to open it I think we should call Forensics. We can't rule out the possibility that it's a bomb.'

'Yeah, OK.'

'By the way, have you touched it?'

'The only people who've touched it were the officers who went to pick it up, but they had gloves on.'

'Where exactly did they find it?'

'Behind the statue of David in the Piazzale Michelangelo, just where the anonymous caller said it would be.'

The perfect place to leave something compromising that you wanted found, Teresa thought. There were no houses nearby, just a restaurant on the far side of the square that would be closed at that hour, like all the other restaurants and bars on the edge of the city. And at night there was no traffic except the occasional car driven by someone who lived locally.

He'd been clever, she told herself.

'Have they traced the phone the caller used?' she asked.

'The operator's checking. It doesn't look like it came from the city.'

First, an external examination was carried out.

The technician made every effort to discover fingerprints or biological liquids.

Then he carefully opened the envelope and tipped the contents onto the desk: a folded page from the previous day's newspaper, with something inside it. He unfolded the page to reveal a transparent plastic bag, like those used for collecting evidence.

What they saw in the bag sent a chill down their spines.

Two eyes.

The balls looked like glass jellyfish. The fibres of the muscles and the white filaments of the optic nerves were clearly visible.

'Shit!' the inspector exclaimed in a loud voice, bringing his hand up to his mouth. He couldn't help himself, and ran to the toilet to throw up.

In the meantime, the forensic technician had extracted a piece of white paper, folded into quarters, from the bottom of the envelope. On it were a few typed words:

You were missing these, Superintendent Micalizi.

Followed by a signature:

GENIUS

He showed the paper to Teresa, who was already on the phone to Ferrara.

'There's a message, too, chief,' she said.

'I'll be right there.'

As she waited for Ferrara, Teresa interviewed the switchboard operator.

'Can you describe his voice?'

'I had the impression it was disguised, as if he was talking with a handkerchief over the mouthpiece.'

'Was it a man?'

'How can I be sure of that? The voice was distorted.'

'Any distinctive inflections?'

What kind of fucking question is that? the operator thought. Out loud, he said, 'No, Superintendent,' while wondering why he was being given such a grilling.

'Did you find out where the call was made from?'

'Yes, from a public phone box in San Piero a Sieve.'

'Good. Write up the transcript straight away so that the Chief Superintendent can read it as soon as he gets here.'

35

Operator: Switchboard. Can I help you?

Caller: In the Piazzale Michelangelo, behind the statue of
David, there's something that might interest Superintendent
Micalizi. It's in connection with the Costanza case.

Operator: Who's speaking?

Caller: Genius.

Operator: Genius? Genius who?

Caller: Genius. Are you asleep or what?

Caller hangs up.

Ferrara finished reading the transcript.

This was the second time in twenty-four hours that Genius
had put in an appearance: there was no doubt that he was the
hooded man in the video. Once again, he was claiming responsibility.

It could only have been him, Ferrara thought. Was this
what he had meant when he'd said they would hear from him
again?

His thoughts turned to the place the call had been made from.

San Piero a Sieve was the locality where the Monster of
Florence had posted a letter to the only female deputy prosecutor who had taken an interest in his crimes. Inside it, he had
placed a strand of hair belonging to the female victim killed on a

night of the new moon in September 1985 at Gli Scopeti near San Casciano Val di Pesa. The letter had been sent the very same night the murder had been committed.

It was a disturbing analogy.

PART THREE

HUNTING FOR CLUES

36

Tuesday 31 August

The seven a.m. news bulletin was on, and once again images of Florence flooded the screen.

After a view of Fiesole, there was a shot of Enrico Costanza's villa. Clearly visible on the imposing gates was a sign reading: POLICE HEADQUARTERS, FLORENCE – SQUADRA MOBILE – HOUSE SEALED BY ORDER OF THE JUDICIAL AUTHORITIES.

'There are still no developments in this horrific double murder case,' the newsreader said. 'The general impression is that the investigators are still groping in the dark . . .'

Ferrara, who was getting dressed, turned up the volume with the remote and stood there watching the TV. The whole item lasted just under two minutes, and ended with a brief statement by the Chief Prosecutor.

Luca Fiore had been filmed sitting at his desk in his office in a short-sleeved shirt. He calmly explained that a political motive had been ruled out, since Enrico Costanza had not been involved in active politics for a long time. He also declared that he was quite confident that the case would be solved within a reasonable time frame.

'What do you mean by reasonable?' the interviewer asked him.

'The time required for such a complex case.'

Ferrara switched off the television and finished getting dressed. He was late. He kissed Petra goodbye and went out into the morning light. It was likely to be another hot day.

When he got to Headquarters and started up the steps, he heard the usual voices, the footsteps and laughter coming from the courtyard where the drivers parked the cars from the official pool and hung around arguing and joking amongst themselves. Then he walked along the corridor on the first floor and it was as if someone had suddenly turned the volume down, then off completely.

He was met by a tomb-like silence, and the last few yards before he reached his office seemed very long.

He immediately summoned the key members of his team.

The meeting started less than ten minutes later. Only Guido Polito, the inspector from the SCO team, was absent.

Luigi Ciuffi, the head of Narcotics, had also been brought in to advise on the drugs found in Costanza's villa. Ferrara held him in high regard, both for his professional abilities and his willingness to put in the necessary hours without always having one eye on the clock.

As Ferrara's secretary, Nestore Fanti would take the minutes. Beside him sat Superintendent Gianni Ascalchi, only just back from holiday. Short and thickset, with a crooked chin, he looked like a young Totò. He enjoyed a certain fame among his colleagues for his jokes, which he told in dialect. A Roman by birth, he had been in Florence for several years now and knew the city's criminal underworld well. Four months earlier, a suspected tumour in one of his lungs had scared him so much that he had given up smoking cigarettes for good. He had even started to hate them and found the sight of his chief with a cigar in his mouth hard to take.

By now, they were all convinced that the double murder had been carefully planned down to the last detail. It was impossible to believe that the crimes could have been committed in a fit of rage or without premeditation.

'Now, tell me what you've all found out,' Ferrara said.

They each explained what they had done, including their attempts to reconstruct the last day of Costanza's life.

The former senator had left his villa before eleven in the morning on Saturday 28 August to go to Milan, where he had an appointment with a specialist. The Tumour Institute had confirmed his attendance. He had got back to Florence at about seven in the evening and his driver had dropped him off at the Hotel Villa Medici in the Via Il Prato. He had dined there, although they were still not sure whether he had eaten alone or in company. Then, at about a quarter past eleven, the driver had returned to pick him up and take him home. They had not stopped anywhere along the way.

'Well, at least we know what time he returned home,' Rizzo said. 'It would certainly be useful to check the CCTV cameras along the route. And we shouldn't neglect the speed cameras on the road leading to the villa. It would also be worth checking out any speeding fines that have been issued.'

Florence had become one of the Italian cities with the highest levels of surveillance. There were CCTV cameras everywhere – not that that had helped to bring down the crime rate.

'It's an idea,' Ferrara said, 'though I think it'd be like looking for a needle in a haystack. Still, we have to try everything.' He had opened a file on the desk in front of him, a file that was still quite thin at the moment. But soon this mere handful of papers would be joined by duty reports, witness statements, interviews, photographic dossiers, and so on, until it was bursting at the seams.

Having listened to his team members, Ferrara looked at them all in turn and took the floor.

He recapped the results of their investigations so far.

Then he showed them a computer-generated image of a female

face. It was the face of the woman who had been driving the A-Class Mercedes. The forensics expert had worked for almost two hours to put together an electronic portrait. Not the classic identikit, but almost a photograph.

They all looked at it carefully, but none of them recognised the face. It could have been anybody.

'Do you believe the witness's statement, chief?' Rizzo asked, knowing that Ferrara had a sixth sense about these things.

'He seemed genuine to me,' Ferrara replied with a sigh. 'Whether it helps us at all is another matter.'

'So now we've got a woman to look for?' Rizzo asked. 'It'd be the first time a woman has been wanted in connection with such a horrible crime here in Florence.'

'Yes, the first time,' Ferrara agreed. 'I realise it's hard to believe, but we can't dismiss anything out of hand. I want a copy of this portrait distributed to all the patrol cars in the area, and I want it up on the noticeboard here in Headquarters, in every station, and in the offices of the railway, traffic and airport police.'

Nobody objected. After a few moments, Ferrara drew everyone's attention to the necessity of keeping an eye open for the presence of any A-Class Mercedes cars on the road between Florence and Borgo San Lorenzo, the stretch where the witness had seen the car.

None of the people living in the area had seen or heard anything useful. They had been asked the customary questions, but to no avail. Nobody had seen anyone suspicious, or noticed anything strange. Even if they had, not everyone was prepared to cooperate with the police, either through fear, or to avoid getting involved.

Enrico Costanza's few friends had all stated that, as far as they were concerned, no one had any motive to hate him. In accordance with the maxim that repeatedly cropped up in such investigations, nobody liked to speak ill of the dead. They all stressed the victim's good points and omitted to mention the dark ones. Even if they were aware of them, most preferred not to reveal them. This was an attitude especially common in the circles in which Senator Costanza had moved.

Ferrara was perfectly well aware that among Freemasons, solidarity was paramount, even when one of them had died. And these friends of Costanza's were all Masons, and all fairly well known. They would continue interviewing them, but it was unlikely they would discover anything.

Nobody in Narcotics had heard Costanza spoken of as being involved with drugs. The same was true of his butler Luis Rodriguez, an immigrant who had been working quite legally in Florence for almost five years.

Nothing had emerged from an examination of old recordings from the CCTV camera that protected Costanza's villa.

No technical clues had come from Forensics, but they would soon get the results of the ballistics tests, which were still in progress.

What was the motive? Should they think of the double murder as the work of a killer who had acted purely out of hatred for the victim? Or could there possibly be a connection to the Leonardo Berghoff affair and the Black Rose?

At this point, Ferrara finally made up his mind to tell his men about the contents of Leonardo Berghoff's letter, while emphasising that the information was private and confidential.

'For now, this information does not leave this room. I'll inform the Prosecutor's Department at a later date. The important thing at the moment is to dig a bit deeper and, if we find out anything, that's when we send them a report.'

To all intents and purposes, they were feeling their way in the dark. So far, they hadn't found a damn thing. But now they had to decide on priorities. The first thing was to carry out another search of Costanza's villa to try and find the case that had been used to withdraw his money from the Savings Bank.

'I want you to take charge of that, Francesco,' Ferrara said to

Rizzo. 'Use our colleagues from the SCO. Then you'll have to reconstruct Costanza's movements in the days before he was killed. We also need to find out whether he met anyone, perhaps a guest, at the Hotel Villa Medici on Saturday night.'

'I'll ask the Deputy Prosecutor to authorise a new search warrant straight away,' Rizzo replied. 'Then I'll deal with the victim's last days and go to the hotel.'

'Perfect! We also need to reconstruct the last movements of the butler, Luis Rodriguez. That could be very useful.' Ferrara turned to Venturi. 'I'd like you to question Costanza's driver again. We especially need to know about his last few visits to the bank.'

'OK, chief.'

'Teresa, I want you to continue examining the documents we took from the villa, and keep in touch with the external expert about the video.'

Teresa nodded.

'I'll contact Criminalpol in Rome to find out whether there have been any similar murders in Italy,' Ferrara went on. 'And I'll ask Interpol about the foreign contacts. I'll also ask the Prosecutor's Department for permission to acquire the records of mobile phone traffic in Fiesole on the night of the crime and during the previous forty-eight hours. We've already asked for Costanza's records and we're expecting them shortly. Now let's get to work. I'm going to Costanza's funeral later. By the way, Francesco, are any of our officers already in place there?'

'Yes. Forensics too.'

'Good.'

The meeting was at an end. Everybody stood up and walked out.

'Francesco, wait a minute.'

Rizzo retraced his steps. 'Yes, chief.'

'You know what?'

'What?'

'I always call you by your name, and yet, after all these years and even though we're good friends, you still call me chief.'

Rizzo stared at him, wondering where Ferrara was going with this.

'Doesn't that strike you as odd?'

'To tell the truth, I've never really thought about it.'

'Why don't you drop all this "chief" business?'

'I'd feel uncomfortable, chief.'

'Enough of all this "chief". Call me Michele. That's an order.'

Rizzo laughed. 'All right, but in private, not in front of the others.'

'OK. Whatever suits you.'

37

Alone again, Ferrara settled down to read last night's reports.

He was particularly struck by the fire in the lift. A carabiniere had suffered the effects of smoke inhalation and the residents had had to seek refuge on their balconies.

It wasn't the first occurrence. There had been several similar cases, with a couple of months between them. In the end, thanks to a neighbour's testimony, they had identified the probable perpetrator of at least one of the fires: a thirty-something doctor who specialised in psychiatry. From their inquiries, it had emerged that he had been treated several times for neurological problems, hence the gaps in his activities. The investigation had had to be abandoned for lack of proof. His parents had even provided him with a watertight alibi: they swore that he had been at home with them on the night of the fire.

Could this one be the same person?

He leafed through his files and took out the FBI study he had consulted back then to learn more about the personality of a pyromaniac.

The American experts called such people serial arsonists, and they had sketched a profile: a young male between twenty and thirty, single, introverted but excitable, with few friends and a low IQ. Upper-middle class, often living near where he started the fires. Psychologically, he suffered from sexual and obsessive-compulsive disorders, which drove him to repeat acts he recognised as dangerous to other people, which he simply could not do without. In time, these acts could lead to more serious crimes. In fact, according to the Americans, many serial killers had pyromaniac pasts, just as others began their criminal careers by torturing and killing animals: dogs, cats, birds, and so on.

He read the FBI report a second time, then summoned Superintendent Ascalchi. He assigned him the latest case of arson, advising him to keep in close contact with the Carabinieri, who were officially in charge of the investigation.

'See whether that crazy doctor is free and check any alibi he may have. Hopefully, unlike the other times, his parents won't insist he was at home.' He handed him the folder, into which he had put a copy of the FBI study.

'OK,' Ascalchi replied. 'I'll arrest him at home and give him the third degree.'

'I urge you to use caution and tact, Ascalchi. We've got enough problems already.'

'Don't worry, chief.'

As Ascalchi was leaving the room, the telephone rang.

'Chief Superintendent Ferrara?'

'Speaking.'

'This is the guardhouse. Officer Pizzimenti speaking.'

'What can I do for you?'

'There's someone asking for you. A priest.'

'What's his name?'

'Father Torre.'

'Bring him up to my office.'

A few minutes later, Father Giulio Torre was sitting in front of his desk. Ferrara had met him several months earlier during the investigation into the murders committed by Leonardo Berghoff. It had been his old friend, the bookseller Massimo Verga, who had introduced him as an expert on the occult, especially Satanism. Father Torre had given Ferrara some useful pointers about the rituals in the deconsecrated chapel where Madalena's charred body had been found.

Ferrara had called him the night before to arrange a meeting.

'Thank you for coming, Father.'

'It's always a pleasure, Chief Superintendent. In fact, we ought to meet up for dinner again one of these days.' Father Torre remembered the excellent Florentine steak he had enjoyed while discussing esotericism with Ferrara. It had been an interesting evening. 'This time it'll be my treat. But tell me, were you hoping for my opinion on something else?'

'Precisely,' Ferrara replied.

He told the priest some of the details of Enrico Costanza's death. Then he asked the question which had him racking his brains. 'Father Torre, what do you think is the significance of the victim's eyes being removed?'

The answer was not long in coming.

'It was a punishment, and at the same time a message to those able to understand it.'

'What do you mean?'

The priest explained that historically, the eye was a Masonic symbol meaning enlightenment, which was the means by which the Masons came to know the secrets of the group. He added that on the physical level it also symbolised the Sun, from which Life and Light derived, on the intermediate astral level the Word, and on the spiritual or divine level the Great Architect of the Universe.

What a load of bullshit! Ferrara thought. Out loud, he said, 'Go on, Father.'

'Perhaps the killer was trying to tell us that Enrico Costanza was no longer a Mason, no longer among the enlightened.'

To Ferrara, this interpretation seemed to confirm what he had already suspected: that Costanza had been killed by his brothers. Leonardo Berghoff had suggested as much in his letter.

'Could that gesture have any other significance?'

'Yes, of course, though not in this case, in my opinion.'

'I'd still like to hear the alternatives,' Ferrara insisted.

Father Torre cited the Egyptian tradition, in which the eye had a less sinister meaning. It represented the eye of the Sun God, who was depicted in sculpture and painting as having the head of a falcon and the body of a man.

'The Egyptians decorated their sarcophagi with a drawing of two eyes, because they believed that this would allow the deceased to remain in the world of the living . . . '

Ferrara could have listened to him for a lot longer, but the investigations did not allow him that luxury. He promised Father Torre he would ring him to arrange their dinner.

'This time I'll take you to another restaurant with a really amazing wine list,' he said, thinking of the 1995 Brunello di Montalcino he had drunk on his return from Germany.

'I'll expect your call,' the priest replied. His cheeks and nose had turned red, almost as if he was already savouring one of those excellent wines. He shook Ferrara's hand firmly and left the room.

After a few moments Ferrara left too. He had an appointment, and he was late.

His destination: the offices of the Tuscan Regional Forensics Centre.

The ballistics results were ready.

38

'Do you fancy going for a wander round the centre of town?'

Angelica was driving, and Guendalina was sitting beside her. They were just crossing the Ponte delle Cure. 'We can leave the car in the car park near here, in the Piazza della Libertà, and continue on foot.'

'Oh, yes, let's. We can go for a little stroll and maybe have a pizza at one of those restaurants in the Piazza San Giovanni.'

'No, not there, Guendi. They're tourist traps. The pizzas will be frozen, and so will the starters. I see I need to teach you all about this city.'

'Where shall we go, then?'

'A really nice little place. We'll stop there on the way home. I want you to try potato tortelli made with handmade pasta, and *migliaccio* for dessert.' Angelica gave Guendalina's leg a squeeze and winked at her.

'What's migliaccio?'

'Oh, darling, you've still got so many of our local delicacies to discover. It's a dessert made with chestnuts, sometimes known as *castagnaccio*.'

They had reached the car park. Angelica got the admission coupon and started driving down the ramp.

*

'The same gun was used in both murders, Michele. No doubt about it.'

Ferrara was in the forensics lab, a veritable forest of computers, test tubes and optical and electronic microscopes, looking out onto the Piazza Indipendenza, where Gianni Fuschi was giving him the results of the ballistics tests.

Fuschi ran a hand through his hair. He was wearing a white lab coat over a pair of brown linen trousers and an ivory polo shirt. Tall and elegant, he was a handsome man by any definition, who looked more like a university lecturer than a police forensics expert.

'I've examined the casing and the nose with both the measuring microscope and that optical comparator.'

The optical comparator was used to compare the imprints on ballistic exhibits by making it possible to view two separate objects in the same field. It consisted of two microscopes with identical lenses linked by an optical bridge containing a combination of prisms that channelled the two images into a single eyepiece.

'Did you find anything else?' Ferrara asked.

'I checked the database, but it doesn't look as if the gun was used in any other incidents.'

'What else?'

'It had a silencer, Michele. The signs are unmistakable.'

He explained that they had found semi-circular indents on the nose of the bullet casing, typical of a bullet impacting against one of the metal diaphragms coaxial to the barrel.

Ferrara nodded. He knew that such indents were caused by the elements of a silencer being imperfectly aligned with the axis of the barrel.

'A real professional,' he murmured.

'There's no doubt about it,' Fuschi said by way of confirmation.

'Gianni, I need your report as soon as possible.'

'You'll have it on your desk tomorrow ...' He was about to add 'Gatto', but stopped himself just in time. Now was not the moment to make jokes, and it was best to drop that nickname given to Ferrara by a journalist at *Il Tirreno* who had been struck by the catlike shape of his hazel-green eyes.

The Piazza Libertà, where the company that ran the city's CCTV cameras was based, was just a few minutes away from Headquarters, so Rizzo decided to go there on foot.

A little earlier, Venturi had called Costanza's driver, who had confirmed the route he had followed on Saturday evening: Piazzale di Porta al Prato – Via Roselli – Via Strozzi – Via Lavagnini – Piazza della Libertà – Viale Don Giovanni Minzoni – Cavalcavia delle Cure – Piazza delle Cure – Viale dei Mille – Viale Volta – Via San Domenico – Fiesole.

It was the first time that Rizzo had been here. He had made an appointment over the phone with the manager, who had told him that he would be able to see him that same morning. In fact he was waiting for him: a tall, thin man in his early forties. He shook Rizzo's hand and led him into the surveillance room.

Once inside, Rizzo looked around and was taken aback by the sight of dozens of monitors and a large workforce sitting at long benches of computers.

The manager, who had introduced himself as Giuseppe Aviati, noticed the surprised expression on Rizzo's face and smiled. He was always pleased to see the effect his 'baby' had on the few visitors allowed in to see it, mostly officials.

'We started off with about ten or twenty cameras, almost all focused on key central points in the city,' he said proudly, 'but now we've got about five hundred of them and we'll soon be installing more. We have a direct connection to the city centre police, and arrests are often made on the basis of what my staff see on these monitors.'

'Is there always someone on duty?' asked Rizzo.

'Twenty-four hours a day, seven days a week. Sometimes we're asked to keep an eye open for suspicious individuals, and if we spot them we inform the State Police or the Carabinieri. Follow me!'

He led Rizzo over to one of the monitors.

'This is CCTV Camera 32. It's at the traffic lights near the Ponte Vespucci. If our technician moves the joystick in front of him, he can zoom in on the parked cars or those that are going through. And even on the people crossing the road or walking by the river.' He proceeded to give a quick practical demonstration.

Rizzo was struck by how clear the images were. 'Would you be able to follow the progress of a car from the Hotel Villa Medici to Fiesole by way of the Via Il Prato?'

Aviati smiled. 'I guessed your visit was connected to the senator's murder. On Sunday morning, the technician on duty noticed the police cars and ambulance going down the Viale Volta towards Fiesole with their lights flashing. We've had a look at the footage from earlier, but didn't notice anything out of the ordinary or we would have been in touch before now.'

'We need to confirm the presence of a black Mercedes from about eleven o'clock on Saturday night,' Rizzo insisted, taking a small notebook from his jacket pocket and giving him the licence number of Enrico Costanza's car.

'We'll do our best,' Aviati replied. 'It's a good thing you came this morning.'

'Why?'

'The footage is automatically deleted after seventy-two hours. We keep copies of the useful stuff on video and on hard disk, always bearing in mind the privacy laws.'

'I realise you can't just hand over the information to anybody who asks for it.'

Aviati nodded. 'We can give you the material, but we need a court order.'

'Of course. In the meantime, maybe you could at least check

for the Mercedes. If you find what we're looking for, you'll get the court order straight away.'

'We'll do what we can, but it's going to take time. There are several CCTV cameras to check, because from the Via Il Prato, the car could have gone in a number of directions to get to Fiesole. I'll let you know as soon as I can.'

'We know the route the car took,' Rizzo replied, and reported what they had learnt from the driver.

'Perfect. It's still worth checking the other routes as well.'

'OK. But remember, this is urgent.'

'Don't worry.'

Rizzo was just about to leave when he remembered the A-Class Mercedes, and asked Aviati to also let them know if there were any sightings of that model.

He left the building. He had other things to do, mainly interviewing Enrico Costanza's friends and acquaintances.

His next stop, though, was not Police Headquarters, but the Hotel Villa Medici.

He called Venturi and instructed him to start the interviews. He would be there in about an hour.

39

There were still five minutes to go.

Ferrara got out of the car and looked up at the clock on Fiesole's bell tower. Five minutes to twelve. He looked about him, then walked across the square, filled that day with the stalls of the weekly market. The presence of certain vultures of the press had not escaped him. It was predictable.

There were a number of wreaths and bouquets on the ground on either side of the main door of the cathedral.

He went in.

The two blocks of pews on either side of the wide central nave were already half full. He stopped for a few moments by one of the stone columns near the entrance. Some of the people sitting in the back rows turned round to look at him. He moved along the right-hand nave, turning to look to his left. There were many well-known faces, including several politicians in their requisite black suits, sitting in the front row along with the mayor. No family members. Costanza's only grandson lived in the United States and, from what they had gathered, he had been on bad terms with his grandfather, so Ferrara was not surprised by his absence.

In other words, there was nobody here who would make any effort to stop this death from fading into insignificance, no relative ready to build up the memory of the 'dear departed', if possible through public statements or by taking part in television broadcasts.

Costanza's body had arrived at the church that morning directly from the morgue at the Institute of Forensic Medicine, without being put on display. Now it lay in a coffin in front of the altar.

A forensics technician, positioned to one side of the square and well stocked with cameras, had been photographing the participants as they had arrived over the past couple of hours.

On the other side of the square, a plain-clothes officer was noting down the licence numbers of their cars, most of them big, powerful vehicles.

The priest began the service.

At the end of the mass, the coffin was carried out on the undertakers' shoulders, and in a matter of minutes people started to drift away, apart from the few who set off in procession towards the cemetery. For a while, Ferrara followed them at a distance, then slipped a hand into the inside pocket of his jacket and took a cigar from his leather case. He lit it and took a few puffs to make sure it did not go out. It was his third of the day.

Then he walked slowly back to his car. As he walked, he caught an exchange of remarks between two old men.

'He really is a great loss,' one of them was saying.

The other nodded. 'A death is always painful, especially when it's the death of a brother.'

Obviously two Freemasons . . .

He got back in the car and ordered the driver to take him back to Headquarters.

The Piazza San Giovanni was packed with tourists pointing their cameras at the façade of Florence Cathedral and Brunelleschi's dome, the largest masonry dome ever built. The queue of people waiting to get into the baptistery was so long that it stretched almost the whole way round the building. The sun beat down on them.

Next to the entrance, a woman sat on the floor with a child in her arms, her crossed legs covered by her long, ample skirt. In front of her was an empty cup into which nobody dropped any coins. People's indifference was palpable. They did not even spare her a fleeting glance: it was as if she were a ghost or a plague victim.

Angelica and Guendalina were walking hand in hand, exchanging long glances every now and again. You did not have to be the most observant person in the world to grasp the nature of their friendship.

They walked along the left-hand side of the building and reached the Piazza del Duomo, where they stopped for a few moments to admire the round slab of white marble in the pavement by the apsidal wall of the cathedral.

'This,' Angelica said, 'marks the exact spot where, on 17 February 1600, the huge gold-plated copper ball on the roof lantern fell after being struck by lightning.'

'Seventeen's always an unlucky number,' Guendalina said with a smile, looking up at the dome.

'The ball rolled down along the buttresses, causing a lot of damage, and then stopped right here.'

'And then what happened?' Guendalina asked, her eyes those of a little girl eager to learn something new.

'It was replaced two years later, by order of Duke Ferdinand I.'

'Could it fall again?'

'No. Thanks to the invention of lightning rods, that's impossible now.'

'Well, that's a relief!'

Guendalina looked up again at the dome. She was struck by the number of visitors all the way up there. 'Shall we go up?' she asked. 'I'd like to see the city from above. It must be amazing.'

'Not now, Guendi. We'd have to wait for hours in this heat. We'll go another time, as soon as it opens.'

Hiding her disappointment, Guendalina let Angelica lead her to the Via de' Calzaiuoli. They reached the Piazza della Repubblica with its cafés, then the Via Strozzi and the Via della Vigna Nuova. They walked past extremely elegant but sadly empty shops. Business in Florence was changing: even the tourists were deserting these streets, preferring to travel to factory outlets a few miles out of town.

As they walked, they did not notice a young man with faded jeans, a white T-shirt and a reddish beard who had been following them for some time.

40

The imposing eighteenth-century building had just one entrance. In front of it was a pay and display car park, with a taxi rank about a hundred yards away.

The porter, wearing a grey uniform trimmed in red, was giving directions to a young tourist with a map of the city open in her hands. Meanwhile, a coach full of Japanese tourists had pulled up.

All the hotels in the historic centre were full as usual. There never seemed to be enough beds in Florence for all the visitors.

Rizzo looked around, then walked in through the elegant glass door.

Once in the foyer, he realised why this had come to be regarded as one of the city's top hotels. A huge crystal chandelier hung from the wooden ceiling.

He headed for the bar area. On the way there, he glanced at the inner garden with its swimming pool and saw several people lounging on sunbeds beside it.

The furnishings of the hotel displayed refinement and sophistication. The walls were wood-panelled. There were few paintings. Comfortable armchairs stood around small tables. He sat on one of the stools at the bar and waited for the barman, who was busy making a cocktail, to finish. When the waitress went on her way with the cocktail on her tray, he ordered a coffee. As the man turned to make it, Rizzo studied him carefully, thinking of the questions he needed to ask him.

'Here's your coffee, sir,' the barman said. 'Would you like a glass of water too?'

'No, thank you.'

Rizzo drank the coffee, then took advantage of the fact that it was a slack moment to say to the barman, who had moved over to the bottle rack, 'Excuse me, would you mind coming here for a moment?'

'Not at all.'

The man, who was short, fat and completely bald, was wearing a striped waistcoat and a pale tie. His name badge identified him as Piero. He looked at the ID Rizzo had produced.

'I hope I haven't done anything wrong?' he said hesitantly, in a typical Sardinian accent.

Rizzo took a photograph of Senator Costanza from the inside pocket of his jacket. 'Have you ever seen this man?'

'Of course. He was a customer here. The poor man! What a terrible way to end! I read what happened in *La Nazione*. Have you found out who did it?'

'Had you seen him recently?'

'Yes. Let me just think for a moment.' He took a piece of paper out of a drawer. 'Oh yes, I was on duty on Saturday night. I remember now: the Senator came in here after dinner and sat down at that table there.' He pointed to a table to his left, the one furthest from the bar.

'What time was that?'

'Ten thirty, ten forty-five.'

'Was he alone?'

The barman waited a couple of seconds before replying. 'No, he was with someone.'

'Who?'

The man shrugged. 'Someone . . . '

In the meantime, the waitress had returned with a new order.

'Excuse me a moment. Our guests around the pool are waiting for their drinks. With this heat . . . '

He poured two glasses of beer and two flutes of champagne, put the champagne bottle in an ice bucket, handed everything over to the waitress, and came back to Rizzo.

'Who was this somebody? A man? A woman?'

'A man. I'd never seen him before.'

'Can you describe him?'

'Not really. I only saw him for a moment when I took two whiskies over to the table.'

'Was he young or old?'

The man hesitated. 'In the evening we turn the lights down . . . there were other customers and I was on my own. But I did get the impression he was middle-aged, maybe a bit older.' He shrugged his shoulders, as if to apologise for not being more specific.

'What exactly do you mean by that?'

'About sixty. Younger than the Senator, anyway.'

'Tall? Short? Thin?'

'I couldn't tell you anything about his height, but I think he was of average build. What struck me was how lined his face was.'

'Beard? Moustache?'

'No, neither.'

Rizzo had taken his notebook out of his jacket pocket.

The barman started to look worried. 'What are you doing? Is this an interrogation?'

'For the moment, I'm just making a few notes. After that, we'll see.'

The barman seemed to stiffen.

'I should explain that I'm investigating a murder, in fact two. Senator Costanza was killed the same evening he came here for dinner. This is a serious case and I urge you to tell me the truth and not hide anything from me, or I'll have to send for a patrol car and continue this conversation at Headquarters.' This time Rizzo had assumed a more resolute tone.

'But I don't know that other man, I swear,' the barman said, looking around as if wanting to reassure himself that no one was listening. 'Why don't you ask the waiters and the maître d'? One of them might know who he is.'

'Did they leave together?' Rizzo asked.

The barman shrugged. 'Yes, they did.'

'Do you have CCTV?'

The barman shook his head. 'Can I get you a drink?'

'No thanks. The coffee was enough. How much was it?'

'Nothing, it's on me.'

'I insist.' Rizzo took a ten-euro note from his wallet and put it on the counter, then walked out of the bar area and over to reception.

'I need to speak to the manager,' he told the girl at the desk, showing his police ID.

'I'll call him straight away.'

The manager introduced himself as Fabrizio Gentile. He was wearing a dark grey suit with a smart white shirt and a pale grey tie.

'To what do we owe this visit?' he asked once he had examined Rizzo's ID. 'Is there some kind of problem?'

'I'd just like to ask you a few questions.'

'Go ahead.'

'I'm investigating a double murder.'

'A double murder?' the manager echoed, his face turning red.

'Senator Costanza was killed a few hours after he was here in the company of another man. To all intents and purposes, the staff who served him in your restaurant and bar were the last people to see him alive.'

'But—'

'All I'd like to know is whether the man who was with the senator was one of your guests?'

'What's his name?' the manager asked, turning to look at the register.

'If I knew his name, I wouldn't be here.'

'In that case, if you don't mind waiting, I'll have to ask my staff.'

'I've already talked to the barman.'

'What day was it?'

'Last Saturday, between seven and eleven in the evening.'

'Please bear with me a moment.' He went behind the reception desk and leafed through another register. 'They're on duty tonight, between six and midnight.'

'Can you give me their names?'

The manager seemed undecided at first, then resigned himself. Rizzo made a note of the names of the maître d' and two waiters in his notebook. Then he took a business card from his wallet.

'I'd like you to contact them and tell them to come in to Police Headquarters this afternoon, before they go on duty.'

'They won't miss their shifts, will they? I'd have real trouble replacing them. We have several staff on holiday at the moment.'

'No. If they come in by three o'clock, they'll be able to start their shifts as usual.'

The manager nodded.

Rizzo said goodbye and started towards the main entrance, but turned back after a few steps. 'Did you see the senator that evening?' he asked.

'No. It was my day off. I normally have Saturdays off when I'm working on Sunday.'

'Thank you.'

Once outside, Rizzo looked at the front of the building for a moment and saw that there was a CCTV camera to the side of the entrance.

And they'd told him they didn't have CCTV . . .

He wanted to go straight back, but decided to question the barman's colleagues at Headquarters first.

Maybe he had been hiding something.

41

The meeting was not at all pleasant.

Having been summoned by the Commissioner, Ferrara found him particularly agitated.

There and then, he assumed Adinolfi must have received a dressing down from the powers that be in Rome. That was fairly predictable: everything pointed to the fact that 'the Romans' were putting pressure on the Commissioner to serve up the culprit on a plate as soon as possible. It didn't really matter if the accused person was acquitted after his trial due to lack of evidence or, worse still, released by the Prosecutor's Department during the preliminary investigations because of a lack of clear pointers to his guilt. All that mattered was to provide the public and, most of all, the media with an immediate answer.

But this time, Ferrara was wrong.

Yes, Adinolfi was preoccupied, but by something else. Having remained completely silent, with an absent expression on his face, the whole time Ferrara was giving him the latest updates on the investigation – unfortunately, they still weren't making much headway, apart from the ballistics results – the first thing he said, when it was his turn to speak, was: 'Chief Superintendent, I would urge you not to waste your time making prison visits.'

Ferrara stared at him, wondering how on earth he knew about

that. He certainly hadn't told him and, apart from the staff at the prison, only his closest colleagues were aware of the visit.

'You also need to get the men from the SCO more involved,' Adinolfi went on. 'Further reinforcements will be arriving this evening. The Head of the State Police is sending them. Don't just have them going round in circles, do you understand? Use them, then you'll be able to concentrate on your other cases.'

'But Commissioner—' Ferrara started to reply.

Adinolfi cut him off immediately, raising his voice. 'There are other things getting our citizens upset, especially the shopkeepers. Thefts, bag-snatching, muggings, the sale of counterfeit goods in the main streets in broad daylight. Think about the state of the Via de' Calzaiuoli. It's a real mess. Quite intolerable. You can't even walk straight down it these days, you literally have to zigzag to avoid treading on the merchandise. And what have you got to say about the arson attack on that lift? We could have found ourselves faced with a mass murder. If we don't find the culprit or culprits, people will be killed and we'll all be in the firing line, me in particular.'

Adinolfi's eyes were blazing. Ferrara said nothing for a while, unsure whether or not to defend himself. He would have liked to point out that it was the job of the city centre police to prevent the sale of illicit merchandise – that same body whose one goal seemed to be to hand out as many parking tickets as possible, singling out the vehicles of the State Police in particular.

'But Commissioner—' Ferrara tried to reply again, but once again he was not allowed to finish.

'No "buts", Ferrara. Those are my orders. You should never concentrate on just one case. Be content with your recent successes, don't go chasing ghosts. It's a waste of time. There aren't any.'

Ghosts? Ferrara thought. What was Adinolfi raving about?

There was a brief pause while the Commissioner picked up some of the papers in front of him and locked them away in one of his desk drawers. At that moment, the telephone rang. Adinolfi was so nervous that the receiver slipped from his fingers as he was lifting it to his ear.

'Just a moment,' he said to the caller. He put his hand over the mouthpiece and asked Ferrara in a whisper to wait outside.

Ferrara nodded, got up, and joined the Commissioner's secretary.

He was filled with anger and bitterness. The same old thing, he thought. There were certain people you just couldn't touch. Damn this job!

Just over five minutes later, Ferrara was back in front of Adinolfi's desk.

'Tell your staff they need to show the witnesses more respect,' the Commissioner resumed, even before Ferrara had sat down. From his tone, Ferrara realised that this was not just a request, but an actual warning.

He stared at Adinolfi and realised that his face was even redder than usual. He would have liked to ask for clarification, but right now he could not find the right words. He had never imagined, not even vaguely, that he would ever be subjected to such a reprimand.

'I have been informed that you've been giving Senator Costanza's friends a rough ride, and actually have further interviews planned. Some have already received a summons.'

He seemed on the verge of exploding with rage.

A rough ride? Ferrara thought. What was he talking about?

He decided to be tactful and answer with generalities. 'We're doing what we normally do in such cases, Commissioner. Asking questions and comparing testimonies is part of our job.'

'Your job? Is that how you do your job? I've heard that you've been questioning them for hours on end, almost giving them the third degree. Some of them must have felt they were actually under investigation themselves.'

'None of them are under investigation, or even under suspicion. I can assure you of that.'

'Call off your deputy, Superintendent Rizzo. And leave the Freemasons alone. All these questions about the lodge. I'm informed that you've approached Interpol for further details about certain names you found in Costanza's papers. Foreign citizens – English to be precise.'

So that was why they hadn't heard back from Interpol yet.

'Well, Commissioner, our initial investigations seem to point in that direction. Enrico Costanza was a Freemason and the head of a secret lodge here in Tuscany.'

'If it's secret, how do you know about it? Who told you?'

At that moment, Ferrara realised that he had made a mistake and gone too far. Adinolfi did not know about Leonardo Berghoff's letter.

'An informant,' he immediately replied.

'An informant? The usual informants who talk nonsense. Drop them. There are no more informants. There are only criminals who turn State's evidence. They're the people who get us the results we want. The world has changed, investigative methods have changed, and you have to adapt. You have to change too.'

'But Costanza's foreign contacts, especially the English ones, could be useful to us. At the very least they could help us get to know the victim better.'

He would have liked to add what Father Giulio Torre had told him and the conclusions he himself had drawn from Berghoff's letter, but he preferred not to go into detail, both to avoid revealing his sources and to keep his remaining cards close to his chest. His instinct told him to keep things vague, especially because this conversation was giving him a strange feeling. Did he need to be wary of Adinolfi? Maybe the less he knew the better.

Moreover, the Commissioner's brief was not really criminal investigations, but the maintenance of public safety, which meant he did not have the right to know what Ferrara and his men were doing. No, he certainly wouldn't be telling him any secrets.

'Chief Superintendent Ferrara, I'm telling you what's come down to me from higher up. I have been strongly advised to treat these people with the respect they deserve and to leave woolly theories about the Freemasons alone. I don't think I need say more.'

This time, unusually, he had lowered his voice: maybe he didn't want even his office walls to hear what he was saying.

Absolute silence fell in the room.

From higher up? Woolly theories? Some things never changed, Ferrara thought. Once again, the upper echelons in Rome were trying to interfere in his investigations and keep him under control. How on earth was he supposed to work like that?

'All right, Commissioner.'

'Good, Chief Superintendent. I'm sure you're not going to cause me any problems. You're an intelligent man, you've understood what I've said. Let's draw a veil over this Freemasonry business. As I've already said, let the men from the SCO do more on the murder investigation while you take more of an interest in your other cases. Especially the arson attacks. That's a time bomb that could blow up at any moment.'

Ferrara nodded a few times. He knew he had no choice. He was at fault. He hadn't managed to solve anything, which meant that he was in no position to protest.

'Of course,' he replied with a barely contained sigh.

'One last thing, Chief Superintendent – you're an excellent police officer: resolute, creative, capable, cunning, all useful qualities in our institution. The competition may be getting tougher every day, but don't let it get the better of you.'

Ferrara nodded again.

'If you want to progress in your career, the qualities I've mentioned aren't enough. You have to back the right team. That's the only way you can win. And the right team is Guaschelli's team.

Have I made myself clear? Nothing is gained by opposing him. Don't try and be like David fighting Goliath.'

'You've made yourself very clear, Commissioner.'

'Now, get to work and bring in whoever started that fire. If you do, I'll put you forward for an official commendation, which will do wonders for your career.'

As he went down the stairs, feeling more frustrated than he ever had, Ferrara told himself that the conversation he had just had was proof of what kind of official Adinolfi was. A bureaucrat. A slave to the system. A nonentity. Was that how you became a commissioner? he wondered. If so, they could all go to hell! He was, always had been and always would be, a free man.

But there were people above Adinolfi, people with the right contacts in both the police and the judiciary, people who had developed a complex system of protection that allowed them to keep out of trouble, to make everything go away. Unfortunately, this was nothing new in Florence, a city in which there was a secret world determined to give the orders and decide what could and could not happen in politics, the law, and even criminal investigations.

The Black Rose.

There was a risk that nobody would pay for the double murder, especially now that the investigation, through the increased involvement of the SCO, would be subject to the long arm of Armando Guaschelli.

No, he wouldn't let that happen, not while he was head of the *Squadra Mobile*.

He was all the more determined given that, according to the law, he was in charge of criminal investigations for the whole province. It was to him that the Prosecutor's Department had to report. Yes, he would give the men from the SCO a more positive role in the investigations from now on, but he would make sure they were always supervised by himself or one of his most trusted men.

A number of thoughts began to torment him, one more than the others: did they want to see him transferred?

It would not be the first time.

It had happened before when he had poked his nose where it was not wanted, including his investigations into the possible masterminds behind the Monster of Florence killings.

There were certain circles that were untouchable.

It was just after seven in the evening when he received the results of the forensics tests on the envelope and its contents that the killer had sent Teresa.

There wasn't a single print on the page from the newspaper or on the note. The one thing that was certain was that the note had been typed on a computer in twelve point Times New Roman, except for the signature, which had been written in bold twenty-point lettering.

The paper was a common brand, widely available in super-markets. The note had been printed on an HP inkjet printer. Also quite a common make.

It was a dead end.

42

That evening, Sir George arrived at the Tuscan residence he had inherited from his family: one of his ancestors, a bishop, had bought it back in 1618.

The villa was in the countryside between San Gimignano and Certaldo, the area where Boccaccio was born.

His trusted retainer, who had acted as his gamekeeper for more than twenty years and lived in a cottage on the estate, had been waiting for him at Pisa airport.

After a relaxing hot shower, he went straight to his favourite place.

He had a long torch in his right hand as he opened the iron gate and switched on a series of fluorescent lights on the side walls. He went down a dozen stone steps to a large space where two walls facing each other were lined with enormous wine barrels, some covered in spider webs. He looked around. Everything was just as he had left it last time. He could go on.

There were several passages, all with vaulted ceilings made from bricks or very old stones. The damp got into your bones.

He went to a wall and pushed a button hidden in a niche behind stones and earth. A moment later a doorway opened. He went through it.

Holding the torch straight out in front of him, he started to descend the stairs, misshapen now through years of use. As he advanced, he lit big wax candles, two on each side of every step. At the bottom of the stairs was a series of passages and spaces of varying sizes. It was like a labyrinth of galleries and vaulted areas, some of them so low you had to bend your head to avoid touching the ceiling. It was a fearful place, reminiscent of medieval torture chambers.

He took the longest of the passages.

Halfway along it, he turned right into a spacious room with a high domelike ceiling. The air was damp and stale. The floor was of earth and the walls were made of great blocks of natural stone.

Once, a very long time ago, the place had been a Roman temple. A number of relics bore witness to this, including the iron crucifix planted in the ground, behind which, on the wall, was a drawing of a shell: the coat of arms of the bishop from whom he had inherited the property.

Sir George was fully aware of the history of his family and knew that this had been his predecessors' favourite place, starting with the bishop. Now, though, the crucifix had been turned upside down. It was his father who had done that.

He sat down on a large stone, switched on an old record player and closed his eyes to savour a piece of music that was very familiar to him. It was Bach. He loved to listen to it in this place; he loved the sensations it aroused in him, which he only felt here and nowhere else.

He concentrated and started to think – as he had done before at difficult moments, far from the hubbub of the world.

No one knew about this hiding place, except his eldest son, who had promised to keep it a secret after his death. It was a jealously guarded secret, to be passed only from father to son.

Time did not matter here; it slowed down, came to a halt.

He knew he had decisions to make before the situation got out of hand.

As it was starting to do.

43

'Does this face mean anything to you?'

Inspector Venturi had returned to the restaurant near Costanza's villa, accompanied by Officer Carlo Rossi. The owner had been joined by his son, Alessandro, who was wearing a pair of jeans and a flowery shirt. They were all sitting at a table in a private room.

The father took the identikit of the woman and stared at it without moving an inch, then shook his head to indicate that no, the face didn't mean anything to him. He had never seen the woman before.

'Are you absolutely sure?'

'Absolutely. Who is she, if you don't mind my asking?'

'Somebody a witness saw in the area,' Venturi replied, without going into more detail.

The picture was passed to the son. After looking at it carefully, he also categorically denied knowing her.

'That face means absolutely nothing to me,' he said firmly.

'So can you rule out the possibility that she might be one of your customers?'

The two men nodded.

Venturi asked the younger man a few further questions, trying to discover more about the regulars and, in particular, who had visited the restaurant in the days immediately before the double murder. The man seemed irritated by this questioning, and merely nodded or shook his head in response. Venturi asked him to give clearer answers, but soon realised that he was not going to obtain any useful information, so he asked to show the picture to the waitresses.

The owner got up to go and call them, and when the girls entered the room Venturi and Rossi recognised them immediately.

One of the two, who had long curly hair, took her time over the identikit, as if the face wasn't completely unfamiliar to her – or at least that was the impression Venturi got. But, in the end, she denied having ever seen the person in the picture.

'Does this woman have anything to do with what happened near here?' she asked. She was slim, in her early twenties, with a pale, intelligent face. Judging by her accent, Venturi thought, she could well be a foreign student working as a waitress to pay for her studies.

'Why do you ask?'

'No reason, it's just that . . . ' She turned to look at the owner. He gave her a fierce look, making no attempt to hide his disapproval.

'Oh, I forgot to mention, this woman drives an A-Class Mercedes,' Venturi said.

This detail did not garner any more positive response.

Venturi stood up. 'In case you do remember anything, ring me.' He looked at the older man. 'You've already got my business card.'

'Yes, I kept it,' the man replied. 'Aren't you going to stay and eat? We have excellent porcini mushrooms on the menu.'

'No thank you, we have to get on with our work.'

The two policemen said their goodbyes and left. The first thing Officer Rossi said to his superior was, 'Inspector, did you see the look the old man gave that waitress?'

'Of course, it was hard to miss. I think we need to speak to that young lady again at Headquarters. If she does know something, she'll be more likely to tell us when she's away from those two. Don't you agree?'

'Just let me know and I'll come and get her.'

'You like her, don't you?'

'She's cute.'

'All right, I'll let you take her the summons.'

Carlo Rossi smiled and put the car into first gear. 'Where next?'

'To the other restaurants and bars in the area. Everything from here to Borgo San Lorenzo.'

'What about food?'

'You're always thinking about food, you are. Get going, then we'll see.'

'At least a pizza, Inspector ... ?'

44

Teresa was exhausted.

She had spent the entire day examining and cataloguing the exhibits from Costanza's villa. In the afternoon she had telephoned Fabio Biondi and asked him if he had managed to get any more interesting images from the video. He had told her he was still working on it and would let her know as soon as he had anything.

By the time she left Headquarters, she had no wish at all to go straight home, so she decided to go for a walk. There were crowds of people in the streets. The cafés, pubs and restaurants were full to bursting, and a lot of tourists were hanging about on the pavements waiting for a table to become free.

Thanks to the warm weather, small groups of young people had formed outside the bars along the riverbank, putting their drinks down on the low walls and listening to rock music at ear-splitting volume.

Having reached the area near the British Consulate, Teresa stopped for a few moments to look at these youngsters. They all seemed cheerful and carefree, oblivious to the hate and rage simmering just below the surface of the city, ready to explode at any moment. Like young people anywhere, they had dreams. She almost envied their light-heartedness, their faith in the future, their sleep untouched by nightmares.

For the first time, she wondered whether she had made the right decision in joining the police, or whether she would have been better off choosing a different profession that would have allowed her to live a quieter life. Perhaps, she told herself, the mistake had been to choose Florence as her place of work, attracted as she had been by the city's beauty but unaware of its other face.

She dismissed these thoughts. It was time to go home. She set off again, her face caressed by the evening breeze, accompanied by the voices of the tourists who crossed her path, a murmur that reminded her of a swarm of insects. She walked past historic buildings that bore witness to a prestige that had long been forgotten, and wondered what was hidden inside them. She thought about her cat, Mimì, who was waiting for her, and imagined her curled up on her usual chair.

She went into a snack bar near the Piazza del Mercato Centrale to buy something to eat. She had to make do with a quarter of roast chicken and potato croquettes, the last five in the place. There was nothing else. She would reheat them in the microwave she had bought just a few days earlier and had not yet used. It was the perfect opportunity.

As she was about to open the door to her building, she saw a group of young immigrants under the portico to her left, their voices raised in animated argument. She went in and climbed the stairs to her top-floor apartment. As she got to the door, she froze.

It was ajar. Someone had forced it open.

The second nasty surprise in less than twenty-four hours.

She had to stay calm.

She took her gun from its holster, pulled back the slide release, and inserted a bullet in the chamber. Then she took a deep breath and went in, her heart pounding in her chest. Gritting her teeth, she immediately flicked the light switch to her right. As she did so, her bag slipped from her hands and she felt her heart beating faster than ever. She was starting to sweat. She advanced step by step.

What if it was a trap?

But it wasn't. There was nobody here. Just complete chaos: objects strewn over the floor, her travelling bag open in the living room, the tap left running in the bathroom. The typical signs of a burglary.

Why here? What had they been looking for? Certainly not money or valuables.

Her breathing returned to normal and she put her pistol back in its holster.

Now she would have to do an inventory of the missing items. She looked everywhere and established that the thieves had taken her stereo, her camcorder and the family photograph album which she always kept on her bedside table so that she could look through it often, sometimes just before she went to sleep, to bring back happy memories and drive away the nightmares.

Devastated, she slumped onto one of the kitchen chairs.

What about Mimì? she suddenly wondered. Where had she gone? Had she taken advantage of the half-open door and run away?

She stood up abruptly and started looking for her.

No, she hadn't run away.

Teresa found her curled up in a ball under the bed. She reached her arms in and pulled her out. She hugged her tight and gently stroked her fur. The poor thing was trembling.

She took out her mobile and dialled Rizzo's number.

'I'll be right over,' Rizzo said, reassuringly.

The apartment was a small one, and the two forensics technicians took just over an hour to search for prints. They found a few, but were unsure whether or not they would be useful.

In the meantime, a patrol car had checked out the immigrants under the portico. They were still arguing, although their voices were noticeably more subdued now. They were Moroccans, and only one of them was without an up-to-date residence permit. When asked whether they had seen anyone go into the building, they all said no.

'It's a strange burglary, Francesco,' Teresa said to Rizzo after listing the stolen items.

'Yes, it is.'

Why on earth had the burglar taken the photograph album? he wondered. What did he intend to do with it? Could someone have been trying to intimidate Teresa?

And he couldn't help remembering Costanza's eyes.

Before leaving with Rizzo, the forensics technicians did a temporary repair job on the apartment door. Once she was alone, Teresa decided to call it a night. She was too tired and upset to do anything. She took a quick shower, got into bed, huddled beneath the covers like a little girl, and switched out the light. She closed her eyes and fell into a restless sleep.

She woke with a start just after five. Her mouth was dry and she felt really thirsty. She had dreamt that she was in a swimming pool and someone was trying to strangle her.

When she realised that she wouldn't get back to sleep, she got up. She was hungry. She remembered the chicken and the potato croquettes. She had left them in the kitchen, still wrapped. She reheated them in the microwave and ate them. The chicken wasn't bad at all. She looked at Mimì. Strangely, the cat lay curled up on the chair, staring at her without moving. She must still be traumatised by that unexpected visit, thought Teresa.

How many of them had there been? Just one, or more than one? What a pity Mimì couldn't tell her.

After a while, the cat shook herself, jumped down from the chair and ran towards the bedroom, as if she were being chased by a huge dog. She had never done that before.

The poor thing was terrified.

Teresa put her Neapolitan coffee pot on to boil. She didn't feel like going back to bed, and she wouldn't feel safe until there was a new lock on the door. Right now, she needed at least two cups of coffee.

She also needed to think about what had happened.

Sitting there, with her gun beside her on the kitchen table, she came up with hypothesis after hypothesis, but each one ended up collapsing like a sandcastle battered by the waves. There was only one possible conclusion: it must have been a straightforward burglary, carried out by one of the many small-time crooks who operated in the city centre and grabbed only what they could easily take away with them.

The coffee aroma, which smelled of a brand new day, made her feel sad. There was nobody sitting opposite her. She longed for a companion, someone she could share her life with: both the good things and the bad. And she realised that this was something she had never thought about seriously. She was single, in spite of having been the object of her colleagues' attentions on more than one occasion. There was one in particular, Maurizio, who worked at Headquarters in Rome. He'd been in touch several times lately, asking to see her again, and she had put him off with one excuse or another. Now, though, she would have liked to have him here, next to her.

What an idiot she'd been to turn him down!

It was time for a change.

PART FOUR

FURTHER MYSTERIES

45

Wednesday 1 September

It was first thing in the morning and they were already pestering him.

Ferrara recognised the Commissioner's number on the screen of his mobile. He pressed the green button and answered.

The call was a brief one, but Adinolfi was clearly agitated.

'Headquarters, straight away,' Ferrara ordered his driver as soon as he had hung up. 'And fill her up with petrol as soon as we get there, there's no time to lose.'

There had been another death.

And they would have to go out of Florence this time.

Barely twenty minutes later, the Alfa Romeo 156 set off along the A1 autostrada in the direction of Rome.

In addition to Rizzo, Commissioner Adinolfi was on board. He had insisted on coming in person. With the light flashing on the roof and bursts from the siren when they hit traffic jams, they reached the Magliano Sabina junction. From there, they travelled along a series of A-roads until they got to Lake Bracciano.

The lake, which had volcanic origins, had once also been known as Lake Sabatino. It was here that, whenever he could, at weekends or on periods of leave, Inspector Antonio Sergi, Florence's Serpico, would get away from the accumulated fatigue of his work and forget his problems. At least that was what he had always told his colleagues. 'I'm going fishing,' he would say. 'There are plenty of fish in those waters. And don't even think of calling me. I'm not picking up my phone for anyone.'

He would actually switch off the phone, making himself completely unreachable. At Ferrara's request, Rizzo had discovered that Sergi had been spending the last few days there, making up for all the overtime he had worked and not been paid due to lack of funds.

During the journey no one had said a word. They found it hard to believe that anything could possibly have happened to Sergi.

Of them all, Adinolfi seemed the most pensive. From the moment he had got in the car he had been completely silent, his eyes fixed straight ahead. He had turned them to look out of the window at the countryside once or twice, but only for a few moments.

Ferrara and Rizzo on the other hand, sitting in the back seat, had exchanged a number of troubled glances. They would have liked to talk, but Ferrara had decided that it was best to say nothing.

Maybe because he had stopped trusting Adinolfi.

The body was lying on the beach, surrounded by police officers, some uniformed, some in plain clothes.

Some thirty feet away stood a group of men dressed in suits and ties, looking alternately towards the corpse, then towards the waters of the lake.

Somewhat further off was a crowd of onlookers. They had been attracted by the flashing lights of the police cars and Carabinieri, which had been left randomly on the road, some double-parked.

The car carrying the Commissioner, Ferrara and Rizzo pulled

up at a spot where the road widened slightly. As soon as he got out, Adinolfi gave his clothes the once-over and hurried towards the group of men in suits and ties.

Ferrara glanced around. In the distance, he could make out the Castle of Odescalchi, one of the most beautiful aristocratic residences in Europe. His eye fell on a poster advertising an event to be held locally: a three-day Buffalo Bill-style contest between cowboys and the *butteri*, herdsmen from the Maremma, involving two hundred horses.

He was just about to go over to the body when he looked at the group and froze. What were the National Security Coordinator and the Head of the State Police doing here in person?

He exchanged a quick look with Rizzo, then said, 'Come on, let's go and find out what happened.'

Rizzo nodded. He had also recognised Guaschelli, Head of the State Police, but said nothing. He did not know the other official.

They introduced themselves to the officers from the Rome *Squadra Mobile* and the Carabinieri from the local barracks.

'Two fishermen found him in the water this morning,' one of the Roman officers said. 'He went out yesterday afternoon and didn't return. That's according to the man who looked after his motorboat. He's being questioned at the barracks right now.'

Ferrara took a closer look at the body. It was Sergi. He was wearing jeans and a T-shirt and was quite bloated. The T-shirt had rolled up almost to his neck.

'Did he drown?' Ferrara asked.

'We think so,' the marshal in command of the barracks replied. 'It must have been an accident.' He had been the first on the scene and, in line with standard procedure, he would be in charge of the investigation, which would be coordinated by whichever deputy prosecutor was on call.

Ferrara looked at the lake. Its waters were dead calm. At Headquarters, Sergi was known to have been an excellent swimmer. Ferrara found it hard to believe that he had drowned, unless he had suddenly been taken ill. It was puzzling to say the least, but he said nothing for the moment.

'Which deputy prosecutor is handling this?'

'Someone from the Prosecutor's Department in Civitavecchia,' the marshal replied. 'This is their patch. He was here with the pathologist who carried out the external examination of the body. Right now, we're waiting for the body to be taken to the morgue for the post-mortem. There are a few marks on the body, but they could be the result of an accident or the length of time he spent in the water.'

'When will the post-mortem be carried out?'

'I heard the deputy prosecutor ask the pathologist to do it in the morning.'

'What about the boat?'

'It's been recovered, but there was nothing on board apart from his sunglasses and a wallet with his boat licence.'

Ferrara's concerns were growing minute by minute. He knew perfectly well that an accident could be used to hide a murder.

He might have yet another mystery to solve. And he felt guilty, because they had not had time to investigate the possible role played by Sergi in the secret lodge.

Luck really wasn't on his side at the moment.

46

'Florence,' Adinolfi ordered the driver.

The body had just been taken away and he had said goodbye to the others and got in the car, followed by Ferrara and Rizzo.

And that was the only word that left his mouth for the entire journey. When they got back to Headquarters, he asked Ferrara into his office, alone. There, in the strictest confidence, he told him what he had just learnt: that Inspector Sergi had been involved with the Secret Service, working undercover to infiltrate an international criminal organisation.

Ferrara was surprised to hear this, and blamed himself for not having had the slightest suspicion about his colleague's secondary activities and for having suspected him of being a mole. Never for a moment had it occurred to him that he might actually be a double agent working for the State: a dangerous role, and one that only officers with special – and increasingly rare – qualities were able to play.

'Why on earth was I kept in the dark about this?' he asked.

'Even I didn't know about it until today. The information was restricted to the Director of the Secret Service and the Head of the State Police. As an undercover agent, his role would only have been known to those who absolutely had to know about it. I'm afraid you weren't one of them, Chief Superintendent.' He sighed. 'Did he have a wife? Children?'

'He had a wife, but they were separated.'

That was where all that money came from! Ferrara thought. It all made sense now: Serpico had been in the pay of the Secret Service and benefited from their special funds, which let him live the high life, quite unlike a normal police officer.

'How long had he been working undercover?' he asked.

'About a year. According to the Director of the Secret Service, he was doing an excellent job.'

'And now that he's dead?'

'It was all for nothing.'

'But he must have gathered some evidence, surely?'

'Yes, but everything depended on his future testimony. Things he had been told, things he had been in a position to see . . . He could have been a witness in a possible trial, but now that he's dead there's nothing left that could be used as evidence.'

A long silence fell over the room, during which Ferrara thought about the difficult situation Sergi must have found himself in recently.

'Now get back to work,' Adinolfi said at last, 'and I strongly urge you to keep this information secret. Don't tell anyone, not even your deputy. Do you understand? That's an order.'

'You can count on me, Commissioner.' He stood up and left the room, grim-faced, his mind filled with foreboding.

Rizzo was waiting anxiously for Ferrara in his office, agog to know what the Commissioner had had to say.

As soon as Ferrara came in, he sat down behind his desk, lost in thought. Rizzo waited for his boss to speak.

Ferrara wasn't sure what to do. Not telling Rizzo, whom he had come to regard as a friend, made him feel almost like a traitor.

Rizzo waited.

It was a long, almost interminable, wait.

At last, Ferrara spoke. He had made his mind up, and he would take full responsibility for his decision. He didn't give a damn about the promise he had made the Commissioner. Commissioners came and went, but colleagues stayed. It was his colleagues who ran risks alongside him, who had to swallow the occasional failure, who spent their lives looking for clues, collecting evidence, tracking down criminals. His promise to Adinolfi didn't matter. He needed to tell Rizzo.

And he did.

The agitation was increasing minute by minute in the corridors of the *Squadra Mobile*. Sergi's death had shaken everyone and the meagre account of the discovery of his body had been passed from mouth to mouth without any extra details being added, as might otherwise have been expected.

All the members of the team were present. Even those who had a day off had come in to Headquarters to discuss what had happened and wait for any news from Bracciano, especially the results of the post-mortem.

Officer Pino Ricci was visibly the most shaken. He had been Sergi's partner for quite some time, and they had become almost inseparable. Between them they must have weighed over five hundred pounds. And between them they had successfully carried out many operations, in particular against drug dealers and traffickers. They had used the classic good-cop, bad-cop technique, with Ricci as the good cop and Sergi the bad. With his impressive physique – made even more intimidating by his thick beard – Sergi had often resorted to drastic methods. On occasion, these means had even been violent, harking back to the old school of policing, learnt on the street.

The bar on the corner of the building opposite Headquarters was filled with police officers. Even the barman was unable to hide his sadness.

47

At last they had the telephone records.

It was late afternoon, and Inspector Venturi was sitting in front of Ferrara's desk, holding the first records for Enrico Costanza's landline and mobile, those for the previous month. In the next few days, Vodafone and Telecom would give them the records for the last quarter.

'Have you already looked at them?' Ferrara asked.

'Yes, though there isn't much activity.'

'Tell me about it.'

Venturi went through the records in detail. With regard to the landline, apart from local calls, he had noticed a few calls to and from England.

'But we still don't know who the English account holders are. The numbers are the same ones we found in his diary and passed to Interpol.'

'Have we heard anything?'

'Not yet.'

'Chase it up!' he ordered, ignoring the Commissioner's request.

'I already have, by priority dispatch.'

'Well done.'

Venturi moved on to the mobile phone records. Not many calls there either. Only two during the whole of Saturday, 28

August, both outgoing: one to the Tumour Institute in Milan at 9.12 in the morning, the other to another mobile phone user in the Bologna area at 6.15 in the evening. That had been the last call made or received that day. The last call before he was killed.

'Do we know who the owner of the other mobile is?'

'Yes, of course. The phone used a TIM pay-as-you-go sim card registered to Cosimo Presti.'

'The journalist?'

'That's right, the journalist. Should I question him, Chief Superintendent?'

'Not yet. Get hold of a photo, maybe from his passport application or his identity card, and give it to Rizzo. He can show it to the staff at the Hotel Villa Medici.'

Maybe Lady Luck was giving them a helping hand . . .

The interviews with the hotel's manager and barman the previous afternoon had not yielded positive results. Neither of them knew the Senator's companion, and the CCTV camera outside had not been working for several days.

Ferrara's instinct was telling him that they were on the right track.

Suddenly Fanti came in, visibly agitated. He had a piece of paper in his hand, a fax that had just arrived from Headquarters in Rome.

And it contained a piece of information destined to cause even greater agitation in the corridors and offices of the *Squadra Mobile*.

It was about Sergi.

His death had not been an accident. Antonio Sergi had been strangled. The post-mortem had uncovered irrefutable evidence.

A fracture of the cartilage to the left of the hyoid bone had been discovered, a typical sign of strangulation. In addition, no water had been found in the lungs, as would have been the case if it had been a drowning. The pathologist had been categorical about that, and had sent a brief preliminary report to the Prosecutor's Department in Civitavecchia and the investigating officers in Rome, and it was the latter who had informed Florence.

The death had occurred the previous night.

The news left them speechless.

It seemed impossible that someone could have got the better of a solid, astute and, above all, physically strong officer like Sergi. Several of them wondered if there had been more than one killer. But who? Of course he had made enemies in his line of work, but usually such a serious act was preceded by some fairly clear signals. Had Sergi mentioned anything to anyone? Maybe to Ricci? No, nobody had been told anything like that.

Some speculated that Sergi had been leading a double life. Ricci, though, had other ideas. He would never ever believe that the colleague he'd loved so much could have been corrupt in any way. He would have sworn on his own life that Sergi had been a man of total integrity.

He remembered so many incidents. He had seen him perform great exploits, arresting groups of dealers and fugitives. He had seen him dodge bullets when a pimp opened fire on them. And how could he forget the day he had tried to save the life of a dangerous criminal, giving him first aid and driving him to hospital at top speed along a perilous road?

No. These were not the actions of a dirty cop who had failed in his duty.

But they were all united now, not only in their grief, but also in their determination to ensure that those responsible for this death that affected them so intimately were brought to justice. They would examine all the operations in which their colleague had been involved, starting with the most recent. That was where they needed to dig around, in his work, not in his private life. They were all sure of that. And if by any chance a dark side of him did emerge, they would shine light on it so that no shadows remained.

Serpico had been the best.

Ferrara called a meeting of his most trusted colleagues.

He had clarified his ideas about Costanza's diary entry for 20 August.

Sergi had realised that he was at risk, perhaps because someone had discovered his double game. Wanting to get out of whatever he was involved in with Costanza, he had been killed for posing a threat.

The word that kept echoing in Ferrara's brain like a pneumatic drill was the one the Senator had underlined: *Stupid*.

If only Sergi had confided in him, he thought, he might still be alive.

Everyone needed someone to talk to, damn it! Could it really be that he hadn't told anyone his secret, or confided the dangerous situation in which he had found himself?

Even if it meant having to face Adinolfi's wrath, he had decided that his colleagues should also know the truth about Sergi. That was the only way the investigation could proceed according to the plan he had in mind.

'Let's try and work on parallel lines,' he told his team. 'On the one hand, we'll carry on as if there's no connection between the murders of Costanza and Sergi. On the other, we won't rule out the possibility that we're dealing with the same killer.'

He assigned them their new tasks.

Ascalchi would go to Rome and help their colleagues who were investigating Sergi's death. As a Roman himself, he knew the area, which made him the best man for the job.

'Check the records for his mobile and his landline,' Ferrara suggested, hoping there might be a clue in his recent calls.

Ascalchi nodded, making notes on a piece of paper. 'What about the arson investigation?'

'I'll take care of it,' Ferrara said. 'By the way, are there any developments on that case?'

Ascalchi shook his head. 'No. The original suspect, the mad doctor, died six months ago in a car accident. I've spoken to some of the tenants and neighbours, but it was useless. No one knows anything.'

'Bring me the file.'

They got straight down to work.

All of them were teary-eyed.

48

She was really beautiful.

Without her waitress uniform, she looked like a different person. She wore a close-fitting cotton dress, which showed off her slim figure. She had a waist like a wasp. Her face was framed by blonde curls that made her look like a character from a fairy tale.

Officer Carlo Rossi had summoned her to Headquarters for an interview with the *Squadra Mobile*. Now he sat at his computer, ready to type what Venturi dictated. This time they would need to draw up a transcript.

First came the routine questions.

The girl's name was Kirsten Olsen. She was nineteen years old and had been born in Copenhagen, where she lived with her parents. She had been in Tuscany for about a year, studying Italian language and literature, and had been working in the restaurant to support herself.

Rossi typed everything out, deleting and rewriting the words several times. He was nervous, distracted by the witness's beauty. He would have liked to invite her out to dinner, but he didn't know how, or when, to ask her.

'Do you have a boyfriend, Signorina Olsen?' Venturi asked.

'No, I don't.'

What a relief, Rossi thought.

Venturi took the identikit from the desk drawer and showed it to her. 'Look at this picture carefully, please, and tell me if it reminds you of anyone.'

The girl looked at it for a few moments. 'It's the long hair that doesn't seem quite right to me,' she said.

'Why?'

'Based on the shape of the face, and the thing you mentioned about her driving a dark A-Class Mercedes, she does remind me of a woman I've seen in the restaurant a couple of times. But she had a very short haircut.'

'Was she alone?'

'No, she was with another woman on both occasions and . . .' She hesitated.

'And what?'

'I got the impression they were quite affectionate. They kept touching each other, and the other woman was looking at her in a certain way. I'm not sure I'm explaining myself very well.'

'You mean they were lesbians?'

'I wouldn't say that, but if you're asking was there something more than just the usual friendship between two women, then yes.'

'When did you see them?'

'The first time must have been in July.'

'This year?'

'Yes. And when they left I was curious so I watched them, and saw them get into a black A-Class Mercedes parked in front of the restaurant in one of the spaces reserved for our customers.'

'Who was driving?'

'The one with the short hair.'

'What about the second time?'

'That must have been July as well, or maybe early August.'

'Do you know where they live? Are they from the area?'

'I don't know.'

'Can you describe the two women in a bit more detail?'

The girl thought about it for a moment or two. 'The one with the Mercedes was tanned, and in good shape. She looked like someone who works out at the gym, if you know what I mean.'

'How tall was she?'

'About five foot six.'

'Did she have any distinguishing features?'

'Not really. Nothing I could see, anyway.'

'What colour was her hair?'

'Reddish.'

'What about the other woman?'

'She was an attractive woman too. She had long black hair, tied up in a ponytail. A bit of an Amazon.'

'Anything else you remember about either of them?'

'No.'

'If you happen to see them again, could you please let us know?'

'Yes, who should I call?'

Venturi gave her his business card, getting in before Rossi, who was about to pull his out of his wallet.

Rossi felt as if he'd been robbed.

He stamped the transcript and, once Venturi had read it aloud, gave it to the girl to sign and told her she could go. She said good-bye and Rossi walked her to the exit, keeping as close to her as he could, intoxicated by the scent of her skin.

In the meantime, Venturi was reflecting on her statement, thinking that, if the woman in the identikit was the one this girl had seen, she must have been wearing a wig when D'Amato, the mechanic, had seen her. Her hair could not have grown that much since early August.

He decided he would comb the Mugello area even more thoroughly the next day, since, according to D'Amato, the woman had been driving in the direction of Borgo San Lorenzo.

Having received orders from Ferrara to search Sergi's desk and locker, Fanti was now back in front of the Chief Superintendent with all the material he had gathered.

'Everything's recorded under different headings,' Fanti began. 'Petrol, travel, motorway tolls, hotels, lunches. Sergi made a note of everything. Absolutely everything, down to the last cent. He was almost fanatical about it.'

Because he was claiming expenses from the Secret Service, Ferrara thought.

'There are also cash deposits into the bank round about the end of each month. Between two and five thousand euros at a time. And I found something else, chief.'

From the top of the desk where he had put the material, already sorted with the precision for which he was known, Fanti picked up a folder labelled MISCELLANEOUS NOTES in black marker pen.

'Go on.'

'They're all reports, unsigned, and on unheaded paper. Some pages have *Confidential* written at the top. And they seem to refer to meetings he held with various private sources.'

'Does it mention the Black Rose?' Ferrara asked.

'No, it's never referred to. But on some pages he does mention that his "source" belonged to a secret organisation with foreign branches, especially in England.'

'And what does he report?'

Sergi's source, Fanti explained, had promised to exert serious pressure on the Minister for the Interior to have him promoted, in return for information on the status of certain investigations. And he had provided it, because he needed to win their trust, although on some occasions he had passed on credible-sounding but false information.

'But what really seems important to me, chief, is something else.'

'What's that?'

'Sergi was in contact with someone here in Florence. He indicates several times that he would pass his information to a source known as "the Archivist", who worked from home.'

'The Archivist? Is there anything to tell us who that is?'

'No, chief. I've examined every page.'

'Leave them with me. Well done, Fanti, you've done a great job.'

Fanti put everything back in the order in which he had found it and left.

It seemed to Ferrara that at last there was light at the end of the tunnel. The darkness in which the investigation had been shrouded would disappear sooner or later. The important thing was to be ready when it did and seize the moment.

49

Teresa looked around, then got out of the car from the Headquarters pool. The driver kept his hand on his holster until he saw her go in through the front door.

Ferrara had insisted that she should not take the short walk home from Headquarters alone and on foot this evening, in case someone was lying in wait for her.

He had not yet figured out why the killer had chosen this particular member of his team, the newest arrival, as the recipient of the envelope containing Costanza's eyes. Nor whether the burglary at her apartment was linked with their current investigation.

Teresa went quickly up the stairs, panting at the top.

But there was no surprise waiting for her this time.

Only her cat was there in her silent apartment. She was on her usual kitchen chair and when she saw Teresa, she jumped down and started rubbing herself against her legs. Teresa picked her up, bowed her head and received the usual hair-licking. Mimì was back to normal.

That night, a shadowy figure emerged from beneath the Loggia dei Lanzi in the Piazza della Signoria, walked quickly to the statue of Perseus, wrote *E. G.* on the base with a big red marker, and disappeared.

Rizzo burst into the room right in the middle of a meeting.

Ferrara was assigning tasks to the SCO and discussing the situation with Inspector Polito. So far they had only been involved in the new search of Enrico Costanza's villa, looking for the briefcase in which the victim had put the money, but to no avail.

Ferrara only had to look at his deputy to realise that something had happened. He hoped it wasn't more bad news. He had only just arrived at his office when he had been subjected to a talking-to from the irate Commissioner about the defacing of the statue of Perseus. He could have done without vandals further complicating his life.

'Now who's going to talk to the mayor, the city prefect and the Romans?' Adinolfi had shouted at him down the phone. 'We might as well pack our bags right now!' He had finished by slamming down the receiver.

'Excuse me,' Ferrara said to Polito and moved towards the door, followed by Rizzo. They stopped in the outer office.

'What is it, Francesco?'

'Beatrice Filangeri was found hanged in her cell this morning.'

Ferrara's face clouded over. He took a few steps, then leant back against the wall. He felt as if he had suddenly been punched in the stomach. He could not breathe.

'Go on, Francesco.'

Rizzo told him the details he had just received from the prison administration. Beatrice Filangeri had cut up her sheet and fixed one end to the bars over her window and the other round her neck.

'She had her hands tied behind her back, although not very tightly. According to the prison doctor, the way they were tied is quite compatible with suicide.'

'Why would she have tied her hands?'

'Maybe to avoid having second thoughts. At least that's what they told me.'

Ferrara would have liked to send Rizzo straight to the scene, but he dismissed the idea. He knew that the investigation of such deaths was the responsibility of the penitentiary police, who tended to play things close to their chests. His one obligation was to inform as soon as possible whichever deputy prosecutor was on call, and take any orders from him.

He let a few moments pass, then looked at Rizzo and said in a low voice, 'Inform the deputy prosecutor and make sure you're kept informed of the post-mortem results. Then remember to show the photo of Presti to the staff at the Hotel Villa Medici.'

'I'll do it this morning, chief.'

'You're still calling me chief, even though we're alone.'

'Sorry, Michele.'

Polito noticed the drawn expression on Ferrara's face as soon as he came back into the office. Instead of inspiring confidence, it made him worried.

They carried on with the meeting, but Ferrara's mind was elsewhere.

There was one question he really wanted the answer to immediately: had Beatrice Filangeri really committed suicide or had she been killed?

In the past ten years, the number of suicides in prison had risen almost three hundred per cent. This was almost always connected with the poor conditions in Italian prisons, but also the lack of staff, who were unable to be as vigilant as they should.

Ferrara was perfectly well aware of this situation, but there was no way Beatrice Filangeri's death could not strike him as suspicious. Particularly since he had discovered that his visit was more widely known about than he had assumed.

Had they struck even there? he wondered.

The case was slipping through his fingers.

The thought that the woman might have died because he had gone to see her was going to haunt him for a long time now, maybe for ever.

It was like a curse.

50

He was puzzled. For the last seven and a half miles he had been driving down a narrow winding road, wondering whether the SatNav might be wrong, but then he noticed a sign saying *San Gimignano* and realised he was actually taking the shortest route.

It wasn't the first time the machine had selected a less than easy ride just to save a couple of miles, or even only a few hundred yards.

In the vicinity of the Porta di San Giovanni, he found an empty space in a pay and display car park, then set off on foot along a pedestrian street flanked by shops selling ceramic items: plates, vases, lampstands and souvenirs. There were also a few wine shops. As he walked, he glanced briefly into the windows. He really quite liked the local ceramics. Before he left he would like to buy something to take back to England.

He reached the Piazza della Cisterna, just a short walk from the Collegiate Church with its Romanesque façade.

He looked around and decided to take a seat at one of the empty tables in the café and ice cream parlour opposite a branch of the Monte dei Paschi di Siena bank. He checked the time on his Rolex. He was on time. In fact, he had arrived ten minutes early. He ordered an iced coffee.

Sir George had arranged to meet him right here, in this magical piazza. He looked at the octagonal travertine limestone well that had once been used as a source of water but was now just a place for tourists to be photographed. Then his gaze was drawn to the Torre del Diavolo on the south side of the square. As he was staring up at it, Sir George arrived, a bundle of newspapers under his arm. He stood up to greet him, and they shook hands.

'Did you have a good journey, Richard?'

'Excellent, Sir George.'

The waiter came over and Sir George ordered a cup of tea.

Neither of them noticed a couple queuing outside a packed ice cream parlour a short distance away, looking at them in an apparently unconcerned manner: a man and a woman, dressed like so many others in jeans, T-shirts and Converse high tops. And later when they moved away towards the well, ice creams in hand, they walked confidently and were soon swallowed up among the other visitors.

Richard and Sir George discussed the latest developments, particularly those in Rome.

'It wasn't their doing, Sir George. Someone beat them to it, someone who wasn't from an organisation known to us.'

'There must have been another motive. But what? And who could it have been?'

'I hope to be able to find out soon. As regards the other matter, mission accomplished.'

'We knew we could count on you, Richard.'

51

It was no longer a matter of an isolated case.

Ferrara took a piece of paper and wrote:

Murders of Costanza and Rodriguez: night of 28-29 August.
Murder of Antonio Sergi: discovered Wednesday, 1 September.
Suicide(?) of Beatrice Filangeri: Thursday, 2 September.

He went through each death one by one, noting down significant details, a method he had often found useful. He would come back to these notes when necessary.

Once again, though, he was unable to establish a definite link between these events and ended up wondering whether it could all be coincidence. No, there were too many of them and they had happened within too short a period of time to be coincidental. And what about the Black Rose: that, surely, was a common denominator? The only difference between these deaths was the manner in which they had happened.

Costanza and Rodriguez had been murdered by a ruthless professional killer who had planned the crime in detail, without leaving the smallest clue behind, whereas in the case of Sergi, the murder did not seem to have been premeditated.

Filangeri's suicide was extremely suspicious. Beatrice had been

Leonardo Berghoff's partner and had killed Madalena with him and other, as yet unknown, accomplices.

He kept scribbling on the sheet of paper, trying to see his way through the tangle of thoughts in his head. Why had his visit to the prison not been kept a secret as he had requested? Who had spilled the beans to the Commissioner? Who had wanted to keep Beatrice Filangeri quiet?

Regarding Sergi's murder, he wondered how the fracture of the cartilage to the left of the hyoid bone could be explained, given how well-built the man had been. Maybe they'd dragged him by the neck when they pulled him out of the water.

He could not help thinking about an old case: the death of a well-known businessman in another lake. No post-mortem had been performed, and the death had been classified as either an accident or suicide. It was only many years later, when the body was exhumed, that it was discovered, precisely because of a hyoid bone, that the man had been murdered.

He re-read the relevant section of the pathologist's report that had been faxed to him from Rome: *The objective fracture in the upper left cartilage, which is believed to have occurred while the subject was still alive, makes it highly probable that the cause of death was violent mechanical asphyxiation produced by constriction of the neck (either manual strangulation or strangulation by ligature) carried out with murderous intent.*

He underlined 'murderous intent' several times, thinking as he did so that it must have taken more than one person, at least two or three, to overpower a man of Sergi's physique.

He thought again about the Commissioner's suggestions: *Forget about the Freemasons. Don't go chasing ghosts. Stop questioning Enrico Costanza's friends. Focus on your career. Make sure you're on the right team!*

He remembered the sight of Guaschelli deep in conversation at the crime scene at Lake Bracciano, and his presence there now seemed even more suspicious. That dwarf had been putting a spanner in the works for some time now, he was sure of it. It was just a feeling, but his instinct told him to proceed with caution.

The investigation into the deaths of Costanza and his butler had not made much progress. There were still no leads, not even from that identikit of the woman driving the Mercedes, assuming she had even been involved in the crime.

Could he actually be dealing with a perfect murder? No, he found that hard to believe. In reality, the perfect murder didn't exist. What did exist, on the other hand, were imperfect investigations, either where an important detail had been overlooked or misunderstood, or where the investigators were unaware of possible mistakes made by the killer.

He thought about Enrico Costanza's final telephone call to Cosimo Presti. What was the nature of Presti's relationship with the senator?

Maybe *that* had been the mistake.

Ferrara looked up from the sheet of paper on which he had been scribbling, and let his gaze wander round the room. He couldn't get Berghoff's letter out of his mind. The same question kept recurring: should he tell the Prosecutor's Department everything or continue to keep quiet?

The first option would, in all probability, have immediate consequences for his career. He might even have to face disciplinary proceedings. They could reasonably accuse him of failing in his duties as an official of the State Police, let alone as head of the most important criminal investigation department in the whole province.

But if he chose the second option, he would still have to square things with his own conscience. As a man first, as a police officer second.

He couldn't even think of a third option.

It was a real mess, but he had dug himself into this hole with his own hands, and nobody else could help him get out of it.

Perhaps the moment had finally come to write a full report and attach Berghoff's letter to it. If he had done that straight away, it would have been easier to obtain authorisation from the Prosecutor's Department to speed up the inquiries into foreign nationals and continue with the questioning of the victim's friends.

He decided to sleep on it.

Just then, the telephone rang, dragging him from his thoughts. It was Fanti, telling him that there was an international call for him.

Could it be Interpol?

No, it wasn't Interpol. It was the last person Ferrara would have expected to hear from at that moment: his opposite number, Markus Glock, head of the Criminal Investigation Department in Munich. They had met at the beginning of July, when Leonardo Berghoff had fled to Germany.

'What a pleasure to hear from you, Markus,' Ferrara said as soon as he recognised his voice.

After the pleasantries, Glock asked him, in his hesitant Italian, about the latest events in Florence. 'Are all these murders still linked to Berghoff? I read about them in the *Münchner Merkur* and the *Süddeutsche Zeitung*.'

'We still don't know. They could be.'

'If I can help by checking out anything here in Germany, just let me know, Michele.'

'*Vielen dank*, Markus.' Then he had a sudden flash of inspiration. 'Actually, there is something you can do for me.'

'What?'

'Email or fax me a report, if you have one, of the investigation so far into whoever killed Berghoff. I'm right in thinking you haven't caught them yet, aren't I?'

'Yes. And there is a report, which we wrote for the Prosecutor's Department.'

'Could you send me a copy?'

'Yes, of course.'

'Thanks, Markus.'

'Say hello to Francesco for me, Michele.'

'I will.'

Ferrara sat there with the receiver in his hand for a while. What a pity, he thought, that there wasn't another Markus in London. He still had vivid memories of how helpful his colleague had been, the way they had worked together to track down Leonardo Berghoff, the night the shootout had taken place, the daily visits as he was recovering in the hospital at Füssen . . .

They had developed a good relationship, which was fundamental when circumstances required cooperation between police forces, especially across borders. And now this telephone call was like an act of divine providence.

While speaking to Markus Glock, he had suddenly realised how to solve the problem of the letter. He added it now to his list of things to be checked out.

Luck was finally on his side.

52

He came out of the bedroom.

Angelica was sitting on the living room sofa with several news-papers resting on her lap.

He went over and stroked her hair. She stood up, put her arms round him, and kissed him on the lips. She loved kissing him. As cold as ever, he did not respond but slipped out of her embrace as soon as he could. He was too focused on what he had to say to her, and he wanted to say it as soon as possible. He did not care how she reacted. His mind was made up.

'You could have slept a bit longer,' she said. 'I brought you the papers. You would have found them here.'

'I'd have been late. You know I have to go and see someone. Tell me . . . ' He broke off, turned and went into the kitchen to get a drink of water: his throat felt terribly dry. He had slept on and off for four hours, three of which had been hellish. More nightmares. They had even made his bones ache, as if someone had taken him and given him a beating. No, it wasn't possible, he told himself. Those things were a long way in the past.

He walked slowly back to her.

'What did you want me to tell you?' she asked.

'Who's that friend who lives in your house?'

She wondered how he could have known. She waited a

moment, then said, 'She's the same one you saw me with in the Piazza San Marco on Sunday. I'm helping her out.'

'Just a friend?'

'Yes. Don't tell me you're jealous.'

'Who's jealous?' he retorted, raising his voice. 'You don't understand a fucking thing. You should stay well away from that girl. I don't want to have to tell you again.'

He was really starting to lose his temper. He could feel his rage building inside him, and he had to make a considerable effort to control it.

'She's only staying with me for a while, just a few days, a week or so at the most. She's looking for somewhere to live in Florence, and you know how hard that can be. The rents are ridiculous.'

'Our business is ours alone. I'm not going to tell you again.'

'But—'

'No buts. I don't give a fuck about your *friend*'s problems. You should be more careful. Especially now.'

He started back towards the kitchen. It was whisky he needed now.

She cut in ahead of him and barred the doorway. 'Let's talk about this.'

'I've got nothing more to say, Angelica, so just fuck off.'

She went out, slamming the door behind her. She was furious. She wasn't going to let anyone control her life like that! Not now that she had found someone she really liked. No, there had to be a solution, she needed to make him see that they weren't kids any more, that behaving the way he did jeopardised their relationship. If he didn't change, their ways would part forever.

She got in her car and set off with a screech of tyres. Guendalina was waiting for her at home.

Gradually, the further she got from him, and the more she thought about Guendalina, the more she realised that the situation was becoming untenable. This double life couldn't continue. She had to stop pretending. Sooner or later, the woman she loved would realise she was hiding something from her. And she did not want to lose her.

'He can fuck off,' she murmured as she turned on the radio. She immediately recognised Amy Winehouse's voice singing 'Stronger Than Me'. She turned up the volume and started to sing along. She knew every word by heart.

In the meantime, he was thinking it was time to put another piece of the jigsaw in place. A new one, not part of his initial plan.

He didn't need her. He could get everything he wanted through his own efforts. He had no limits. He could find a solution to every problem, like the mathematical genius he was.

He would make her pay dearly.

But he had to hurry.

By Sunday, or Monday at the latest, he would have to leave Florence.

Maybe forever.

53

'Any news, Francesco?'

As soon as Ferrara, who was trying to get to grips with Sergi's papers, saw his deputy come in, he set them aside and motioned him to sit down. He looked at his watch. It was five past two in the afternoon.

Rizzo told him about his conversation with the director of Sollicciano Prison. An external examination of Beatrice Filangeri's body had not revealed any signs of violence. And there had been no traces of poisonous substances or barbiturates in her blood.

'Did he tell you whether she happened to leave a note?'

'No, Michele.'

'What about the post-mortem?'

'They're doing it later.'

'How did it go at the Hotel Villa Medici?'

'Fine.'

'Were they able to tell you whether the person with Costanza that evening was Cosimo Presti?'

'Yes, it was.'

Piero, the barman, had been in no doubt. The man with Costanza had indeed been Cosimo Presti. The maître d' had confirmed it. Costanza and Presti had dined in one of the hotel's two restaurants, the Lorenzo de' Medici.

That left them with several options. Should they question Presti straight away? Or would it be better to wait and keep him under surveillance for a few days? Should they acquire his telephone records? Tap his phone? Get a warrant to search his home?

It was a difficult choice to make, and they had to trust their intuition. But whatever they decided, they needed to keep one important thing in mind: Presti was a journalist, and they all knew that, when it came to the media, the Prosecutor's Department acted with extreme caution.

'Michele, do you think they'll authorise us to get hold of his telephone records and tap his phones?'

'We'd have to really justify our request, and even then I have my doubts. Unless . . . ' He broke off for a moment and when he resumed he told Rizzo about the telephone call from Glock.

In the end, they decided to send Deputy Prosecutor Vinci a detailed report, attaching to it Leonardo Berghoff's letter along with the other documents sent by their German colleague.

They could well be coming to a decisive moment. One that might also clarify the position of the Prosecutor's Department.

'Where were you? You have to tell me where you were!'

Angelica had got home to find Guendalina sitting on the sofa, grim-faced, her hair tangled. In her hand she was clutching a half-empty glass of cognac.

'And you have to tell me why you haven't replied to my text messages!'

As Guendalina spoke, she continued to stare at Angelica, her big black eyes now swollen and brimming with tears. She had been lying on the sofa for a long time, brooding over some imagined betrayal.

'Calm down, darling,' Angelica said, dismissing her anger. 'Have a glass of water, instead of this stuff.' She picked up the almost empty bottle from the coffee table and took it into the kitchen. Then she tossed her handbag onto an armchair and headed straight for the bathroom. She did not feel like answering, at least not straight away. There would be time. In the meantime she would try to think of what she was going to say.

She could tell her she'd gone for a drink with colleagues after work. Or been to a meeting about the planned exhibition. Both were plausible excuses, but she knew that Guendalina would not believe either of them. She was too sensitive. Angelica realised that she could not continue lying to her. For now, she would hold her tight in her arms, caress her and kiss her. Just as she had done the previous evening when she had come home and found Guendalina sulking and ready to accuse her of being unfaithful. She had sworn to her over and over again that she didn't have anyone else. Later, in bed, they had kissed and caressed and made up. And Guendalina had pretended to believe that her friend had really been somewhere near Siena, working on a painting project.

Meanwhile, Guendalina had stood up, grabbed Angelica's handbag, and taken her mobile out of the outside pocket. Her fingers moved quickly. She pressed the button for recent calls, and the one for text messages. She saw the usual numbers, which were familiar to her. Among the texts she saw the ones she herself had sent which had gone unanswered. There were also a couple that struck her, though. Short, almost telegraphic messages. They had come from a number that hadn't been saved in the contact list, a number that was completely unknown to her.

Another thing she found in the handbag, wrapped in a paper tissue, was a small quantity of marijuana.

These two discoveries hurt her: she had believed that Angelica had no secrets from her and that she had been sincere when they had promised not to lie to each other.

She would have liked to ask her immediately, about both the texts and the grass, to confront her, to make a scene. But she reined in the impulse. A little voice inside her, a voice of caution, told her to pretend that nothing had happened, to feign indifference.

She put the mobile back in place and stretched out again on the sofa.

She told herself to relax when she saw Angelica come back into the room.

She pressed the button of the CD player on the sideboard next to the TV and the room was filled with Ricky Martin singing 'Livin' La Vida Loca'.

Angelica sat down next to her on the sofa, took her hand, and held it tight. Sobbing, Guendalina threw herself into her arms. She needed to be held. She dismissed her fears and suspicions and started to take her clothes off.

54

Fabio Biondi pressed the button to open the door as soon as he heard the bell.

He was expecting Teresa. He had called her an hour earlier to let her know the news.

Now she was here, curious to hear what he had to say.

Fabio looked away from the monitor and announced with a smile of satisfaction, 'I've managed to extract two more images. Come over here, Superintendent!'

Teresa went closer. On the screen, charred remains lay on a floor, recognisable as Madalena's body. There could be no doubt now about the nature of these images.

'Something awful must have happened in that place, Superintendent,' Fabio said. 'The crucifix . . . those burns . . .'

'Madalena,' Teresa said, and immediately regretted letting the word slip out. Fabio was an external technician, and had no official role, which meant that he was not bound by rules of professional secrecy.

She tried to correct herself, telling him that she was just speculating at the moment.

In reply, Fabio merely said that he would continue working on the video.

'Thanks Fabio, we're counting on you.'

*

There were few names in the small phone book with its soft leather cover, and the contents were written in a way that only he could interpret, thanks to his amazing mathematical memory. It was the only thing he had been able to show off about in front of his classmates. He had cultivated his talent over time, and had reached a professional standard at the game Salto del Cavallo. With the appropriate modifications, he exploited these skills to demonstrate his own genius.

The game consisted of moving the knight in the typical L-shaped move as defined by the rules of chess, in such a way as to touch each square once and once only. It was a real brainteaser, which had been attempted by a number of mathematicians.

He leafed through the phone book until he found what he was looking for. He had changed her first name to a man's name. He had changed the area code too, so that, if some nosy parker had tried to call that number, a complete stranger would have replied.

He had just got out of the shower, a towel around his waist. He could see her in front of him as he dialled the number. A few inches short of six feet, long black hair, dark eyes, small breasts with pointed nipples. He remembered every detail perfectly. He saw her kneeling in front of him, submissive and ready to give him pleasure, so aroused that she did not feel his nails digging into her back.

He became aware of his erection beneath the towel. The woman answered on the fourth ring. 'Hello?'

It was the warm, sensual voice he remembered.

'Florinda?'

'Yes.'

He imagined her naked: her firm thighs, her long legs, her black pubic hair.

'It's Stefano, do you remember me?' It was a name he had only ever used with her. 'I've just arrived in Florence . . . '

'Oh, yes, Stefano. Of course I remember you.'

She waited in silence.

'Would it be OK if I came over? I told you I'd see what I could do, and I've got some really good news for you ...'

'Not right now,' she replied. 'I'm expecting my sister. Come in an hour. But can't you tell me the news now?'

'I'll tell you when I see you, and I'll bring a bottle of champagne, because this demands a celebration.'

'OK, then. I'll see you later.'

When the call was over, he switched off the phone, took out the sim card and put another one in immediately. It was a precaution worth taking. They would never be able to identify him, never track him down. He always used mobiles without GPS.

He looked at his watch. It was almost eight in the evening. In just sixty minutes, he would be at her apartment, right on time. Punctuality was one of his obsessions. As he put on his black tracksuit, he let his fantasies run wild.

When he was ready, he looked at himself in the mirror. He liked the devilish gleam in his eyes. He went to the drinks cabinet, took out the bottle of whisky and half-filled a glass. He felt the alcohol moving down into his stomach, the burning sensation there, the warmth spreading through his whole body.

Tonight he would add another piece to his jigsaw.

From the big underground room, he got a five-inch double-bladed knife with a mother-of-pearl handle. He had bought it some time ago for a special occasion, just like the one that was taking shape in his mind.

He went out.

On the way, he thought with growing excitement about their meeting a week earlier.

He had approached her in the Giubbe Rosse, the historic café in the Piazza della Repubblica, founded at the beginning of the nineteenth century by the Reininghaus brothers. The café, which owed its name to the Viennese-style red jackets worn by the waiters, had started out as a focal point for the German community and had become the heart of intellectual and artistic Florence during the twentieth century.

He was familiar with the history of the café, and loved to spend time there, looking up at the drawings and paintings covering its walls.

One day, he had noticed an extremely beautiful girl who was a regular and had started looking out for her. They would often sit beside each other and before long they were exchanging a few words.

She told him she had done modelling work abroad and had come to Italy with one dream: to be a catwalk model for a famous Florentine fashion house.

'But it's not as easy as I thought,' she said, with a slight grimace. 'I guess I don't have the right connections. It's a closed shop. Someone advised me to try Milan instead.'

He had listened to her attentively, unable to look away from her stunning black eyes, which had struck him from the first moment he had seen her. 'You're right,' he had said. 'You do need the right connections to work here, but today's your lucky day.'

'Really?'

'Oh, yes!'

He had told her he worked for an American film production company and could certainly help her out.

'I can get you into films, maybe only as a walk-on to start with, but that could lead to other things. There are great opportunities in the fashion world in New York too.'

He was very good at inventing new identities for himself, and it had never for a moment occurred to her that he might be telling her a pack of lies. She had trusted him and had told him how entranced she was by the beauty of the Florentine hills.

'That's why I rented an apartment in Pontassieve. It's beautiful and cheap, too.'

'It's such a long way out, though,' he had said. 'Do you have a car?'

'No, but there are plenty of trains and buses.'

'Are you doing anything right now?'

'No.'

'Let me take you home, then. On the way I can tell you what I'll do when I go back to the United States.'

'Thanks very much.'

'And you know what we can do?'

'Tell me.'

'We'll go via Mugello. It's not too much of a detour, and there's something I want to show you I'm sure you haven't seen before.'

She had smiled.

After driving for about an hour, they had reached Vicchio del Mugello, the birthplace of Giotto and Fra Angelico.

They had had a snack just outside the village, at the Casa del Prosciutto, and when they resumed their journey towards Pontassieve he had taken an unpaved side road. He had told her that the river Sieve, a tributary of the Arno, flowed nearby. The river was almost dry, and they had walked along the bank. Then they had stopped and sat down to enjoy the peace of the countryside.

There was not another living soul about, and the silence was total.

He had talked to her about Giotto and his art, then about Michelangelo and the statue of David that he liked so much.

After a while he had taken her hand and she had squeezed his tightly. He had brushed her cheeks with his lips, then kissed her on the mouth, and she had responded eagerly. It was at that moment that he had felt a kind of explosion inside. It was his dark side aching to burst out.

'No, not here,' she had said when she'd felt his hand slipping inside her T-shirt. 'Let's go to my place.'

Fate had come calling for her.

And for him, too, when he thought about it. Because he had planned this new piece of the jigsaw, but at a different time.

Now, though, was perfect. Right now.

He was ready to let his fantasies run wild.

That night, the Rohypnol had no effect on him. Maybe he needed to increase the dose. He had opened his eyes and was surprised to find himself in his own bed. Nobody had tied him to a chair, gagged him and dragged him away, nor were the words he had heard his own: 'At this point I should confess that I have been seriously considering eating your wife.'

He remembered now: it was a scene from Ridley Scott's *Hannibal*, which had been set in Florence. In it, Chief Inspector Rinaldo Pazzi, played by the great Giancarlo Giannini, was the object of Hannibal Lecter's attentions. The scene was still vivid in his mind.

Hannibal Lecter was one of his idols.

He closed his eyes and tried to get back to sleep, telling himself how great he was.

Lies, disguises, fantasies. Perfection. He was a true genius.

He fell asleep with this one last thought: the climax to everything would soon be here.

It was a matter of days, maybe even hours.

He would keep the promise he had made himself.

55

Friday 3 September

It was eight twenty-five in the morning when the car from the Carabinieri barracks in the Via Aretina turned into a dead-end street in Pontassieve, about seven miles from Florence. The driver stopped outside number seven, a small, three-storey, ivory-coloured apartment building dating from the beginning of the twentieth century. It was the address that a woman, her voice shaking with emotion, had given the 112 operator a few minutes earlier.

Two carabinieri, one superior to the other, got out and walked quickly towards the front door, looking around without noticing anything out of the ordinary – either because it was still early, or maybe because the woman on the phone had lied. At least that was what they were hoping. It wouldn't be the first time that they had responded to a tip-off that had then turned out to be false. There were always plenty of attention-seekers, and plenty of young kids killing time.

The front door was ajar. They went in and climbed the stairs, taking care where they put their feet. You could never be too careful. But there wasn't anything strange here either. They stopped on the first floor.

The door to the apartment was wide open, and a young girl was sitting on the landing outside it with her back against the wall. She was crying softly and wiping her tears with the back of her hand. Her eyes were filled with horror. A young man was crouching beside her, trying to comfort her. When she saw them, she turned her head and mumbled a few words, 'Inside ... inside ... oh my God ... go inside.'

The two carabinieri went in.

The small, shabby, barely lit entrance led to a narrow corridor. A tracksuit top was hanging from an old coat peg attached to the wall. To the right was a kitchenette and to the left a room with a sofa, an armchair and a round table with four chairs pushed up against a wall. Everything looked second-hand. Even here, though, there was nothing unusual.

At the end of the corridor was a small bathroom. The superior officer stuck his head in. Nothing. Just the smell of talcum powder. Next came a wide-open door. The bedroom.

The furniture had been kept to a minimum: a wooden chest of drawers with a television and VCR on top, a dresser, a small wardrobe, and a double bed with an imitation leather headboard. Everything appeared to be in order, apart from one of the dresser drawers, which was open, the dishevelled bed, and the red marks on one of the walls.

Next to the bed, between the bedside table and the wall, was the body of a young woman. She lay on her back, in a pool of blood. Her stomach was covered with a sheet, and one foot was half inside a slipper, but the rest of her was naked. Her legs were splayed open. On the exposed part of her body were a number of wounds, almost all concentrated around the left breast. They looked as if they had been inflicted with a knife, or at least a very sharp object.

She must have been about twenty. Even in death, her face was very beautiful, with prominent cheekbones, full lips, now turning purple, and long black hair. Her mouth was wide open, as were her eyes.

How had she reacted to the fury of the attack? Had she frozen with terror or had she defended herself with all her might?

The officers stood looking at her, but without going too close. Their first thought was that, in all probability, this had been a sexually motivated murder.

'Go downstairs and call the barracks,' the superior officer said to his subordinate. Then he went out to the weeping girl and the young man consoling her and said, 'Come on, signore, signorina, let's go inside.'

They went to the living room, where the young woman, still overcome with shock, collapsed into an armchair. She was the victim's sister. The young man introduced himself as her boyfriend. She could not stop crying and was only able to speak every now and again in a strong local accent while the young man tried in vain to calm her down.

Soon they were joined by other carabinieri.

Patrol cars and unmarked vehicles filled the street, double parking. Among them was the commander of the barracks, Marshal Vincenzo Moretta.

One of the officers who had found the body came to meet him on the stairs, and from the expression on his face Moretta could imagine the horror of the scene awaiting him.

He had seen a lot of bodies in his time, but the one he now saw sent him back years into the past.

The terrible wounds, almost all concentrated around the left breast, the blood on the floor, the splayed legs: they were like a language that spoke directly to him. A distinct language, reflecting the modus operandi of the Monster of Florence, who had killed a young couple in their car in a secluded spot just a few miles from here, back in 1974. The girl had been stabbed over ninety times with a sharp object, particularly in the area around her left breast.

For a while, the marshal said nothing, unable to accept the idea that one of that band of perverts, still at large, had struck again.

He dismissed these thoughts. He mustn't jump to any conclusions in the heat of the moment. He knew perfectly well how much that could prejudice or even impede the progress of an investigation and delay the discovery of the truth.

After a while he heard voices on the stairs. It was the pathologist and his assistant.

In the meantime, a couple of the carabinieri had been checking the windows. They all looked out onto an internal courtyard and all had shutters that had been closed from the inside. Nobody had forced them open. Nor had anyone forced the wooden door.

This meant that either the killer had been in possession of a key and had let himself in, or had been let in by the woman because she knew him.

'Ranieri,' the marshal said to the officer from the patrol car, 'establish the names of all the tenants here and interview those who are at home. We need to know as much as we can about the victim, her life, her habits. Then question her sister.'

They had no time to lose.

The pathologist put on his plastic overshoes and latex gloves, approached the body, crouched down and lifted the sheet.

Piero Franceschini was a pupil of Gustavo Lassotti, director of the Institute of Forensic Medicine. He had been in Florence for just over two years. He was in his forties, at the height of his professional career, and there was every reason to believe that he would soon follow in Francesco Leone's footsteps.

He stood up and moved aside so that the photographer from the forensics team could record the scene and document the exact position of the body.

The thing that had most horrified all of them was the large wound that went from the pubic area to the navel. The killer had made a cut more than four inches long and opened the skin, leaving part of the intestines exposed.

There were other cuts, some deeper than others, around the pubic bone.

Just like Jack the Ripper ... or the Monster of Florence!

There could only be contempt and hatred behind such cruelty. The killer must be a sadist who got pleasure from torturing his victim, seeing the terror in her eyes, watching the blood flow from that violated body. It was like an unusually severe punishment, and maybe that was what it was meant to be.

Since they did not have hi-tech equipment in this district, other technicians had come from Florence and were now moving about the room in white coats, examining the bloodstains. There were lots of them and they were spread over a considerable area.

The technicians noted the position and shape of the various spatter marks. This was in order to establish the exact place where the attack had begun, the height and strength of the assailant, not to mention his position in relation to the victim and, above all – a detail that could be particularly useful during the investigation – whether he was left- or right-handed. The post-mortem would then provide the key by revealing the angle of the wounds.

Naturally there was a greater concentration of blood near the body, where the woman's life had ended. However, there were also some marks present on the wall where the chest of drawers was. Some suggested dragging, as if the victim had walked along that wall after being wounded, leaning against it to support herself before collapsing to the floor.

Could they be bloodstains that the killer had tried to erase? the marshal wondered. In that case, maybe he had left a trace of DNA behind.

One of his men came over to him and said, 'Marshal, there's more blood on the floor near the sink in the bathroom.'

Moretta went to the doorway of the bathroom and saw the marks immediately. Maybe the killer had washed himself before fleeing the scene, he thought. Given the amount of blood spilled during the murder, that was a reasonable assumption. Samples were being taken from all the stains to be analysed later in the lab.

On the floor, just inside the bathroom door, they found a light print from a rubber-soled shoe measuring ten inches by three inches. There were also several hairs in the sink. Collected and sealed according to international protocol, they would be handed over to the pathologist for examination.

As Moretta was overseeing the work, he heard the pathologist calling him. 'Marshal, could you come here, please?'

Franceschini was crouching next to the body and holding up, for Moretta to see, what looked like human hairs. They were light brown in colour.

'She was clutching these in her right hand and some of them have the bulbs attached. She must have fought her attacker. That's also shown by the wounds on her left forearm and some of her fingers. They're typical defence wounds.'

'Was there any sexual violence?' Moretta asked.

'From an initial examination, I'd say no. But I can only confirm that after the post-mortem.'

'When are you thinking of doing it?'

'In the morning. What I can tell you now, for certain, is that there are no signs of recent sexual activity.'

As he said this, he stood up, moved away to take off his latex gloves, then added, with his back still to the marshal, 'The body can now be taken to the Institute of Forensic Medicine in Florence and you can continue with your work.'

'Thank you, Doctor,' Moretta said. 'I'll expect your phone call after the post-mortem.'

'OK.'

Franceschini said goodbye and started to leave, with his typical shambling gait, but stopped in the doorway of the bedroom and turned.

'Marshal.'

'Yes?'

'Who's the deputy prosecutor on call?'

'Vinci. We informed him straight away but he said he couldn't come. He's busy with the murders in Florence. He delegated the crime scene investigation and the initial inquiries to us.'

'Thank you,' Franceschini said and walked out.

The body was put in a waxed fabric body bag, then into a zinc coffin, and carried outside, where a hearse was ready to take it to the Institute, escorted by a patrol car.

At last they were free to carry out their search.

They combed every corner, looking for clues, hoping to recover the murder weapon.

The bedroom was full of papers of various kinds: business cards, handwritten notes, a 2004 diary, a few magazines, and a lot of photographs stored in a cardboard box. They seemed to be part of a professional portfolio. Many of them featured the victim in a variety of poses, and some showed her on the catwalk wearing a swimsuit.

There was nothing, though, that could be linked to the crime, let alone the murder weapon, or any clothing belonging to the perpetrator. This led them to believe that the killer had not changed his clothes before leaving. Which could mean only one thing: the murder had been planned down to the last detail.

Finally, the apartment was sealed and placed under a sequestration order. Chalk marks had been left on the floor to indicate the position of the body, and everywhere were traces of the silvery powder used to lift fingerprints from the furniture, doors and light switches.

56

As was to be expected, a crowd of curious bystanders had gathered outside the building behind the red and white tape put in place by two carabinieri to prevent people milling about the front door.

Some, horrified by the rumours that had immediately begun circulating, were discussing the incident in low voices. Others, more cynical, were declaring that the girl had had it coming. How had she ever thought she could avoid attracting attention, dressing so provocatively all the time?

Naturally, reporters from the newspapers and the local television stations were there, waiting impatiently for the marshal to come out so that they could bombard him with their questions. As soon as he stepped out of the front door, he started walking quickly, eyes fixed on the ground. That did not stop the more aggressive reporters from pushing past the tape and encircling him as if he were a hunted animal. Unfazed, he simply said, 'No comment,' and pushed away a microphone that had been thrust in his face. He had always been reluctant to release statements, preferring to respect the rule that it was the public relations office at Command Headquarters in Florence, under whose authority his barracks fell, which handled all that kind of thing.

'Can you at least tell us her name?' one of the reporters asked him. 'Is it true she was Cuban?'

The marshal gave the victim's name and age – Florinda Olivero, twenty – and confirmed her nationality.

Then he managed to force his way through the crowd, walked briskly to his car and got in. The driver set off at top speed.

Pontassieve would be on all the front pages the following day.

Meanwhile, Ferrara had been having a long conversation with Teresa about the break-in at her apartment.

Neither of them could find a plausible explanation for the theft of the photograph album, an object of merely sentimental value. For some reason, the burglar seemed to have wanted to target her soft spot: her memories. But why? More importantly, who?

Being the good observer that he was, Ferrara had noticed that, in spite of her efforts to hide her emotions, Teresa was tense and preoccupied.

'From today,' he ended by saying, 'you'll be accompanied by an officer wherever you go, at least until we have a clearer idea about this whole thing. And don't worry, you're not alone.'

By now it was almost two in the afternoon.

Ferrara lit the unlit cigar he had been clenching between his teeth – his second of the day – and waited for the two o'clock regional news.

Inevitably, the first item was the murder in Pontassieve. Equally inevitably, it emphasised the horrific state in which the body of the young Cuban had been found. It was clear that, in spite of the marshal's reticence, certain details had leaked out to the media. The second item was a fatal collision between a heavy goods vehicle and two cars in a tunnel on that terrible stretch of the A1 between Florence and Bologna that crossed the Apennines.

Ferrara switched off the television, with the reporter's conclusion to the first item echoing in his head: 'An act of violence that threatens to plunge the whole province back into the nightmare of a homicidal maniac at large.'

Suddenly, he heard a commotion in the corridor. He leapt to his feet, rushed out of his office, and saw two uniformed officers struggling with a young, dark-skinned man in handcuffs who was trying to break free. They had caught him in the act of stealing a wallet from a tourist's bag in the Piazza della Signoria. The city was full of these petty thieves.

'We're putting him in a cell,' one of the officers said.

Ferrara nodded, while thinking it was probably a complete waste of time; within a few hours, or the next morning at the latest, the man would be sentenced but then be back out on the streets anyway.

He was about to go back into his office when he saw Rizzo, who had been to the Prosecutor's Department, coming towards him with an envelope in his hand.

'Let's go to a bar and get a coffee, Francesco.'

He'd had a sudden desire to get away from the four walls of his office. He needed a coffee anyway, even if it was his fourth or fifth of the day. His cigar would taste better afterwards.

They left Headquarters. As they walked, Rizzo told him that Vinci had hesitated for a bit, then granted them authorisation to acquire copies of Presti's telephone records.

'Just for the last fortnight, though, Michele.'

'What about the phone tap?'

'He said he'd let me know. I suspect he'll talk about it with his boss.'

'When will we know for sure?'

'I'll call him tomorrow morning.'

'Yes. You have to keep on at him, because with all his other commitments – tennis, jogging – he'll never get back to you.'

'We know what he's like by now. I'll actually go to his office at nine tomorrow morning.'

'Better still.'

Then Rizzo told him about the results of the post-mortem on Beatrice Filangeri.

The pathologist's report stated that the death had occurred between one and two in the morning. The cause was asphyxia. There was no indication of a struggle or anything else untoward.

'Who performed the post-mortem?' Ferrara asked.

'Francesco Leone.'

By now they had reached the bar. They ordered a couple of tuna and tomato sandwiches and a weak coffee each for lunch. They wolfed down the lot and walked back to Headquarters.

There was work to be done.

57

He was on the A11 autostrada linking Florence and Livorno via Pisa. The traffic had suddenly come to a halt.

He felt his back growing increasingly sweaty against the seat.

The radio announced that there had been a collision between two cars. So it wasn't a police road block.

Now a man came walking between the two lines of cars, looking from one to the other. When the man drew level with his car, he saw that he was wearing a bib with the word *Police* on it and seemed to be taking a close interest in him. Just as he was about to take his right hand off the wheel and slip it under the passenger seat, he realised that the policeman had moved on.

He gave a sigh of relief and rubbed his eyes. Gradually, everything came back to him.

He had slept for ages. The pills had worked.

Everything was going according to plan. Although it was possible he had made a mistake. His first one.

Had the images in his dream, which were becoming hazy now, been premonitions?

That bitch had turned out to be stronger and more cunning than he had anticipated. She had defended herself like a wild animal. And, once he had got back home, he had had to treat and bandage his right hand, which had been injured in the fight.

That Cuban whore hadn't wanted to die.

But no one would ever pin the killing on him, he had told himself when he woke up. He was safe.

He had drunk a large glass of cold milk in the kitchen, then gone down to his big underground room.

It was time to add another piece to the jigsaw.

Angelica had become a loose cannon. He had tailed her and her lover; he had spied on them constantly, even when they were having sex, listening to the words they used, their moans of pleasure.

Hiding two miniature cameras in that house had been child's play. He had planted one in the bedroom and the other in the living room. He knew everything, including the fact that that slut of an ex-convict had secretly checked Angelica's mobile.

An act that would cost her dear.

He had to do something.

He sent a text, a code word they had agreed on which meant that he expected Angelica to keep watch in San Gimignano by herself tonight. They needed to find out if that Englishman who was travelling in a rented car was still there as a guest of Sir George, or if he had finally left. It was something he absolutely had to know if he was going to put the final piece of the jigsaw in place.

Then he'd be able to forget about Florence – the Florence he loved so much – for a good long time.

58

'A homicidal maniac!'

Marshal Eduardo Gori, commanding officer of the Carabinieri's Criminal Investigation Squad in Florence, had just finished informing the colonel. He was forty-one, tall and thin, with prominent cheekbones and thick dark hair, greying at the temples. He was a man of great experience.

His colleague in Pontassieve had sent him a report with all the essential details and Gori had immediately called him to assure him that the team in Florence would do everything they could to help. It was a courtesy call, not strictly necessary, since the area covered by his squad included the whole of the province anyway.

'This was all we needed,' Colonel Arturo Parisi went on, his medals on prominent display on his impeccable uniform. 'What do you think, Marshal? Are we dealing with a serial killer?'

Gori shook his head. 'It's a bit early to say that after only one murder, sir.'

'But there have been similar murders in this very province in the past. Don't you remember the cases of the courting couples and the prostitutes?'

'Yes, sir, but those are old cases.'

'Well, it's best not to rule out anything, especially at the start. Make sure your colleague Moretta is aware of that. In fact, you know what I think? Send a team to back them up, I think they're going to need one.'

'Absolutely, sir, I'd already thought of it and told Moretta. I'll send Sergeant Surace and some other men immediately.'

'Perfect. And make sure you solve this case as soon as possible.'

Gori nodded, gave the ritual military salute and click of the heels, and hurried out.

Surace was standing in the outer office, waiting for him. He was only young but already weighed over fifteen stone. In his hand he held some papers that had just been faxed from Pontassieve.

It was the statement made by Florinda Olivero's sister.

'Come into my office, Domenico!'

They sat down opposite each other and Surace handed him the statement. The marshal took it and started to read it carefully. They both had the same feeling: in the end, the case would be dumped on their shoulders.

The young woman's name was Alicia Olivero. She was twenty-two and worked at a bar in the central square in Pontassieve. Every day, before and after work, she would spend a few hours with her sister. She lived in a small apartment in the same area with her boyfriend, who worked in the same bar.

That morning, she had arrived at her sister's just before eight and, having rung the bell a few times and got no response, had run home to get her copy of the key. She was very worried because her sister lived alone and she was afraid something serious might have happened to her. She had called her name several times as she walked down the corridor, then had gone into the bedroom and seen her. She had started screaming. A neighbour, alerted by her screams, had come running, and she had asked her to call the Carabinieri. In the meantime, she had called her boyfriend on her mobile and he had come as quickly as he could.

This was followed by some more specific questions.

Had her sister told her about anyone who'd been causing her trouble? Any incidents in the past few days that had scared her?

Was her sister seeing anyone? Did she have a boyfriend?

All the answers were negative.

With regard to Florinda's work, her sister said she had been trying to get a foothold in the fashion world. It was her great passion. In fact, a few days earlier she had told Alicia that she had met a film producer who had said he would help her out.

Gori raised his eyes from the statement and looked towards the window. He was thinking. In his phone call, Moretta had told him that the young woman was very beautiful and that they had found several photographs of her on the catwalk. Clearly someone capable of turning men's heads. God alone knew how many of them had tried to get her into bed with promises of giving her a job, or helping her find one. And God alone knew how many times the poor girl had had to give in to a man's advances in the hope of fulfilling her dream!

Gori wondered who this film producer might be. Could he be the killer?

'Domenico, take a team to Pontassieve and work with Moretta's men. Question Alicia Olivero again. We need to find out more about this film person. If he's from Florence, we should be able to track him down. There aren't that many film producers here.'

'Providing the information's correct, Marshal.'

'Of course. In any case, it's worth a try. Is there anything else in those papers, Domenico?'

'Nothing. Just a brief report by Moretta on the action they took after the neighbour called 112. He also asks if someone from our office could attend the post-mortem. He doesn't have many men and he's very busy.'

Just as Gori had imagined.

'We'll send one of our men along. The colonel ordered me to give them our full cooperation. He's worried about this murder.

He mentioned the killings of the courting couples and the prostitutes. Do you remember them?'

Surace nodded. 'How could I forget them, Marshal?'

They were quiet for a while.

'The victim's telephone records could be useful,' Gori suggested.

'If Moretta hasn't already made the request, I'll do it,' Surace replied before leaving the room.

Gori picked up his pen and a piece of paper and started writing notes. He jotted down the words *serial killer*, followed by a question mark. In the last few years, several cases of serial killers had been recorded in Italy. At the start of 2000, for example, there had been the playing-card killer in the Veneto, a man named Michele Profeta who had spread an enormous amount of terror before he was captured. There had also been the man who had killed prostitutes in the Prato area.

And anyway, in Florence anything was possible.

59

It was five in the afternoon when Rizzo came into Ferrara's office with the records for Cosimo Presti's mobile. It was a TIM phone, and he had contacted the director's executive secretary, who was a friend of his wife's. Thanks to her, he had been able to jump the queue and obtain the data for the last fortnight.

'Michele, there's just one contact with Costanza,' he said before he had even sat down. He leant across the desk and showed Ferrara. He had underlined the call with a yellow highlighter.

It was the call they had already noted on the evening of 28 August in the Bologna area, which also featured in the Senator's telephone records. There could be no doubt it was the same one.

'Then there are two calls to numbers in Rome,' Rizzo went on.

'Who to?'

'It's the switchboard number for the Ministry of the Interior.'

'So we have no idea who he spoke to,' Ferrara said.

'Precisely! It's a pity, it would have been interesting to know.'

'Francesco, go back to Vinci tomorrow morning and urge him to give us authorisation to tap Presti's phones. Try and convince him to fast-track it, the judge can validate it later.'

'I'll give it my best shot.'

They both knew that, in most investigations, only the first conversations, those recorded directly after the phone tap was set up, were of much use. Later, when the people under surveillance began to suspect their phones were being tapped, the content became increasingly incomprehensible, if not downright cryptic.

Be that as it may, Ferrara was convinced that the connection between Presti and Costanza could point them in the right direction, so it was essential to back it up with other evidence, and the only things that could provide that were phone taps and a thorough interrogation.

Ferrara suddenly had an idea. He summoned Fanti and told him to call a meeting of the local press for six-thirty.

It might turn out to be a fruitless endeavour, but it was worth a try. Nothing could be left to chance.

Gori had just finished reading the pathologist's preliminary report.

No semen had been found on the oral, rectal or vaginal swabs. In addition, there were no signs of inflammation or lacerations. In other words, no evidence of rape.

Analysis of the stomach contents had yielded only a small quantity of brown liquid. Clearly, Florinda Olivero had not eaten for several hours.

According to the initial toxicological tests, there were no traces of pharmaceutical or recreational drugs.

The analysis of the wounds had shown that the killer had stabbed the victim with extraordinary ferocity. It was a kind of overkill, using excessive force and inflicting an excessive number of stab wounds, definitely more than were necessary to cause death.

But Gori found the most interesting result in the report's conclusion.

The victim's blood type was AB, which matched the blood samples collected from the body as well as various areas of the bedroom and the bathroom.

It was the rarest blood group, present in only five per cent of the population, as the pathologist noted.

The light brown hair found clutched in the woman's hand, however, belonged to a person with blood type A. Furthermore, the tests had revealed that the hair had undergone cosmetic treatment and had been dyed. The presence of the bulb indicated that it had been pulled out by the root, and confirmed their hypothesis about the victim's reaction, as demonstrated by the wounds on some of her fingers and her forearms.

Gori closed the report and picked up the phone to call his colleagues at the RIS, the Carabinieri's forensics department, in Rome and request a DNA test, the only test that remained to be done.

Could this be the turning point?

'We're looking for this woman.'

Ferrara began with these words as he stood in front of the journalists in his office. Some of them were sitting with their notebooks on their laps, others were standing around the desk.

They all stared at the identikit, which Ferrara had had blown up. The cameras clicked rapidly. He had decided to release it in the hope that someone might see it on television or in the papers and recognise the woman.

'She's probably between thirty and forty years of age. Her hair is long, but' – here he remembered young Kirsten Olsen's statement – 'may also be very short and reddish in colour. She drives a dark, possibly black, A-Class Mercedes.'

He had spoken slowly to give the journalists time to note down all the details. After a while, one of them raised a hand.

'Questions at the end, please,' Ferrara said.

The journalist apologised and Ferrara smiled. He had recognised him: he worked for the ANSA agency and Ferrara respected him for his decency and the accuracy of his articles. He had not seen him for a while and was happy he was there.

'We believe this woman may have something to do with the double murder of Senator Costanza and his butler, Luis

Rodriguez. I would ask anyone who may have information to contact my office or call 113, and I hope that this time *omertà* will not win.'

'*Omertà?*' came a chorus of voices.

'Are you telling us, Chief Superintendent, that you believe there's a code of silence in Florence, just like in Sicily?' The question came from a woman journalist, as short and thin as a breadstick, who worked for a private radio station.

'I'm only saying that anyone who knows anything needs to talk. And you all know that hasn't always been the case in other investigations.'

'Are you by any chance referring to the conspiracy theories surrounding the Monster of Florence case?' the woman insisted.

'Yes, of course. And now you'll have to excuse me, I must go. Thank you.'

This abrupt conclusion triggered a reaction in the journalists, who raised their voices, firing a volley of questions at him. 'Chief Superintendent! ... I have a question, please ... I must ask you ... *Omertà* ... conspiracy theories ...' Ferrara ignored them, thanked them once again, and asked them to leave him alone.

He had not even considered the possibility that he had just unwittingly lit the fuse of a truly enormous bomb.

60

He lay on the sofa, waiting for the local news. When the usual baby-faced newsreader, who always ended up doing the late night bulletin – he must be putting in the hours while his colleagues were at home with their families – appeared on the screen, he picked up the remote and turned up the volume.

'There are new developments in the investigation into the murder of Senator Enrico Costanza,' the newsreader began, while the now-familiar image of the villa in Fiesole appeared in the background.

He sat up. What were these new developments?

'Thanks to a witness, the police have put together this identikit of a woman seen at the wheel of a dark, perhaps black, A-Class Mercedes in the area where the crime was committed.'

On the screen, the image of the villa was replaced by a drawing that could almost have been a photograph.

'The police are looking for this woman and are asking the public for their help. Anyone who recognises her or can provide further information is asked to call 113 or make use of the contact details below.'

A telephone number and email address scrolled across the bottom of the screen.

'One further detail,' the newsreader added before moving on to the next item. 'The woman may have very short, reddish hair, rather than long hair as shown in the picture.'

Angrily, he pressed the OFF button on the remote. He was no longer interested in hearing what they said about the murder in Pontassieve.

She couldn't have seen the news bulletin; she was keeping watch in San Gimignano. Damn it, he had warned her to be careful, not to make mistakes. She'd really blown it, thanks to that fucking ex-convict!

He had to make a move. His plan needed to be modified. And from now on, he would have to act alone.

61

That evening, Ferrara received a visit from his friend Massimo Verga.

They sat opposite one another on the terrace, enjoying the breeze. It was the first time his friend had come to see them since their return from Germany.

Petra poured them each a small glass of Slyrs, a whisky they had been given by a good friend from Germany. It was a Bavarian speciality and Michele only drank it on special occasions.

'Excellent!' Massimo exclaimed after the first sip. He lit his pipe and Ferrara lit his cigar. Each of them maintained that his form of smoking was the nobler: it was one of the few subjects on which they did not see eye to eye. They enjoyed the first puffs in total silence, looking up at the glorious star-filled sky.

Massimo was the first to speak. 'Who would ever have thought that one day we would find ourselves up here smoking and drinking whisky?'

On the rare occasions when they managed to meet up, the two old friends always ended up reminiscing over their high school days. After school, Massimo had chosen to study Philosophy and Ferrara did Law. He had wanted to become a police superintendent and he had done so. Meanwhile, his friend had opened a bookshop in the Via Tornabuoni that in the space of just a few years had become a focal point for cultured Florentines. They had lost touch, as often happens when friends go their own ways, far from their home town, but had met up again by chance right here in this city: a gift of fate.

Ferrara knew that his friend might help him understand the various meanings of the word *Genius*. When he heard the question, Massimo could not help laughing loudly. He was convinced that, while rising through the ranks of the police, Michele had fallen into an abyss of ignorance.

'What are you laughing about, Massimo? I need to find out why a killer might have used that word to sign his message.'

Massimo immediately turned serious and nodded. He launched into an explanation, although he took a roundabout approach. 'Well, you know that Latin was always my strongest subject. The word derives from *gignere*, which means to generate or create, and was given to the deity that represented man's creative spirit . . .'

In the Roman religion, he went on to explain, the *dies natalis* was dedicated to Genius, while for the Greeks he was the *daimon*, a divine being inferior to the gods, but superior to mankind.

He stopped to take another sip of Slyrs. Ferrara did the same, then took a few more large puffs on his cigar, which was going out.

'This whisky really is very good, Michele,' Massimo said.

Below them was the gentle glow of the lights on the Ponte Vecchio. It was a priceless view.

'Moving to the present day,' Massimo went on, 'and in a more down to earth sense, a genius is of course a special being, someone with exceptional gifts, like Dante, Leonardo da Vinci, Einstein. But in this case it could be what's called an "Evil Genius".'

All this was what Ferrara had expected to hear. But he had thought it was worth a try, in case the word hid some other secret meaning, one which might have a significance for Satanists, whom he had encountered in recent investigations, or for Freemasons – another world that remained something of a mystery to him. No, the killer probably just thought of himself as a criminal mastermind, an evil genius. That had to be the meaning of the two letters written on the base of the statue of Perseus.

Now it was his turn to explain the mystery. He took a deep drag on his cigar, and at that moment felt a surge of confidence. A confidence that came from the presence of a true friend he could always rely on.

San Gimignano

It was almost midnight.

The ground floor rooms were all lit up as if it were day. And the lamps along the tree-lined avenue that led to Sir George's villa had not been switched off yet.

Everything looked as if an all-night party that would finish in the first light of dawn must be in full swing. But such was not the case. There were only two people in the house: Sir George and his guest, Richard, sitting in comfortable armchairs, sipping a highly refined grappa, Riserva da Vinacce di Chianti.

Far from prying eyes and ears, the two men were weighing up the pros and cons of a decision that should resolve the situation in Florence forever.

Richard had already informed Sir George that the contents of Costanza's safe-deposit box in Lugarno had been confiscated by the police.

'I'll get our Brother, the "fake beard", involved,' Sir George said. 'He knows how to deal with such things.'

Richard did not object. He was in no position to do so. It was up to Sir George to make the final decisions. That was how it had always been, and how it would be in the future.

It was after two by the time all the lights were switched off, but no car left the villa.

Clearly the guest was sleeping there tonight.

It was an unfortunate inconvenience.

PART FIVE

A CURIOUS DISAPPEARANCE

62

Night of Friday 3 to Saturday 4 September

Guendalina was half asleep.

She thought it had been Angelica waking her. Then she remembered that Angelica was in the Siena area on business – dinner with an aristocratic lady who was thinking of commissioning a portrait from her – and would be back late.

And anyway, Angelica was usually very careful not to wake her.

For a few moments that seemed like hours, she lay there motionless, holding her breath, her heart pounding fit to burst. She looked at the window. The moonlight cast disturbing shadows into the room.

She listened carefully.

Nothing.

But she was still sure she had heard something. A noise, a slight rustle.

Perhaps it was just the power of suggestion, fuelled by the news she had heard on the radio: a young Cuban woman had been brutally murdered in her apartment in Pontassieve, probably by a maniac.

She raised herself to a sitting position.

Could it have been an animal?

She steeled herself: maybe it would be best to go and check all the windows and the front door. It was only now that she realised how much she missed Angelica. She would have felt safe with her. She reached out a hand to switch on the bedside lamp. But the light did not come on.

She got up silently, put her feet on the floor and groped her way to the switch for the overhead light. But that did not come on either. A shiver ran down her spine. Her fear turned to terror.

At that moment a gloved hand covered her mouth and nose, and a tall figure grabbed her and threw her to the floor. She tried not to lose control, but felt as if she could not breathe. She was afraid she was going to pass out.

She made a quick movement to the side and managed to break free and stand up.

'That wasn't a good idea, Guendalina.'

It was a man's voice, hard and cold. A man who knew her name.

'Don't try and resist, it'll only make things worse.'

She started to kick out at him. But her attacker managed to dodge her kicks. Then he was on top of her again, holding her still with his hands. He slapped her hard across the face, making her stagger.

'Help!' she cried, with all the breath she could muster. But no sooner was the word out than she realised that nobody could hear her. She was alone in the middle of the countryside.

'Don't h-hurt ... me ... I ... b-beg ... you,' she stammered.

She jerked free again and ran down the narrow corridor to the living room. Everything was dark here too. No glimmer of light came in through the blinds, which, unusually, were closed. He must have closed them himself: it was now clear that he had planned it all. She staggered, lifting a hand to her face. Her cheek seemed to be burning from the impact of his slap. She remembered that poor Cuban girl. She must find a way out at all costs. But a cabinet had been pushed against the front door. In a fit of desperation, she shouted Angelica's name.

'Quiet, Guendalina. Nobody can hear you.' The voice was calm now, as if trying to reassure her.

Next, she tried to get into the kitchen, but slipped. Her strength was fading, she could not feel the ground beneath her feet. She swayed and almost fell.

The man laughed. 'Can't you see it's useless? Why don't you give up?'

She spun round. 'Who are you?' she cried.

At that moment she was dazzled by the light of a torch. She blinked. He was six feet tall, and he was right in front of her. He was wearing a balaclava. Then she saw the gun in his hand.

'Noooo!' she screamed with all her remaining strength.

'Sit down!'

She obeyed.

'Now write!' He took a pen and a piece of paper from his pocket, put them in front of her on the table and dictated a few sentences to her, which she wrote with a trembling hand by the light of the torch.

He ordered her to stand up.

As she did so, he shot her in the chest.

63

Angelica was driving along the Siena–Florence road.

It was an isolated stretch, and she could put on as much speed as she wanted. She was in a crazy rush to get home to Guendalina. She would look in on her quickly, then sleep on the sofa so as not to wake her.

After the Certosa tollbooth, she took the A1. That way she could avoid having to drive through the city. Her itinerary was: Florence South exit, Bagno a Ripoli, Pontassieve, Dicomano, and home.

She had no idea of the surprise that awaited her.

I'm going and don't try and find me. Maybe I'll get in touch when I understand myself and most of all, you, better.
Goodbye!
Guendi

It was three twenty-five in the morning and Angelica, head bowed, eyes swollen with tears, was clutching Guendalina's note, which she had found on the bedside table.

It wasn't possible, she kept repeating to herself, shaking her head. It wasn't possible that Guendalina could have just gone like that!

She looked at the piece of paper again. It was definitely Guendalina's handwriting, even though it looked a little shaky in places.

There couldn't be any doubt about it. Some of her clothes were missing from the wardrobe, and her make-up was gone from the bathroom. Her suitcase was gone too.

Why had she done it? Angelica wondered. Surely it couldn't have been jealousy . . .

She realised that she had thought she knew her well, but she really didn't. They had met in prison. How could she have known what kind of person Guendalina would be once she was released?

For the moment, she told herself, it might be best to wait.

In her heart, she hoped that the door would suddenly open and reveal her Guendi.

That was all she had: hope.

64

Saturday 4 September

SUPERCOP MICHELE FERRARA ACCUSES FLORENCE OF OMERTÀ was
the headline in *La Nazione* that morning.

Florence has reacted angrily to the accusation of *omertà* made by
Michele Ferrara, the head of the Squadra Mobile, who is currently
investigating the murders of Senator Enrico Costanza and his butler
Luis Rodriguez on the night of 28–29 August. The bombshell came
after Ferrara summoned some journalists to his office yesterday
afternoon to ask for their collaboration in tracking down a woman
whose identikit picture he showed them, and in providing information about the car she is believed to drive, a dark-coloured
A-Class Mercedes.

By yesterday evening, after the news had spread courtesy of private radio stations and local TV news, Florentines in bars and
piazzas throughout the city reacted, accusing the supercop of crossing the line with such a grotesque and defamatory claim.

The mayor, Umberto Pintacudi, has released a brief statement,
saying: 'Florence will not accept this. There is no room for *omertà*
in Florence, it is foreign to our culture. If someone knows something about these crimes and does not speak out, they should be
prosecuted for withholding information, but it is unfair to lay the

blame on an entire city. I shall be consulting the legal department of the city council to consider whether or not to take legal action against Chief Superintendent Ferrara.'

Ferrara closed the newspaper. Someone, he thought, had wanted to create a fuss by twisting the words he had spoken during the press conference. But who?

It was the same old story! There was always somebody pulling strings from behind the scenes.

The day had certainly got off to a bad start.

He imagined the reactions of the Commissioner and the Prefect. He probably would not have to wait long to hear from the Head of the State Police in Rome.

Luigi Vinci's meeting with Francesco Rizzo had been arranged for nine o'clock on the dot.

While he waited, he re-read the words Chief Prosecutor Luca Fiore had written in his own hand in the right-hand margin of the *Squadra Mobile*'s report: 'Don't do anything, this is just speculation!!!'

It was a real mess. How could he explain away the fact that the previous day he had given Ferrara's deputy an emergency warrant to acquire Cosimo Presti's phone records? He wished now that he hadn't.

He looked at his watch. It was just after nine and Rizzo had still not appeared. Then, at last, he heard a knock at the door.

'Come in!' he yelled.

The door opened and Rizzo came in.

'Good morning, Deputy Prosecutor.'

'Take a seat.'

Rizzo moved some sheets of paper off a chair and sat down in front of the desk.

Looking at Vinci, you would never have guessed that he was so fond of physical exercise. Every one of his fifty years showed on his face: he looked tired, his eyes pensive, almost dejected.

'Superintendent Rizzo,' he said, 'I'd like you to give me back the warrant I issued yesterday.'

'What!'

'Yes, you heard what I said. It's quite unnecessary.'

'But I've already informed the legal department at the telephone company. It's too late now.'

'I want you to get that warrant back immediately.'

'That's not possible now.'

'You're putting me in a difficult position . . .'

'Me?' Rizzo stared at him in astonishment. In the *Squadra Mobile*, they called Vinci 'No Balls'. Right now he was in a real panic.

'If you don't get it back, you're going to cause me a huge problem!' he yelled, losing control completely. He grabbed the papers Rizzo had given him the previous day. 'As for your other requests – phone taps, interrogations – you can forget all about them!'

'Why?'

'Orders from above. There's not a scrap of evidence. To tap a journalist's phone, you need a bit more than a call in a victim's phone records and a dinner with the victim. Best case scenario, we have the media on our backs. Worst case scenario, they could actually take us to court. I don't need to tell you where that could lead.'

'But with a phone tap we could—'

'I've said no. Now go and get that warrant back. I don't want to hear anything more about those phone records.'

Rizzo took care not to reveal that he had already obtained them. It could get his wife's friend in trouble. He stood up, said a curt goodbye and left the room.

Orders from above! As he went down the stairs, he kept repeating those three words to himself. As he reached the ground floor, he saw Chief Prosecutor Luca Fiore come in through the front entrance and make straight for the lifts, looking as arrogant as ever.

Fucking Freemasons! he said to himself.

65

She opened her eyes slowly, feeling as if she had just woken from the strangest dream she had ever had, and looked around.

Nothing. Only darkness.

Was it night or day? Where was she?

For about half an hour, she drifted in and out of consciousness. She felt as if she was as light as a feather being blown hither and thither on the wind. Little by little, she recalled the figure of the attacker with the gun. He was tall and his face had been covered. She tried to remember more, but it was all very vague.

Then she tried to stand up. She wanted to go to the toilet, to take a pee, to drink lots of water. Her throat felt dry. But she could not summon the strength. Her body ached all over. Then she remembered her break for freedom, the slap that had almost knocked her senseless, the note she had written at his dictation, the shot to her chest . . . It couldn't have been a bullet, as she had thought at the time, but an electric shock.

She was alive!

She wondered whether Angelica had already discovered that she was gone. She might be looking for her right now, might even have guessed where she was . . .

Then she closed her eyes and slipped back into sleep.

*

'He spent the night there.'

They were at the Florence North service station, opposite Eurogomme, the best stocked repair shop in the city. He had had to replace two of the tyres on the four-by-four.

Angelica had just told him about the lights, including those along the drive, going out. She had waited for a while after that, but no one had come out of the villa.

'Have you read the paper?' he asked suddenly.

'No, why?' As she turned to look at him, Angelica noticed that he had a small cut on his hand.

'Read it! And make sure you change that fucking car.'

Angelica's face clouded over. 'Why?'

He told her about the identikit and the A-Class Mercedes the police were looking for. 'In the identikit, the woman has long hair, but the police believe she may actually have very short hair. Do you know what that means? They must have witnesses.'

Who could have alerted the police? she wondered, panicking. Guendalina? But Guendalina didn't know anything . . .

'What should I do?'

'Hide it somewhere in the countryside, there must be lots of places near where you live. And get yourself another car, maybe a Fiat Panda that won't attract attention. It has four wheel drive, which you might find useful on these roads. And make sure you use a different kind of wig.'

'I'll do it today.'

'I'll give you the money later, in cash. And buy it at Fiat Car, from that young guy we know. He'll find you a good used one, no problem.'

'OK. I'll text you later.'

As she got in behind the wheel, she realised she had goose pimples all over her body. They might already be looking for her.

Had she underestimated Guendalina? Was love really blind?

66

Orders from above!

Ferrara was still reflecting on these words, which Rizzo had passed on to him.

They were further proof that the justice system was like a delicate net that was capable of catching the little fish but stretched or even broke when it came to the bigger fish.

He remembered what had happened on 1 July, when their informant and expert on the occult, Silvia De Luca, had been murdered at her apartment in Galluzzo, not long after he had spoken to her. Luca Fiore had summoned him immediately, in order to warn him in no uncertain terms against taking unauthorised initiatives. He had also questioned his search of Madalena's club, carried out by his men on their own initiative.

Entering Fiore's office that day, he had passed an extremely refined older man in the doorway. He had later discovered – what a surprise! – that the man was none other than Enrico Costanza.

A real bastard, Ferrara repeated to himself, thinking back to that conversation with Fiore, and the words echoed in his head as he listened to Rizzo.

'It's obvious to me, Francesco, that it's Luca Fiore who's blocking the investigation into Cosimo Presti. He must have been put under pressure to do so, don't you think?'

'Pressure, or blackmail.'

'In either case, he's a piece of shit. I've never liked him.'

'You don't need to tell me. I can't stand the sight of him either. The Prosecutor's Department has lost all credibility since he arrived. He may just be trying to protect his old friends and schoolmates in the city's elite. But I think he's actually being blackmailed over some little vice or other.'

Ferrara nodded. He knew what Rizzo was referring to: the rumours that Fiore frequently used underage prostitutes.

'Francesco, a man who has a certain position, an important role to perform, like the head of a Prosecutor's Department, shouldn't be doing such things in the same city where he was born or grew up and where he has relatives and friends. Do you get my drift? That's really one of the biggest problems among the judicial authorities, but the politicians just turn a blind eye.'

'You're right, Michele. They ought to transfer every three or four years at the most, like we do, or the Carabinieri do.'

'I think we should change the subject, Francesco, it's not getting us anywhere. Right now, we have to think about what to do.'

Not even ten minutes had passed when Fanti burst into the room, holding a piece of paper. Ferrara and Rizzo could tell from his expression that it was not good news. It was a fax from Rome.

```
Confidential
For the attention of: Chief Superintendent
Michele Ferrara
Squadra Mobile, Police Headquarters
Florence

cc.
Luca Fiore
Chief Prosecutor
Florence
```

Subject: Written Reprimand

Following items in today's newspapers, which
carry statements made by you judged by this
Ministry to be imprudent and with serious
implications, you are herewith cautioned
against giving interviews or making any kind
of statement in relation to ongoing
investigations without the prior approval of
the Prosecutor's Department.

Should you choose to disregard this caution,
disciplinary procedures will be set in motion.

pp. The Head of the State Police

Deputy Commissioner Giulio Parlato
Director, Press and Public Relations Office

Ferrara picked up a pen and a piece of paper and began to
write. Maybe he should just ignore it, maybe he should throw
what he was about to write straight into the bin, but he couldn't
stop himself.

The truth was the truth.

67

Guendalina woke up.

She felt more clear-headed, even though she had lost all track of time. She had no idea what day it was, let alone what hour.

She saw a dim light in the distance, from which she gathered that she was in a very large room. She realised that she was lying on a mattress on a concrete floor. She touched her body. She was completely naked but her hands and feet were not bound.

Where were her clothes?

Slowly, she got up and tried to take a few steps, but her legs were so weak, they could barely support her. She told herself that she had to try and walk. She moved slowly forwards, looking all around her. There were no windows. It was a strange room, with that rough floor, as if the house was still under construction.

She approached the source of the light and saw an iron door with no handle. It was like being back in prison.

In her mind there was just one thought now: escape.

There had to be a way, and she would do everything she could to find it.

Ferrara was in front of the Commissioner. Standing. He had not even been invited to sit down.

Adinolfi picked up a page from the newspaper on his desk and waved it at him. He was beside himself.

'A short while ago,' he thundered, 'I left the mayor outside the Prefecture. There's going to be an extraordinary meeting of the city council tonight, at which they will vote on whether or not to pass your name on to the judicial authorities. If the decision goes against you, we can expect a claim for damages because of the way the image of the city has been tarnished.'

Ferrara tried to reply but Adinolfi would not let him.

'I think it's best if you keep quiet, Chief Superintendent. Now is not the time, and in any case I haven't finished yet.'

In the meantime, the secretary had come in with a bottle of water and a glass. She filled it and handed it to the Commissioner, then dashed off as if the air in the room was full of poison.

After gulping the water down in one go, Adinolfi continued: 'You will write a public letter of apology to the citizens of Florence immediately and provide a copy to *La Nazione* so that it can be published in tomorrow's edition.'

Ferrara's head was starting to spin.

'Now go,' Adinolfi said, thumping on the desk with his fist. 'I have to call the office of the Head of the State Police.'

Ferrara turned without saying a word. He walked quickly downstairs, grim-faced. He already knew what he had to do.

It was absurd to even think he had to justify himself. Why should he? Over something he hadn't even said? No, he would never write that letter, never. Not even if they took him to court. In fact, let them take him to court: then he'd be able to stand up and defend himself.

For now, though, he would have to hope that one of the journalists would be willing to give him an unedited copy of their recording of the whole press conference. And if he couldn't get one, he would ask the Prosecutor's Department for a warrant.

Providing Luca Fiore authorised the warrant. Because his instincts told him that Fiore was the person behind this new obstacle, as well as all the others. Who else could have made an official complaint to the upper echelons of the police in Rome? As luck would have it, Fiore had been sent a copy of the written reprimand. This time, the Head of the State Police hadn't been able to wash his dirty laundry in private.

But if he fought back, would he be merely tilting at windmills?

68

At last, the long-awaited responses had arrived.

It was afternoon when all the paperwork demanded in the official warrants arrived on Rizzo's desk in rapid succession. Under the circumstances, there was something quite improbable about it, as if everyone had agreed at the same time.

He wasted no time in beginning his examination of the documents.

The staff at the company that operated the CCTV cameras had identified Enrico Costanza's black Mercedes. On the evening of Saturday 28 August it had been filmed at the traffic lights in the Viale Don Minzoni. Then, a few minutes later, in the Viale Volta, heading towards Fiesole. The times coincided perfectly with what Rolando Russo, the Senator's driver, had told them. There was no suspicious car following it, certainly not a dark A-Class Mercedes.

The speed cameras had recorded a great many speeding violations. The local police had sent a printout, hundreds of pages long, with details of place, day, time, make of car and licence number.

Rizzo leafed through it and saw that the word Mercedes appeared several times, but without details of the model. They would have to develop the data. Maybe he would pass the printout on to Venturi to cross-check it against the civil motor authority's database, to which they had access.

On to the telephone records.

Unsurprisingly, there were lots of them, all relating to calls made to or from mobile phones in the Fiesole area during the time frame when the two murders took place. It had been a Saturday night, when young people stayed out later. It would take ages to check the records thoroughly. And it was highly unlikely that anything would come of it.

He thought about asking Ferrara to delegate this task to Fanti, who would be only too happy to do it and would do a meticulous job.

Ferrara listened attentively to Rizzo's updates, but his main concern at the moment was Cosimo Presti. If they could neither question him nor tap his phones, they would have to tail him. It might not have been the best solution, but they didn't have many options, and at least it wasn't expressly forbidden by law.

'I'll get that set up from tomorrow morning, as soon as he leaves his house,' Rizzo assured him.

'Let's keep it going twenty-four-seven. Change the men over every six hours.'

She had heard something. Or was it just her imagination?

There it was again. This time the sound had been more distinct.

Then the iron door opened, the room lit up, and he came in.

He was wearing a balaclava. She took that as a good sign: if he didn't want her to recognise his face, it probably meant he wouldn't kill her.

But then why had he taken her? And why her in particular?

She got up from the mattress and watched him as he slowly approached her. He was as tall as she remembered. When he got closer, she looked at his hands. The fingers were long, the nails well-tended. They weren't a labourer's hands. She tried to memorise the details. She noticed a small bandage, then saw that he was holding something that looked like a remote control.

'Why have you brought me here?' she asked him.

'Now's not the time for questions,' he replied in a calm, courteous voice.

'Why not? I want to know why I've been kidnapped, because that's what this is, isn't it, a kidnapping? But I don't have—'

'I told you this isn't the time,' he cut in.

Suddenly he put his free hand, his right hand, into his tracksuit pocket and pulled out the taser.

'What are you—' She did not have time to finish before she received another electric shock. She fell to the floor, banging her head on the wall as she did so. He threw himself on her, crushing her beneath his weight.

He undid his trousers and let them slide down to his ankles, then grabbed her breasts. His grip was so strong, Guendalina was left breathless with the pain. Her eyelids felt heavier and heavier. She moaned as she lay there. She was trembling. Then her gaze moved to his penis. It seemed quite small, but it was erect, the veins swollen. Immediately afterwards she felt it against her own body.

'Open your eyes!' he said. 'I want to see them, they're very black and very beautiful.' His body moved snakelike above her. Then he penetrated her violently.

She passed out.

Darkness.

She did not even hear him say as he left, 'Don't worry, I won't kill you!'

Feeling satisfied, he closed the iron door behind him.

The bitch should not have come between them. But with her firm, well-toned figure and scared expression, she was even prettier without clothes: sexier, more of a turn-on. It was very exciting to have a woman available for every eventuality, every urge, every fantasy . . .

69

At the Carlo Corsi barracks in Borgo Ognissanti, long the Carabinieri's provincial headquarters, Marshal Gori was still dealing with the murder in Pontassieve. It was almost eight in the evening, and Sergeant Surace, who had returned to the office after spending the whole day looking for clues, was sitting in front of him.

Gori was tired. He was thinking about his wife, who was waiting for him at home, ready to go and see the last show at the cinema. He had promised to take her and did not want to disappoint her.

But Surace still needed to update him on his work. First and foremost, on the latest interview with the victim's sister. The evening before the murder, Florinda Olivero had told her sister that she had received a phone call from an acquaintance of hers, a famous producer who had promised to help her get into films, and she was planning to meet him later.

'Sounds suspicious to me,' Gori remarked. 'What did you find out from the phone company?'

Surace started sifting through the papers in the file.

'Well?' Gori urged him on, having glanced at his watch.

'Here it is!' Surace said, holding up a paper. The call had been made using a cloned sim card, like those used by criminal organisations.

'I think we can assume that it was the killer who called her,' Gori said.

Surace nodded several times. 'He could have been a hacker, Marshal, instead of a film producer.'

'Indeed. Now I'll need to ask for the results of the DNA test. Science could well be the determining factor in this case.'

'Let's hope so.'

'You can go now, Surace, thank you.'

Alone once more, the Marshal immediately called Rome. His colleague reassured him he would have the results by Monday morning.

These scientists certainly took their time, he thought.

PART SIX

A CURIOUS FIRE

70

1.57 a.m. Night of Saturday 4 to Sunday 5 September

The smell was unbearable.

Ferrara extinguished his cigar beneath the sole of his shoe.

It was Teresa Micalizi who had summoned him. In spite of the late hour, she had still been in her office. Along with Officer Alessandra Belli, who had finally been seconded to the *Squadra Mobile* less than twenty-four hours earlier, she had been continuing Fanti's work on the records of calls made to and from Fiesole. When she had received the telephone call from the Operations Room, she had wasted no time in calling Ferrara at home. Next, she had called Rizzo, and now all three of them stood outside the apartment building, with bewildered looks on their faces. The apartment on the third floor – the top floor – was a gaping hole. The windows had been blown out and a good section of the roof had also been destroyed by the flames, which had caused panic among the residents of the neighbouring buildings as they had grown.

That third floor was where Fabio Biondi lived.

The firefighters were still trying to put out the last few flames, but then they would have to make sure the whole building was safe, which was likely to take some time.

'Can we go in?' Ferrara asked a fireman standing next to a fire engine, behind which an ambulance was parked.

'You'll have to ask my chief, Fossati,' he replied.

In the meantime, other firefighters were coming out through the front door. They had already taken off their masks and were trying to wipe the sweat from their foreheads with handkerchiefs. On the other side of the street, the usual crowd of bystanders had gathered. Some were waiting to be able to go back to their homes, others were just trying to find out what had happened. A few, perhaps not locals, were standing a bit apart from the others.

'Is there a lift?' Ferrara asked Teresa.

'No, I had to climb the stairs to the third floor.'

'Have you tried calling him on his mobile?'

'Yes, but there's no answer, it just goes to voicemail. I've left him a message.'

'Can you see him anywhere?'

'No, I've had a look, he's not here.'

Just then Rizzo winked at Ferrara and tilted his head slightly to his right. Ferrara looked in that direction and saw the journalist Cosimo Presti with his mobile phone pressed to his ear. Behind him was a press photographer, ready to start snapping.

'Anything for me?' Presti asked, drawing level with them. He had already put his phone back in his pocket.

Ferrara shook his head, and Presti looked around, perhaps in search of another source of information. Then he looked back at Ferrara and asked, with a sneer on his sunken and horribly disfigured face, 'Is the elusive arsonist behind this one too?'

Ferrara avoided rising to the bait and walked away. Presti did not follow him, but took a pen and notebook from his pocket.

Ferrara looked at the crowd. It seemed to have grown even bigger. Nobody would be able to sleep tonight.

Venturi now joined them after questioning some of the people standing on the pavement. 'I've spoken to the neighbours. They're all shocked. Fabio Biondi's aunt, who lives on the floor below, told me she heard him come home about eleven last night. After that she didn't hear anything until the neighbours started shouting just after one this morning. I also spoke to one of the firemen, and he told me the technical apparatus in the apartment probably acted as fuel for the fire.'

At that moment, the fireman who had been standing by the fire engine came over. 'Chief Superintendent, our boss has just come out,' he said, pointing.

Ferrara thanked him and he and Rizzo made their way over to the man, who was tall and distinguished-looking.

'Chief Superintendent Ferrara,' he introduced himself. 'And this is my colleague, Superintendent Rizzo.'

'Nice to meet you. I'm Eugenio Fossati, Provincial Commander of the Florence Fire Brigade.'

'What can you tell me, Commander?'

'At the moment nothing's certain about the cause of the fire. But I can tell you a bit about what we still have to do.' He explained that his men's work would consist of locating possible victims, making the apartment and the rest of the building safe, and determining the cause.

'So am I right in thinking you haven't yet found anyone inside?'

'Yes, Chief Superintendent. But now we're going to have to take a closer look.'

Ferrara told him that the man who had lived in that apartment was known to the police.

'A criminal, Chief Superintendent?'

'No.' He did not add anything further, despite the fact that the Commander's curiosity had clearly been aroused.

'If you'll excuse me, I need to supervise my men,' Fossati said.

And he walked briskly away and crossed the street.

'It's difficult to see this as an accident,' Ferrara said.

He had moved off to the corner with Rizzo, away from prying eyes. Teresa joined them.

'First Costanza,' he went on, 'then Sergi and Beatrice Filangeri, and now, just a few days later, Fabio, who was doing a tricky job for us.'

'It could be a coincidence,' Teresa said. 'We still don't know the cause of the fire.'

'When there are so many coincidences, it's hard to believe that's what they are. There's really no room for them in our work. But anyway, we'll wait for the fire brigade's report. Commander Fossati seems to have his feet on the ground. He didn't want to speculate about the cause, quite rightly. In the meantime let's see if they find the body.'

He had barely finished speaking when Venturi ran over to them again, took a deep breath and announced, 'They've found a body. They think it's a male. It was in the living room, under a piece of the roof that had fallen down. That's why they didn't notice it sooner.'

'His laboratory,' Teresa said.

'The fire brigade will take photographs and transport the body to the morgue,' Venturi went on.

'One of us should go to the morgue too,' Ferrara said, looking at Rizzo.

'I'll go,' Rizzo said.

By now, it was almost five in the morning.

Their attention was caught by the cries of an old woman who was being supported by two of the firefighters.

'Who's that?' Ferrara asked Venturi.

'Fabio Biondi's aunt.'

Teresa ran over to her and saw that Officer Alessandra Belli had already beaten her to it.

She seemed even thinner than when they had first seen her. She kept her sad, swollen eyes on Teresa. In her hands was a photograph of her nephew.

Teresa and Officer Belli had brought her to Headquarters to comfort and, when possible, question her. They had managed to establish that her name was Rosa Biondi. She was Fabio's paternal aunt and his only relative in Florence. Fabio's parents had emigrated to Switzerland and ran a laundry in Basel. Somebody was already trying to contact them and tell them the tragic news.

In the photograph, Fabio was wearing a white suit and was standing to attention like a toy soldier, with his arms down by his sides. 'He was eleven when this was taken,' the woman said, gently caressing the corner of the frame, as if trying to stroke that clean, innocent face. 'It was the day of his first communion. The man beside him is my poor husband, his godfather, who always wanted the best for little Fabio.'

Her voice broke.

Teresa felt a lump in her throat. That smiling little boy did not look like someone who would end his life burnt to death. In addition, the photograph reminded her of her own first communion. An unforgettable occasion, a day when they had all been so happy together as a family. She too had kept a photograph of that moment, showing her standing between her own parents, the shadow of misfortune still a long way away. Now, though, some of her photographic memories were no longer hers, but in the hands of whoever had stolen the album from her.

Now the woman's eyes were filling with tears. They looked like drops of glass.

There was a light knock at the door and a uniformed officer came in with a cardboard tray holding three hot cappuccinos. He put it down on the desk and went out.

'Help yourself to a drink, Signora Rosa,' Teresa said.

'No, thank you. I couldn't get it down.'

'Please try,' Teresa said gently. With one hand she lifted the cup to the woman's mouth, and with the other gently stroked her back. The woman took a tiny sip, perhaps just to humour her.

'Do you have any idea what might have happened?' Teresa asked her after a few moments.

The woman shook her head several times. 'I don't know,' she

replied. 'I was always telling him all those wires and machines were dangerous, but he never listened to me. Poor little Fabio.'

And she burst into tears again.

Teresa did not insist. She realised that this was not the moment, and she already regretted asking her the question. And anyway, they still did not know what the true cause of the fire was, whether it was arson or not.

The old woman's face had become even stiffer with grief. Teresa saw her eyes closing.

'I don't feel well,' she said in a low voice.

A moment later, her head fell forward onto the desk.

'Alessandra, call an ambulance right away,' Teresa said.

Barely ten minutes later, two paramedics were laying her on a stretcher and taking her away. She had not regained consciousness.

'A heart attack,' the police doctor who had arrived within minutes to administer first aid had declared.

Teresa was silent as she listened to the ambulance siren fading into the distance.

71

Sunday 5 September

It was seven in the morning and they were still in the office, all except Rizzo, who had gone to the morgue.

And, just as he did every day, Fanti arrived exactly on time.

He was always the first to arrive, always at the same time, even on those Sundays when he was on duty. He still needed to finish his work on the telephone records and he could not wait to give the results to the Chief Superintendent. But his mood changed abruptly when he heard that Ferrara was already in his office. That was a sure sign that something serious had happened.

He went first to the wardrobe and put away the rucksack he always had with him – even after all this time, his colleagues still wondered what it could possibly contain that was so precious – and then put his head in the doorway of Ferrara's office and said, 'Good morning, chief.'

Fanti was even more upset when he saw Ferrara's face. It was obvious he hadn't slept a wink all night.

'Fanti, come in!'

'Yes, chief. I haven't yet had time to check the reports from the patrol cars, or the post.'

'Leave that for now.'

Fanti's expression grew ever more worried. He wondered if by any chance he had made some mistake.

'First of all, tell me how far you've got with the telephone records.'

'I still have to finish going through them. Last night before I went home, Superintendent Micalizi asked me for them, saying she'd give me a hand.'

'Actually, I've only checked a few of them,' Teresa said.

'You carry on with them, Fanti, Teresa's busy. Try and finish this morning.'

'I'll get straight on it.' He went out.

Ferrara was just resuming his conversation with Teresa when the telephone rang. It was one of the officers from the guardhouse, asking him if Superintendent Micalizi was there as there was no answer from her office.

'She's here,' Ferrara confirmed, passing her the receiver.

'Yes?'

'There's a friend of Fabio Biondi's here, who says she really must speak to you.'

'Take her to my office.'

'I'll go and see what she wants, chief,' Teresa said. As she was on her way out, she passed Fanti who was coming back in.

'I've brought you a cup of coffee, chief.'

'Thanks, Fanti. I was just about to ask you for one, but I see you've already thought of it.'

Teresa ran a hand through her hair and looked at the girl for a few moments. Officer Belli was sitting to one side of the desk with a notebook open in front of her, ready to take notes.

The girl sat leaning forward in the visitor's chair, her hands clasped in her lap. She was short and thin, with a dark complexion, and did not look older than eighteen. When she had entered the office, Teresa had been struck by the pallor of her lips.

'What's your name?' Teresa asked her.

'Alba Cecchi.'

'And how old are you?'

'I'll be twenty-two on the first of December.'

'What's the nature of your relationship with Fabio Biondi?'

'I love computers, and he's taught me a lot, all kinds of tricks.'

Her accent was typically Florentine. Looking at her more closely, Teresa noticed a small gemstone in the middle of her tongue.

'Had you known him for long?'

'We'd been meeting up for a couple of years.'

'Often?'

'Quite often.'

'Why have you come to Police Headquarters?'

The girl shrugged and half closed her eyes, as if dazzled by headlights. 'Because of what's happened. But I don't want my parents to know I've been here.'

'They won't find out, unless there's a good reason for them to know. But if you're so scared, why have you come?'

The young woman looked at Teresa with questioning eyes and grimaced. 'I'm scared after what's happened. People knew that Fabio and I spent time together. I could be in danger too.'

Her voice betrayed her fear.

Teresa wondered how the young woman had guessed that the fire had been a criminal act, given that the fire brigade had still not established the cause.

'Why do you think you're in danger? Did something happen that worried you and Fabio?'

'No,' the girl replied, her gaze fixed on the middle distance. 'Well, except that yesterday afternoon we had the feeling some-one was following us.'

'Please tell me more.'

Alba Cecchi told them that they had gone to the Parco delle Cascine at about four to stretch their legs, and that as they were walking they had noticed a man who seemed to be following them.

'And what happened to this man?'

'We lost sight of him after a while.'

'Why did you think he was following you?'

'Fabio told me he was probably just a peeping Tom. There are lots of them who hang around the park.'

'How long was your walk?'

'If you're asking how long we were out for, I'd say about an hour and half, no more than that.'

'What time did you get home?'

'About half past five, quarter to six at the latest.'

Teresa and Officer Belli exchanged glances.

'Why exactly did you ask for me?' Teresa asked.

'Fabio told me about you.'

'What did he say?'

'That he knew you. He showed me your present. He really liked it. He told me that you were a very nice policewoman.'

There was a pause.

Teresa looked her straight in the eyes for a moment. 'Is there anything else?' she asked.

'He hinted that he was doing something urgent and difficult for you.'

'Did he tell you anything more?'

'No, I realised it was something he couldn't talk about and I didn't ask him any questions.'

The telephone rang. It was Ferrara.

'I'll be there right away, chief,' Teresa said. 'Please wait here,' she said to the girl. She exchanged a knowing glance with Alessandra Belli and stood up, sure that the girl was hiding something important.

72

She shivered.

She was feeling really nauseous.

The room seemed out of focus and her head was spinning like a top. She was sure she had been drugged. But she had no idea with what. An anaesthetic?

There was a metallic taste in her mouth. She remembered a few things: the electric shock, the way he threw himself on her, his swollen penis, the pitch darkness . . .

The bastard! she thought. *Why me?*

She ran a hand over her body, which was still aching. The bastard had raped her. A man, another fucking man. Slowly, she sat up. She noticed there was a plastic bottle next to her, its seal unbroken. She opened it. It was water. She lifted it to her lips and drank it down in one go. There was also a packet of biscuits. She left it untouched. She didn't want anything to eat. All she wanted to do was pray.

Our Father who art in Heaven
Hallowed be Thy name,
Thy kingdom come,
Thy will be done,
On Earth, as it is in Heaven . . .

She knew her prayers. She had attended mass in the prison chapel every Sunday.

I don't want to die! If I get out of here alive, I'll be loyal to You forever, Lord!

After a while, she stood up. Her head was still spinning, but she was thinking more clearly now. She kept her body under control. She felt dirty.

Then she moved.

She looked at one of the walls and noticed that two lamps were on. The room was quite big. Some of her clothes had been flung untidily onto an old bench. She went over and saw a toilet in the gloom. She could hear nothing – no sound of cars or horns. No din of people in the street or children playing. She must be underground.

She held back a sob as she dressed and then went back to the mattress. She curled up, feeling like a little girl terrified of monsters. After a while, exhausted, she fell asleep.

She did not hear him come in.

He was wearing a black silk dressing gown decorated with large hand-sewn designs. Over his face was a balaclava.

He shook her, and she slowly opened her eyes.

It was not a figment of her imagination or a dream. Her heart started pounding madly.

She wanted to beg him not to hurt her again, but the only thing that escaped her lips was a little sigh. She heard him say a few words, but could not make sense of them.

'I'm not well,' she managed to splutter. 'I need to vomit.' She was trying to memorise as many details as possible. Details that might be useful to her later. She wanted to see this man behind bars.

He seemed to pierce her with his icy gaze. 'It'll pass. If you need to throw up, bitch, just throw up.'

'Why did you do it?'

He did not reply. He seemed distant, ice-cold. He had moved closer to her.

'Please don't hurt me again, I beg you!'

'Go put on a short dress and high heels. I'll show you what real pleasure is, you perverted slut!'

'What the fuck are you talking about? I'm feeling dizzy, leave me alone!'

He gave a loud laugh, grabbed her by the arm and pulled her roughly to him. She summoned the strength to dig her fingers into his balaclava.

'Stupid bitch!'

In a rage, he hurled her to the floor and started kicking her. Again and again. One kick after another, without let-up. He seemed crazed.

Guendalina realised she would soon pass out, and then he would rape her again.

She prayed. 'Our Father who art in Heaven . . . '

Her vision was clouding over and the monster was becoming more and more blurry until he became just a speck of light.

She plummeted into darkness.

'Stupid bitch!' he muttered, switching on other lights with a remote.

Now he would possess her, and this time he would satisfy his most brutal fantasies.

He pressed another button and the music of Guns N' Roses blasted out at full volume. The sound-proofing, which he had installed himself, made the place secure.

The strong, rebellious voice of Axl Rose filled the room.

'A world that's much too dark,' he sang along.

Yes, much too dark. He remembered the concert he had attended many years earlier in the United States, remembered Axl Rose in a blue bandana, with his dark eyes and long blond hair. Just as he had worn his at that time.

The air was vibrating with electricity. He let the dressing gown slip to the floor.

She was incredibly beautiful, such a turn-on with her body covered in bruises. So defenceless as she slept!

He threw himself on her.

73

Should she continue being tactful? Or should she be more forceful in her questioning? On her way back to her office, Teresa decided on the first option.

The girl was still sitting with her elbows on the desk, her head between her hands. Officer Belli had not moved either.

'Let's start again from the beginning,' Teresa said, resuming her seat behind the desk. 'Tell me everything, and I mean everything.' She had dropped her formal tone in the hope that it would make the young woman more at ease. 'I promise your parents won't know anything about this.' She took a piece of paper from the printer and unscrewed the cap from her pen. 'I need to know more about Fabio, because that's the only way I can understand what's happened. Tell me about him.'

She was following a suggestion from Ferrara, who always said that they should not be content with the most predictable information about a victim. A good investigation required a detailed knowledge of his or her personality.

The girl moved her hands to her legs and shrugged, staring at Teresa all the while. Then she turned to look at Alessandra Belli. She waited a few seconds before speaking. From her expression and her new posture, Teresa sensed that she had decided to talk.

'Can I trust you?' she asked in a thin voice.

'One hundred per cent, I give you my word. And I have complete trust in Officer Belli. You can talk freely.'

'I'm going to tell you a secret,' the girl said.

'Go on,'

For a moment, she turned away and looked at another point in the room, then came back to them. 'Look in his bedroom. There's a safe where Fabio kept important documents.'

'What kind of documents?'

'I don't know, because he didn't tell me. He only said that, if anything serious ever happened to him, I should tell you about the safe.'

'Is that really all you know?'

'Yes, I swear.'

Teresa could tell from her eyes that she wasn't lying. 'When did he tell you this?'

'A few days ago.'

As if he really did think something was going to happen to him, Teresa thought.

'Did he tell you whether it has a combination?'

'No.'

'Or its exact location?'

'No.'

Teresa realised there was no point insisting. After a few more questions, she told the girl that her statement had been very useful.

She got up, put a hand on her shoulder and said goodbye.

Alba Cecchi shook her hand, but merely nodded to Officer Belli.

Teresa stood by the door, watching her as she walked slowly down the corridor. She saw her turn to wave goodbye again before going down the stairs.

Even though it was Sunday, Angelica decided to go to Sollicciano Prison that morning. She wanted to look up Guendalina's personal file in the prison records.

She was well respected by everyone, including the warden, Mazzorelli. There wouldn't be any problems.

'Hello, what are you doing here?' Mazzorelli asked her from behind his enormous half-moon desk, a tireless worker even on a Sunday. 'Aren't you still on holiday?'

'I've still got a week left. But . . . '

'What is it, Angelica? Take a seat.'

She sat down. Aware that he already knew a lot about her friendship with Guendalina, she told him Guendalina had left suddenly, without any prior warning.

'I'm sorry to hear that. Do you have any idea where she is?'

'That's why I'm here. I'd like to check her personal file. Maybe I'll be able to find something useful.'

Mazzorelli thought it over for a few moments. Then he picked up the phone and told the person in charge of records to bring him Guendalina Volpi's file.

'Would you like a coffee while you're waiting?' he said after he had hung up.

'Thanks, I'd love one.'

Less than an hour later, Angelica knocked on the door of the rectory. She wanted to see Don Santo, the prison chaplain.

In the file, there had been copies of letters that Guendalina had written him to find out what the Sunday lessons would be. And a few leaflets given out at Mass. Some parts had been underlined in pencil:

Sorrow comes from the devil, who wishes to discourage souls on their spiritual journeys; joy, on the other hand, is a gift of the Holy Spirit and urges us to keep moving forward in spite of our human weaknesses and miseries. The certainty of divine aid increases the need to pray insistently and unceasingly.

The door was answered by the priest's housekeeper, a small, quite well-built old lady dressed entirely in black, with a clothes brush in her hand. Walking with a limp, she led Angelica to the study.

'Don Santo will be here in a moment,' she said in a thin voice and left the room.

While she was waiting Angelica walked up and down and looked around. On a shelf she saw some very old books, and was about to take one down when she heard the door open. She turned.

'Ah, Angelica, what happy wind brings you here?'

Don Santo had white hair and was tall and lanky, with a dark complexion. He was wearing a silk smoking jacket and black cotton trousers. Angelica went to him and they shook hands.

'Don Santo, I need your help,' Angelica said.

He smiled and nodded. 'Just tell me what you want, and I'll see what I can do. But first, can I offer you anything?'

'No thanks, I'm fine.'

'Then I'm ready. What's it all about?'

Coming straight to the point, Angelica told him about Guendalina's disappearance.

'Guendalina's a very sweet person,' Don Santo said, clearly shaken by the news.

'Father, I know Guendalina had a good relationship with you. Do you have any idea where she might have gone? Did she tell you anything in confidence?'

Don Santo interrupted her. 'My child, I have no desire to know anything about the inmates, or their pasts. My only aim is to be a brother to them. And don't forget that I am bound by the secret of the confessional. I can only tell you my impression, which is that'd been very happy recently, and not just because she was due to be released. I never asked her why, but I did notice a new light in her eyes.'

'So you can't suggest where I should go and look for her?'

Don Santo shook his head and looked at her with kindly eyes. 'No,' he said, gently but firmly.

Angelica got up from her chair. She had no desire to waste any more time. Don Santo walked her to the door and gave her a farewell hug. 'Be brave, my child, and don't despair. The ways of the Lord are infinite.'

Disconsolate and full of doubts, she headed home, mulling over the priest's last words.

She could only hope that those ways led Guendalina back to her.

74

Rizzo spoke to Ferrara and Teresa as soon as he got back from the Institute of Forensic Medicine.

The charred body was that of a male, about five feet three in height. There had been a ring on his right hand and his jaw had been broken.

'The details match exactly,' Teresa said. 'It has to be Fabio.'

'Why was his jaw broken?' Ferrara asked.

'According to the pathologist,' Rizzo said, 'it could have happened when part of the roof collapsed on him, but they'll have to do more tests.'

'Who was the pathologist on call?'

'Franceschini.'

'What about the cause of death?'

'Probably smoke inhalation.'

Ferrara was increasingly convinced that this was a highly suspicious death. 'Is there any proof of his identity?'

'Nothing as yet, but Franceschini will do a dental X-ray.'

'What about the ring?'

'We can show it to a family member.'

'Well, we can't ask his aunt, she's in hospital. She fainted while she was in Teresa's office.'

'There's Alba Cecchi, she might recognise it,' Teresa suggested.

'Right. I'll leave that to you, Teresa.'

Ferrara told Rizzo about the safe mentioned by Alba.

'Well, we'll just have to find this safe. But the fire brigade have already sealed the apartment.'

Ferrara ordered him to prepare a request for a search warrant and take it personally to the deputy prosecutor who had been assigned the case.

'Go early tomorrow morning. The Prosecutor's Department is closed today and there's no way the deputy prosecutor on call will authorise anything.'

'I'll go at eight. Do I need to mention what Fabio's friend told us as the reason for the request?'

'Keep it vague, say a confidential source of proven reliability.'

'Right.'

'And don't forget, Francesco, there mustn't be any mention of the fact that Fabio was working for us.'

'OK.'

This investigation, Ferrara thought as he watched his deputy leave, was becoming a minefield.

Angelica was going crazy, unable to find any peace of mind.

Her visit to Don Santo had proved futile, and now, back home, she was moving from one room to another, walking back and forth, sniffing as if seeking out the smell of her girlfriend's skin, then constantly going out and inspecting the garden.

Nothing.

She remembered the sweet words with which she had comforted Guendalina in her saddest moments. She saw her lying asleep beside her with her head resting against her back, heard their sighs and moans during lovemaking, and thought about her doubts and jealousy, their arguments.

It was useless: she could not calm down. She sat down on the sofa and started to cry. The world around her had changed. It had lost its savour.

*

That evening, after dinner, Ferrara sat on the terrace. The heat had subsided a little and a pleasant breeze was coming off the river. After a while, Petra brought him a pullover and arranged it carefully over his shoulders.

'Don't take it off now,' she said.

He lit a cigar and took another sip of the red wine they had been drinking with their dinner. Wine and a cigar, what a great combination, he reflected.

He thought over everything that had happened and told himself that it was no longer possible to speak about coincidences. He re-read the outline of essential information that he had drawn up at the office.

Night of 28-29 August
Victims: Enrico Costanza/Luis Rodriguez. Same 7.65 calibre pistol, fitted with a silencer. Two shots for Costanza, one for Rodriguez.
Clues or useful elements: video with message from Genius. Also contains images of Madalena's death. HP inkjet printer. 2004 diary (20 August): entry with word STUPID. Safe-deposit box. Foreign connections? Bank details. Statement by mechanic D'Amato. Anonymous phone call from San Piero a Sieve (Monster of Florence) informing us of envelope with eyes. Note signed Genius. Statement by Kirsten Olsen, Danish waitress. Identikit.
Suspects: a man, professional. Possible medical knowledge. Likes challenges. Sadist? Probably just under six feet tall. Good knowledge of the area. Woman: drives a dark A-Class Mercedes, long hair (D'Amato's identikit) or short reddish hair (Kirsten Olsen). Lives in or regularly visits Mugello.

Night of 31 August-1 September
Victim: Inspector Antonio Sergi. Strangulation.
Clues or useful elements: worked for Secret Service.

Infiltrated an international criminal organisation. Made reference to the ARCHIVIST (working on same case). Telephone records.
Suspects: More than one person?

Same night, 31 August-1 September
Victim: damage to statue of Perseus.
Clues or useful elements: two letters, E and G, each followed by a full stop. Evil Genius?
Suspects: vandals? Or Genius?

Thursday 2 September
Victim: Beatrice Filangeri. Suicide?
Clues or useful elements: none.
Suspects: None. The Black Rose?

Night of 4-5 September
Victim: Fabio Biondi. House fire.
Clues or useful elements: Statement by Fabio's aunt.
Statement by Fabio's friend, Alba Cecchi. Safe? Search?
Suspects: None. The Black Rose?

He was struck again by the sequence of events. There were too many of them in such a short space of time, too many to all be the work of the same hand at any rate. There did seem to be a connection between the crimes, but in all probability there had been more than one criminal at work. And probably with different motives.

That was the biggest mystery of all.

What did Fabio Biondi have to do with the Black Rose? Was he the Archivist? The contents of the safe might be able to provide confirmation.

Things were sure to become clearer soon.

PART SEVEN

TURNING POINTS

75

Monday 6 September

She woke with a start.

The music, which was coming from hidden speakers, was blasting out at full volume.

She recognised Aerosmith.

She rubbed her eyes, got up and went to the iron door, her heart pounding madly. She was convinced the monster would soon be back.

And she was right.

After a few moments the door opened and she only just had time to move a few feet away.

'Get back on the mattress!' he cried, grabbing her roughly by the arm.

Fear and horror filled the air, along with the deafening lyrics of the song 'Dream On'.

That morning, Ferrara found a note Fanti had placed prominently in the middle of his desk, with the word URGENT in block capitals at the top. The note said that there had been a call from a colleague in the traffic police.

'Fanti!' he called, but there was no reply.

He sat down and dialled the number for the North Florence traffic police.

'Armando?'

'Ah, Michele!' Deputy Commissioner Armando Tucci replied.

'What have you got for me?'

'I have some documents in front of me that you might find interesting.'

Ferrara imagined Tucci surrounded by his colleagues and his maps of the area.

Tucci told him about the speed camera that had recorded a black A-Class Mercedes travelling at about twenty-five miles over the 55mph speed limit on the Siena–Florence slip road on the night of Friday to Saturday. A check on the number plate had identified the owner as a thirty-six-year-old woman living in the Mugello area.

'That's very good. Could you fax me the papers as soon as possible?'

'Of course.'

'Thanks, Armando.'

'If it leads to anything, Michele, keep us in mind for an official commendation!'

'I won't forget.'

Ferrara called Fanti again. And this time his secretary came running in with some papers in his hand.

'I was downstairs in records, chief—'

'Don't worry about that, Fanti. We should be getting a fax from the traffic police any moment now. I want you to bring it to me as soon as it comes.'

Fanti went back into his room, took up position by the fax machine, and stared at it insistently.

The day had got off to a good start. Feeling encouraged, Ferrara picked up the pile of newspapers, knowing the news there was unlikely to be equally encouraging.

The front page of *La Nazione* screamed: MAN BURNT TO DEATH. *The work of the elusive lift arsonist?*

In the middle was a photograph of the building, showing Fabio Biondi's apartment with its windows blown out and part of the façade blackened by smoke.

Next to the story was a feature on all the arsonist's previous crimes, noting the dates and locations of his attacks. The majority had taken place in the area between the Viale Talenti and the Ponte alla Vittoria, very near to the Isolotto. This latest act seemed to signal a new modus operandi, since it had caused the death of a resident and put the lives of other neighbours at risk. They could have been looking at a mass murder.

How many more times must he strike before he is captured? was the question – clearly aimed at the police – with which the piece ended.

After this latest incident, Ferrara thought, the Florentines must be feeling especially jittery. Neighbours would start eyeing one another suspiciously, because it had grown extremely likely that the arsonist was someone living a double life, outwardly ordinary, a maniac inside.

He could imagine the lively discussions that must be going on around the city. People were always interested in the details of such sensational crimes.

He folded the newspaper, hoping it wouldn't be the journalists who solved this case.

76

It couldn't have gone better!

Rizzo had just left the administrative office of the Prosecutor's Department, where he had been told that the case had been assigned to Deputy Prosecutor Erminia Cosenza.

Nicknamed '*La Rossa*' because of her flaming red hair, she was known for her authority, her pragmatism, her stubbornness and her ability to work for up to sixteen hours a day. She was held in high regard, although there were some who accused her of being a prima donna. But this was only because Erminia had never backed down and had taken on cases that no one else would have wanted to be involved in.

He went up another floor and stopped outside Erminia's door. The red light was on, meaning that she was not to be disturbed. He sat down on a chair in the corridor, the envelope containing the request on his lap, and waited.

When the light went out about half an hour later, he knocked.

'Come in!'

Rizzo went in.

Erminia Cosenza was not alone.

Standing in front of her desk, saying goodbye, was Commander Eugenio Fossati, head of the fire brigade. Erminia was wearing a pale blue linen suit and high heels that served to emphasise her lovely legs.

'Come in, Superintendent Rizzo, this is Commander Fossati.'

'We met last night.' He went to him and shook his hand. 'As a matter of fact, I'm here about the fire.'

'Go on, Superintendent.'

Rizzo handed Erminia Cosenza the request and she went back behind her desk and sat down. When she had finished reading, she said, 'The Commander here has just told me the results of the initial investigation. We're definitely dealing with an arson attack.'

'That's right,' Fossati said. Encouraged by a nod from the Deputy Prosecutor, he went on to say that his men had found fragments of glass bottles with traces of flammable liquid. Everything in the apartment had been completely destroyed, including the apparatus, the CDs, the DVDs, and so on.

'It's as if whoever started the fire knew that the victim was in possession of something compromising,' Erminia said. 'So I think it quite proper to accede to your request, Superintendent Rizzo. I'm going to authorise a search of the apartment. If you do discover a safe or any other hiding place, that may help to clarify matters.'

Fossati nodded and said that he was willing to help in any way he could.

'Please wait in my secretary's office, Superintendent Rizzo,' Erminia said. 'I'll have the order ready shortly.'

She stood up and shook his hand.

The DNA results had arrived.

It was quarter past nine in the morning when Marshal Gori found the molecular biology report from Rome on his desk. The expert must have been working on it over the weekend for it to arrive so punctually.

Let's see what surprises this damn test has in store for us, Gori said to himself, with a pang of regret for the days when investigators had little more to go on than their intuition. Now the young deputy prosecutors seemed to give priority either to information from criminals who turned State's evidence – taking their tip-offs, their suggestions, even their hypotheses as gospel – or to the results provided by science.

But it was of vital importance to link this genetic profile to a specific person, otherwise it would just have been an end in itself. Gori was well aware that that DNA results alone could not solve a case.

As a first step, he decided to check if this profile was present on their database.

In Italy, unlike other countries such as Britain, where a database with the DNA profiles of millions of individuals had been in existence since 1995, a single register had not yet been created. However, the Carabinieri had compiled lists of the DNA profiles that had been linked to serious crimes.

The right hand doesn't know what the left hand is doing, Gori said to himself grimly.

And he immediately sent in a request to the central office in Rome, where all the data from the various regional headquarters was collated.

It was worth a try, though it might turn out to be futile.

77

The stink of burnt plastic filled the air.

Having had the seals removed, Rizzo ordered the search to begin. He had only just set foot in the apartment when he realised that what the fire had not wiped out, the water and the efforts of the firefighters had. It would be difficult to reconstruct the sequence of events. The devastation was total. The scene of the crime had been completely destroyed. It would be impossible to find fingerprints, shoe prints, fibres, hairs.

In accordance with the fire brigade's instructions, the officers started to move cautiously around the apartment. They found that only a few CDs and DVDs had survived, along with a pair of miniature digital recorders. They put them in plastic evidence bags, ready to be passed on to Forensics.

They moved on to an inspection of the bedroom. It was there that, after shifting pieces of wood, furniture and fragments of roof tile, all burnt and blackened by the flames, they found the safe. They had not seen it at first because it was covered with charred remains.

Fabio Biondi's friend had told them the truth.

'Commander, can you get one of your men to open it?' Rizzo asked Fossati, who had requested to be present.

'We'll need an oxyhydrogen flame.'

'It's vital we don't damage the contents.'

'Don't worry, Superintendent. I've got just the right man on my team. He'll join us in a few minutes with exactly the equipment we need.'

'Good.'

While they were waiting, the two men talked, the Commander revealing a fair amount of curiosity. He asked Rizzo whether the fire might be linked to the other crimes committed by the lift arsonist, as *La Nazione* called him.

At first Rizzo just shrugged. 'We don't have anything to support that theory, but we can't rule it out. Just as we can't rule out other possibilities.'

His instinct told him that this fire had nothing to do with those other crimes.

On his return from the search of the apartment, Rizzo went straight to see Ferrara, and found him with Teresa.

'Have you got anything for us, Francesco?'

'Some interesting things, I'd say.'

'Go on.'

His deputy explained that they had found a number of folders in the safe, untouched by the fire. Inside were photocopies of documents, some of which had the word CONFIDENTIAL written at the top. They all referred to well-known criminal cases that had either already been solved or were still open.

One folder had on its cover the words THE BLACK ROSE. Inside, all the sheets had been labelled SECRET.

'Michele,' Rizzo said, 'this reeks of the Secret Service. Fabio Biondi must have been a spook.'

'I think you're right. One of those experts that nobody would ever suspect, which is precisely why they're useful. These days they don't just recruit from the civil service, but from the private sector too.'

'But he couldn't join the police because he was an inch too short!' Teresa exclaimed.

'That doesn't mean anything, Teresa,' Ferrara said. 'Being an expert in various areas matters a lot more than height in certain lines of work.'

By far the most interesting discovery was the file on the Black Rose.

There were so many questions without answers.

Why had others known of the existence of the Black Rose when they hadn't? Why had they only discovered it thanks to Leonardo Berghoff's letter?

And why had Fabio Biondi been killed?

'He obviously discovered something he wasn't supposed to, Michele,' Rizzo said.

'Do you think he might have died because of the video?' Teresa asked, feeling guilty.

'It's possible,' Ferrara replied.

'And what happened to it? Was it one of the things destroyed in the fire? Or is it in the possession of whoever killed him?' It was almost as if she were asking herself the questions.

But then the next question had to be – and all three of them were wondering this – how could the killer have known about Fabio's work on the video?

They considered this in silence.

And Ferrara remembered what he had read in Sergi's papers: *The Archivist*. Who worked from home.

He formed a hypothesis: whoever had killed Sergi must have either already known about the role Fabio Biondi was playing or extracted the information from the inspector before killing him. It was pure supposition, but not unfounded.

Ferrara ordered Rizzo and Teresa to search through Sergi's papers, his telephone records, who he had been meeting, even more thoroughly than before. Everything had to be looked at. They mustn't forget Fabio Biondi's telephone records either.

'That's where we have to find the answers to our questions,' he concluded.

They agreed.

78

He had read the online news in the early hours. All the papers were talking about the death of Fabio Biondi. From what he had read, the investigators seemed to be linking it to the lift arsonist.

He burst out laughing. That arsonist didn't have a fucking thing to do with this.

Poor bastards! Let them carry on with their investigations! Let them squander their money – they wouldn't discover anything anyway!

He dialled an international number to say that he would be another couple of days.

'I need to sign an important contract. You know how these people like to play hard to get.'

Then he changed the sim card and sent a text.

We must meet immediately.

Gori could hardly believe it. To think he had asked them to check their records only to be thorough!

The DNA profile did match someone in the records: Leonardo Berghoff, who had died in Germany on 5 July 2004.

How was it possible? The marshal could barely breathe as he read the fax from Rome. What should he do now? he wondered. Call Ferrara right away? Or speak to the Prosecutor first?

As a loyal carabiniere, he chose the second option.

Having first informed his colonel, he hurried to the Prosecutor's Department.

Luca Fiore was sitting behind his desk.

Gori and Deputy Vinci, who had already been informed, took their seats in the visitors' chairs.

'Marshal,' Vinci said, a slight smile hovering over his lips, 'tell Prosecutor Fiore what you've discovered.'

Gori summarised the tests carried out at the biology lab in Rome and the results.

Luca Fiore looked stunned at first. Then he recovered his wits and said in a resolute voice, 'Marshal, I would urge you to exercise the utmost discretion. We must act with caution and check this as thoroughly as possible. I want you to go to Germany in person and confirm what actually happened to this Berghoff.'

'Of course, Prosecutor.'

'If necessary, we'll ask our German colleagues to exhume the corpse that was buried under that name.'

'I'll leave this afternoon, Prosecutor.'

'Thanks, and keep me updated.'

'Of course!'

The marshal left the room. When the two prosecutors were alone, Luca Fiore said to his deputy, 'Luigi, this Ferrara has been telling me tall tales. He's sent us death certificates for a criminal who turns out to be alive and kicking. A criminal who's slaughtered a poor young girl.'

'A monster.'

'Precisely. And then there was that letter about the secret lodge that he sent in with his request. We were right not to agree to it. What would have happened if we'd authorised him to search Cosimo Presti's home and office? We'd have been in real trouble.'

'This whole thing could be a pack of lies.'

'That's what I think.'

'What shall we do?'

'Nothing for now, Luigi. Let's wait and see what the marshal finds out.'

'And then?'

'When we've got the results, we'll decide whether to search Ferrara's office. It's possible we'd find something interesting, perhaps proof that he's been lying all along. What do you think?'

'I'll personally go with the Carabinieri to search it. And I'll leave his office like a brothel after a brawl.'

'I'll come too. All the Head of the State Police has managed to do so far is ask him to write a letter of apology for the press conference, but I'm going to destroy his career. He's really crossed the line this time, and I'm going to make him pay for it.'

A broad smile appeared on Vinci's face.

'And we won't even tell the Commissioner,' Luca Fiore concluded.

'Absolutely not. It has to come like a bolt from the blue.'

79

Ferrara opened the folder.

Inside was the data Fanti had gathered after receiving the fax from the traffic police.

```
COLLATION OF OFFICIAL DOCUMENTS AND REPORT
Angelica Fossi, née Bruno, born Vicchio del
Mugello (Florence), 13 April 1968, currently
residing in Dicomano.
Identity Card: AK7693641
Passport: AA 1985523
Driving Licence: FI 3754210
Weapons licence: None

REPORT:
The subject comes from a family of wealthy
landowners. Both her parents are dead. Her
father killed his wife, who was seriously ill,
and then committed suicide. She was an only
child. After finishing middle school, she
attended a senior high school specialising in
the arts, completing her secondary studies in
1986. She is unmarried. She works as a social
worker on behalf of inmates of the prison at
```

Sollicciano, acting as liaison with their
families. She has a particular interest in
painting.
She lives alone in a farmhouse in the
countryside between Dicomano and Godenza in
the Mugello area.
Report compiled in accordance with your
instructions.
Signed: Sergeant Nestore Fanti
Florence, Monday, 6 September 2004
Appendix A comprises a copy of the subject's
passport application form.
Appendix B comprises various standard reports
provided by Special Ops at the request of the
prison.

Ferrara lingered over the passport photo stapled to the form. He was sure he had never seen that face before: the open, honest face of a young woman no different from many others. But, looking at it more closely, he thought he detected a certain similarity to the identikit.

In the notes from Special Ops, he read that her conduct record was clean, she had no criminal record, had never been reported to the police, and had never been involved in direct political action.

He called his secretary and complimented him on his excellent work.

'It's not finished, chief,' Fanti said, blushing.

'What's missing?'

'I still need to go there and make some discreet inquiries. I might find out more from her neighbours.'

'No, there's no need to go anywhere. You've done an excellent job and now it's finished. Get Rizzo to come and see me.'

'I saw him go out about ten minutes ago, chief. Shall I call his mobile?'

'Yes.'

Fanti withdrew, looking puzzled. Had he made a mistake? But what?

It would torment him for the rest of the day.

They were in San Gimignano again, in a rented car this time.

They were not far from Sir George's villa, taking a lot of photographs: the final details for the last piece of the jigsaw. Later, he would decide what to do with that bitch he was holding prisoner. Maybe he'd set her free. She hadn't seen his face, nor did she have any idea where he had been holding her. It would be a favour to his old friend and accomplice.

A gift, in fact.

It was just after eight in the morning when they saw a car drive out through the gates. It turned in the direction of the town and after a while drove past the car park where they were waiting. They set off after it. Apart from the driver, the only occupant of the other car was Sir George, who got out in front of the Porta di San Giovanni before the car drove on and turned left. They now got out and started following him on foot, keeping at a safe distance. No more than fifty yards, though, so as not to lose sight of him.

They saw him buy a number of daily newspapers, sit at a table at his usual bar in the Piazza della Cisterna, leaf through some of the papers and eat a brioche. Alone the whole time. At that hour, the square was practically deserted. Finally, he paid and stood up, went back the way he had come, and met up with his driver just outside the gate. He got into the car and went back to the villa.

His guest had left.

They set off back to Florence.

'Tonight's the night,' he said to Angelica. 'Nine o'clock, the usual place. Don't be late.'

80

It was almost midday when Officer Carlo Rossi rang the doorbell of Angelica Fossi's house in the middle of the countryside. Venturi had sent him to deliver the summons. She was to come to Headquarters to be questioned about 'matters of interest to the police': a standard phrase that could mean anything or nothing.

The decision had been made by Ferrara in discussion with Rizzo. During the interview they would ask her about the night she had been caught by the speed camera, then about her work and her acquaintances. And, depending on what they found out, they would decide whether or not to search her home.

If they did, they would make use of Article 41 of the laws on public safety. A rule that gave the police the right to search homes, other buildings and vehicles in search of weapons, ammunition or explosives if they had information suggesting that such things might be kept there illegally. It was an old trick, but still useful when it was necessary to act quickly. There was just one condition to be met for it to be legitimate: the existence of an actual item of proof, rather than a simple assumption with no supporting evidence.

As far as Angelica Fossi was concerned, there were certainly elements that linked her to the woman they were looking for: the statement made by the mechanic, D'Amato, her similarity to the identikit, her high-speed journey at night, and, most importantly, the statement made by the Danish waitress, as well as the location of her home.

Rossi rang Venturi and told him that the woman was not at home. He was told to wait there. He was about to get back in his car when he saw a white Ford Escort arriving. The car stopped outside the farmhouse and a woman got out.

It was her. He recognised her from her passport photograph. He went straight to her. 'Signora Angelica Fossi?' he asked.

'Yes.'

He showed her his police ID. '*Squadra Mobile.*'

'Has something happened?'

'I've come to deliver a summons.'

'Why?'

'I don't know. The inspector would like to see you in his office.'

'When?'

'As soon as possible.'

'Right now?'

'Yes.'

'All right.'

'If you like, you can come with me.'

'Thanks, I'll use my own car.'

She climbed in and set off, and Rossi followed in his car.

The first thing he did was call Venturi. 'She's coming, but not in the Mercedes. She's driving a different car.' He gave him the licence number and the model.

Angelica Fossi was in the waiting room, shivering in spite of the heat. In her hands was the plastic cup of coffee that Rossi had given her.

Had they found Guendalina – was she hurt, or dead? No, please, not that!

That morning, as if troubled by a premonition, she had woken at dawn after a night of bad dreams. Now she sat there, lifting the cup to her mouth every now and again – she had put three sachets of sugar in it, but it still tasted bitter.

Meanwhile, Venturi was in Ferrara's office, awaiting instructions. He wanted to know if he would be in charge of the interview. He had found out from the motor licence authority's database that the Ford Escort had been rented from Europcar the previous day.

Why?

What had happened to the A-Class Mercedes?

Officer Rossi had not seen it in front of the house, nor in the surrounding grounds.

It was almost quarter past one when Angelica was led in to Ferrara's office. He would interview her with Venturi present.

'Please take a seat, signora,' Ferrara said, gesturing to the one empty chair in front of his desk. Venturi was already sitting on the other one.

As she sat down, he looked at her closely and noticed fear in her eyes.

'Am I allowed to know why you've summoned me?' Angelica asked, staring at them as if trying to figure out something from their expressions. Even her tone of voice suggested how anxious she was.

'It's a formality, signora,' Ferrara replied.

'But what's it all about? Tell me!' She glanced at her watch.

'Are you in a hurry, by any chance?'

'I'd only just got home when I had to come here. It's not a short distance, you know. An hour to get here and, if everything goes well, an hour back again. I've got a lot to do.'

'In that case I'll get straight to the point.'

'It's not ...'

'Not what?'

'No, nothing, go on.'

'Do you own an A-Class Mercedes?'

'Yes, why?'

'Where is it now?'

'At home. Why?'

'Do you often go out at night?'

'Why? Is it against the law?'

'Just answer the question, please. I ask the questions, you answer.'

'Yes, sometimes.'

'And what route do you normally take on your way home?'

'Sometimes I go through Pontassieve, sometimes along the Via Bolognese, through Fiesole and Borgo San Lorenzo. But why?'

'Perhaps I didn't make myself clear,' he said, an element of steel in his voice now. 'You're here to answer my questions, not to question me.'

'All right.'

'Did you by any chance take the Borgo San Lorenzo route on the night of 28-29 August?'

Silence.

She was obviously uncomfortable. Her posture suddenly changed, and she started shifting her legs and folding her hands. But it was her face that most struck the two policemen. It had turned as white as a sheet.

'May I have a glass of water?' she asked. It was a way of gathering her thoughts and avoiding mistakes in whatever came next.

Venturi left the room.

Meanwhile, in Teresa's office, Teresa and Officer Alessandra Belli were still sifting through the confiscated material, Sergi's papers, and the telephone records.

From their colleagues in Rome, they had received a copy of those telephone records relating to Sergi, as authorised by the Prosecutor's Department in Civitavecchia.

And they had already found something interesting: several calls to Fabio Biondi's mobile phone.

So the two men knew each other.

Was Fabio the Archivist? Right now, it certainly looked like it.

'We'll have to tell the Chief Superintendent,' Teresa said.

Picking up the phone, she dialled Fanti's internal number and asked him to let her know when the chief had finished his interview.

'In the meantime,' she said, after hanging up, 'let's go and get a coffee and a brioche. I've got a feeling we'll be skipping lunch again today.'

81

'You're making a big mistake.'

They had driven up to the restored cottage in two cars. Angelica had unwillingly opened the front door, but now stood in the doorway, trying to stop Ferrara from coming in. But he ignored her: he wanted to get to the bottom of this.

They were in San Godenzo, about twenty-eight miles from Florence. The municipality was named after Saint Gaudentius, a hermit who had retreated into the local mountains with their covering of chestnut trees to lead a life of prayer.

During the rest of the interview at Headquarters, the woman had retreated behind a wall of absolute silence, so Ferrara had decided to proceed with a search of the property. If they found guns or ammunition, everything would be much clearer, but anything at all that could be linked to the double murder would mark a turning point.

'You have the right to request the presence of a lawyer or another trustworthy person,' Ferrara advised her once they were inside the house. 'Provided that they join us as soon as possible. Otherwise, we'll start the search regardless.'

'I don't want anyone,' she replied in a calm voice. 'Just hurry up.'

'Very well then, it's now 3.15 in the afternoon and we're beginning the search. You will come with us into every room. You must always be present. That's what the law stipulates.'

Angelica nodded.

'We'll try not to make a mess,' Ferrara assured her.

She shrugged, a sceptical expression on her face, and followed him to make sure that everything was put back more or less where it had been found.

They moved from one room to another, spending the longest time in the bedroom and in a small room used as a study, which was subjected to an especially meticulous inspection. Venturi took on the task of examining the computer, after requesting the password, while his colleagues emptied the drawers and put to one side notes, receipts, diaries, photographs, and documents relating to her job as a social worker.

Within a little over two hours, they had searched almost everything. No weapons, ammunition or explosives had been uncovered.

To one side of the garden, beneath a wooden shelter, they had found the black A-Class Mercedes. Angelica told them it had broken down, which was why she had had to rent the Ford Escort.

Obviously, they insisted on checking for themselves. Rizzo put on gloves, sat at the wheel and tried to insert the key, but without success.

Angelica found it hard to hold back a smile: unsure of what to do and aware of the fact that the police might be on her trail, she had simply snapped off the key in the dashboard to back up her little story.

Now Ferrara was discussing with Rizzo how to proceed. There was no question this was a problem.

Having made use of Article 41, they could not confiscate any items except those specified by the law: weapons, ammunition or explosives. If they were to do so, they risked their search warrant not being validated by the Prosecutor's Department. They might even be accused of conducting an illegal search. To make matters worse, Angelica had no previous convictions, had never been reported in connection with any offence, and was a social worker.

They were still discussing their options when Teresa came over, followed by Angelica. She and Officer Belli had searched the bedroom even more thoroughly and had found something. So proud was she of her discovery, Teresa could barely contain her delight.

It was a miniature camera, not much bigger than a two-euro coin, with a one-millimetre lens capable of filming the entire room. It had been concealed in the darkest corner of a Gustav Klimt poster.

'What can you tell me about this?' Ferrara asked Angelica.

Angelica had turned white. She was visibly shaking. It had been a surprise for her too. She seemed disorientated.

'I can't imagine who could have put it there,' she replied after a long pause. 'Maybe the woman I rented a couple of rooms to a few years ago. I was only living on the first floor in those days.'

'What's her name?'

'I can't remember, but there must be a copy of the contract among the papers you found in the study. It was only for six months. All I remember is that she was an American student attending the international school of art. She wanted to become an expert on the restoration of frescos and paintings. Then she moved to Florence, near to the main campus, Villa Il Ventaglio. You should be able to trace her there.'

'We're going to have to send this off for analysis,' Ferrara said, holding up the camera.

'If you must.'

Ferrara walked outside and called Gianni Fuschi. He asked him to send a team from Forensics to check whether there were any other miniature cameras or bugs.

The camera might not have anything to do with the murders, but it was advisable, even essential, to carry out further checks.

Fuschi was reluctant to send out a team and advised delaying it until the following day.

'We can't wait until tomorrow, Gianni,' Ferrara said. 'This is urgent!'

'OK, Michele, I'll come,' Fuschi said at last, with a great sigh. 'And I'll also inform Rome and a few expert technicians who work with us.'

In the meantime, a police officer who had been carrying out a closer inspection of one of the other rooms had found another miniature camera.

One was strange enough. Two indicated that something very, very odd was going on.

Angelica said nothing, even when faced with this second item. She looked at her watch. It was almost six and it looked like this might take some time. She did not know whether or not to reschedule their appointment. But she would not be able to call him anyway.

What she could never have imagined was that he already knew everything.

82

I've seen you, Gatto! I've been watching you the whole time. Maybe now you'll realise you're dealing with someone much more cunning than you, and certainly brilliant. No, I don't think your intelligence can help you. And you won't catch me.

Sitting in front of the monitor in his room, he had watched every step of the operation since the police had arrived. He had been amazed to see them and wondered why they had gone there.

Had they been clever enough to link Angelica to the killings?

And why was Ferrara himself there?

Had he really been that cunning?

Or had it been Angelica who had led them there, having told the police about Guendalina's disappearance?

These were the questions buzzing around in his head as he stared at the now-blank monitor.

If Ferrara was the supercop they said he was, he might even track him down.

But, if that happened, he had already come up with a plan. And he had a nasty surprise in store for him.

You have no idea how vulnerable you are! Poor Gatto!

Meanwhile, strange news had arrived from Munich.

Deputy Prosecutor Vinci had received a phone call from

Marshal Gori, who had presented himself at the *Polizeipräsidium* as soon as he arrived in Germany.

His colleagues had provided him with the file on Leonardo Berghoff, and he had gone through it with the help of an official from the Italian Consulate who acted as translator. Then he had got the same man to translate for him the reports relating to the shooting on the Marienbrücke, the bridge below Neuschwanstein castle.

Now Gori was calling to supply further details.

Leonardo Berghoff had indeed been killed on that bridge. The post-mortem report and the documentation relating to the funeral provided irrefutable evidence of that.

'Where was he buried, Marshal?'

'In the cemetery at Füssen, near Neuschwanstein. According to my colleagues here, it's a town near the border with Austria.'

'I'll call the Ministry of Justice,' Vinci said. 'We need to proceed with the exhumation of the body. I'll put the formal request in today.'

'I'll await your orders,' the marshal said, and hung up.

He left the Polizeipräsidium and set off on foot towards the Marienplatz. He was planning to do a bit of sightseeing in the city centre and sample the local specialities at the Spatenhaus restaurant opposite the National Theatre, which a colleague had recommended to him.

It was not often that he was sent on missions abroad.

Darkness was about to fall over the Tuscan countryside, but the police activity at Angelica Fossi's house was unceasing. Following his call to Fuschi, Ferrara had made another one to Headquarters to ask for more men, including officers from the SCO.

At about eight in the evening, when the sultriness that had persisted throughout the search eased off and a gentle breeze which made the work less tiring began to blow, Fuschi said to Ferrara, 'We need different instruments: our colleagues from Rome who are joining us have them.'

Having examined the miniature cameras and identified the make, he had realised that with the equipment he had available it was not possible to locate the receivers. Since they had not been found inside the house, they had to be somewhere else, most likely in the grounds. The technicians arrived in less than half an hour. They got straight down to work, using special machines to take measurements and properly survey the ground, including metal detectors and ground-penetrating radar to search for objects under the surface. These machines could detect cavities as far down as a hundred and thirty feet and so reveal the existence of any underground rooms or tunnels. They were normally used by archaeologists to locate the whereabouts of tombs and underground shelters. The ground was scanned and the image sent to a computer to be analysed using 3D software.

The engineers positioned the equipment on the ground and began to scan it according to a well-established protocol, proceeding in horizontal and vertical lines so that not even the most distant corners were left unscanned. And, while an operator monitored the working of the machine, from which tubes and wires protruded, an engineer at a laptop analysed the images of the subsoil with all its different layers.

Meanwhile, the forensics team, in their white suits, were sifting the air inside and outside the house to establish the presence of possible antennae for the miniature cameras. This was on the assumption that whoever had installed the cameras might have wanted to extend their broadcast range so as to follow the filmed action from a greater distance.

Other officers continued to shift the furniture away from the walls to check the areas of wall and floor that had been covered by them.

Ferrara was following the outdoor operations, convinced that everything that could be done was being done. He had entrusted the supervision of activities inside the house to Rizzo.

Teresa and Officer Belli had stayed with Angelica, who was

increasingly anxious. She kept walking in and out of the house, and they were with her every step of the way.

There was no secret room in the house, nor were there any bugs or any more miniature cameras. They had conducted a meticulous search of every square inch, but nothing had come to light.

Surprisingly, however, the one new development came from the grounds.

It was nine-thirty in the evening when one of the forensics technicians located the transmitter. It had been well camouflaged in a cherry tree and its signal was directed towards the side of the mountain opposite. There could be no doubt as to where exactly: there was only one building within an area of more than a thousand feet.

'Francesco,' Ferrara ordered Rizzo, gesturing to the isolated house, 'run checks on that house immediately. Find out if anyone lives there and, if so, who. Meanwhile, position some men around the house with orders to inform us immediately if there's any suspicious activity.'

He went quickly to Angelica's study. He would have to ask her more questions. The time had come to make her talk, to move things along. In the light of what they had just discovered, she might open up, or at least provide them with something new to go on.

That extremely sophisticated surveillance system suggested the work of someone highly qualified. It was more than just a matter of operating two cameras. There must be something else. Right now, whether or not it was all connected to the double murder didn't really matter. They had to find out, and as soon as possible.

83

Meanwhile, in Munich, it had started to rain heavily. Covering his head as best he could with a newspaper, Marshal Gori answered his mobile. It was Vinci, phoning to tell him that everything had been agreed with the German authorities and that the exhumation of Leonardo Berghoff's body would take place in the morning.

Luca Fiore and his deputy, 'No Balls' Vinci, had kicked up as much fuss as they could with the relevant office of the Ministry of Justice to ensure that the request was granted as soon as possible, effectively cutting through all the red tape. They would decide how to deal with Chief Superintendent Ferrara afterwards.

For Luca Fiore, the time for a showdown was fast approaching. He would at last be able to free himself of that troublesome Chief Superintendent, who was like a dog off his leash, who always acted off his own bat and never looked anyone in the eye. At the same time, he would score points with those powerful friends whom Ferrara, with his usual disregard for anything and anyone, had tried to investigate over the years.

And besides, it was obvious that Ferrara was hiding something in this particular case. A dead man who comes back to kill again? What could he be thinking?

The solution to both problems was just a few hours away.

*

Angelica looked at Ferrara with a shocked expression, wide-eyed, wringing her hands nervously.

She did not know how to behave in this situation, what attitude to adopt, who she should trust – or who she should suspect.

She felt as if she was living in a bad dream. But it was all true. She had proof now that he was the one who had been spying on her, who knew all about her and Guendalina, who had watched them in their intimate moments: kissing, caressing, arguing, making love. He had seen through her in no time at all, uncovering the lies she had told him about her clandestine relationship with Guendalina.

And there was something else, a crucial detail.

Under the chest of drawers in the living room, the police had found the wedding ring and gold chain that Guendalina had been given by her mother shortly before her death. The only things she had left of her, which she would never deprive herself of. She could well remember Guendalina's words the first time she had shown them to her: 'They're the most precious things in the world to me. If I were to lose them ... I don't know what I'd do.'

And now she had disappeared, leaving those pieces of jewellery behind. No, she couldn't have left like that, not willingly. He must have taken her, probably by force.

Damn you, you bastard!

'Signora,' Ferrara said gravely, 'at this point I must ask you to cooperate fully. If you help us, everything will be easier for everyone, including you. We're all exhausted, but now's the time to talk.'

He was looking into her eyes to read her reaction. It was obvious that she was still holding something back. A secret, maybe a shameful one.

After a few moments' silence, Angelica looked away from Ferrara and lowered her eyes to the table, her face twisted in a grimace of pain. She seemed to be on the verge of bursting into tears, as if the weight she was carrying inside was too great and her anguish had got the better of her.

'I can't keep quiet any longer, I can't. All right, I'll tell you what happened.'

'Good. You have everything to gain by telling us the truth.'

Ferrara took his notebook and pen from his pocket and put them down on the table.

Angelica began her story.

She told him how she had met Daniele De Robertis and how they had become friends. They were neighbours: he lived in that former convent on the mountainside opposite. A certain passion had grown between them, she said, but it had never blossomed into a real relationship, because of his sexual problems.

She broke off abruptly, bowed her head and began to cry. Ferrara took a tissue from his trouser pocket and gave it to her. While he waited for her to compose herself, he jotted a few sentences in his notebook: the questions he would ask once he had heard her story.

'I recently met someone and fell in love ...' She hesitated again, unable to hold back her tears.

'Please be brave, signora. If there's something you need to say, just get it off your chest.'

'Guendalina, the woman I love, has disappeared.'

Up until an hour ago, she went on, she had been convinced that her companion had left of her own accord, out of jealousy.

'She was sure I was cheating on her.'

She told Ferrara about how they had met, and about her so far futile efforts to find her.

'Why did you say "until an hour ago"?'

'Because that gold chain and wedding ring made me change my mind. They were the only mementos she had of her mother and she would never be willingly separated from them.'

'And now what do you think might have happened to her?'

There was another pause.

'I don't want to believe the worst, but I'm convinced that he had a part in her disappearance.'

'When you say "he", you mean . . . '

'Daniele De Robertis.'

She started crying again, really distraught now.

Ferrara stood up, went to her and put a hand on her shoulder. 'We'll do everything in our power to get your Guendalina back,' he said gently. 'Please try and calm down.'

Then he called Teresa and told her to stay with Angelica. He left the room, closing the door behind him.

Rizzo was back, looking completely exhausted. It had been a very long day. He had spent the last few hours combing the area, gathering information, in addition to contacting the telephone, gas and electricity companies and persuading the managers to open their offices.

'All right, Francesco, tell me what you've found out.'

The occupant of the house that was receiving the signal from the transmitter, Rizzo told him, was only occasionally seen out and about. He seemed pleasant enough when he went shopping in the village. He lived most of the time in France, in Paris, with a rich heiress: it was she who owned the former convent, which at one time had been used to house young people in trouble who had been taken into State care. One of the locals, an elderly man, remembered him as being one of those children, always bright-eyed and with a gentle disposition.

'Venturi's spoken to one of his informers, and we should know a bit more about him later. From the gas and electricity readings it seems he doesn't use them at all for long periods, but when the house is occupied the electricity consumption is particularly high, especially for a single person. Which means there's something odd going on.'

'Is the owner called Daniele De Robertis?'

'No. The contracts are all in the name of the Frenchwoman

and the bills are paid by direct debit from a current account in Paris.'

Ferrara summarised what he had learnt from Angelica. When he had finished, they discussed what to do next.

Darkness had long since fallen.

84

As he cleaned his gun, he wondered why on earth those police were still there.

Had they found something else? Could it be that Angelica had discovered that he had been spying on her and in her anger was now cooperating with them? Was her love for Guendalina really that strong?

It was quite possible that the police had identified him. That meant they would soon be on their way here to arrest him.

That lesbian had betrayed him!

He quickly reassembled the gun, tucked it into his belt, and went downstairs to Guendalina.

'Get up,' he ordered, taking the gun out again and pointing it at her head. 'Put on your tracksuit and shoes and come with me.'

For the first time she saw him without his face covered. He wasn't how she had imagined. He was no monster, but actually quite attractive.

'Why? I'm not well, I can't get up. Please just leave me alone.'

'Get up or I'll blow your brains out.' He raised the gun and put his finger on the trigger.

She started to drag herself into a standing position and he yanked at her roughly with his free arm. She put on the tracksuit and shoes, then they went up a wooden staircase, consisting of about ten steps, to the ground floor. They walked along a narrow tunnel until they came to a small box room. From there, he dragged her into the living room and tied her to a chair.

'That hurts.'

It was a waste of breath. He had already left her and gone outside to see how the situation was developing. He had anticipated everything.

He even had a nice surprise for Il Gatto.

There were two possibilities.

One was to request reinforcements and carry out a raid, but that would take several hours to prepare, and they couldn't afford to give the killer that kind of advantage.

Alternatively, they could go in straight away. But there were only eight of them. That was too few, given that they did not know who they would find. Was there just one person waiting for them, or more?

Angelica had not said anything about the double murder, but they could not rule out the possibility that she knew something, or had even been involved.

Was that why she had kept quiet? Had she let her heart rule her head in order to save the woman she loved?

They were reasonable questions to ask.

During the search of her house they had found various wigs, some quite long, which seemed to support the testimony of D'Amato, the mechanic.

Perhaps Daniele De Robertis was the key.

Ferrara and Rizzo were starting to get the feeling you get when, after a series of failures, you finally make a real breakthrough.

As they were mulling over the decision they had to make, more officers arrived, including the men from the SCO.

A little while ago, several lights had gone on in the former convent. There was clearly someone there.

Exhausted, but more determined than ever, Ferrara made an urgent request for a pair of helicopters equipped for night flight, with men on board from NOCS, the crack team trained for high-risk situations, in case the man tried to flee. Then he started to work out the specific details of the raid.

They were close to a turning point, he could feel it.

85

Within a couple of hours, Ferrara had assembled his men in an area of thick scrub at the foot of the mountain on which the former convent stood, and now he was explaining in detail how the operation was to unfold.

As he did so, he experienced the special sensation that always preceded an important step forward. A particular kind of shiver down the spine. He spoke for about half an hour, a map of the area in his hand, deploying the men one by one to reduce the margin for error to a minimum.

Then he waited for them all to prepare themselves and take up their positions as he had planned.

They got out of their cars, which they left some distance away, and, after putting on bulletproof vests, they set off silently on foot up the slope with the intention of approaching and surrounding their target.

The excitement was tangible.

On their backs, the men from NOCS carried bags containing equipment useful for getting past obstacles, even fixed ones. They were used to going into action weighed down. Behind them were the officers from the *Squadra Mobile* and the SCO, with Ferrara at their head.

They climbed the ridge, advancing quickly but cautiously so as not to arouse suspicion. Soon they had all taken up the positions assigned by Ferrara, who had carefully studied the area and the potential escape routes – and unfortunately, there were quite a lot of those, if whoever was inside managed to get a hundred yards or so away.

The helicopters, meanwhile, would stay on the ground at the sports field in Vicchio, ready to intervene at Ferrara's request. Some of the NOCS officers had joined Ferrara from there in a four-by-four.

Daniele De Robertis approached the window. He was perfectly well aware of the shadowy figures with torches encircling him. The element of surprise, which they had managed to maintain for a couple of hours, had gone. He lit the porch light, untied Guendalina and dragged her over to the largest window.

'Sit on the floor,' he ordered. 'If you're good, nothing will happen to you. We're going to have some fun.'

Feeling weak and exhausted, she obeyed. She was really scared. She had seen his face. There was no way he would free her now. She despaired of being saved. Her heart was pounding and she feared it might suddenly stop. She began to pray.

He drew back the curtain so that he could be clearly seen from outside. He felt extremely prepared, and he wanted them all to know that they were not in for an easy ride.

He smiled for a moment at his 'audience', which he had followed as they advanced along the ridge and drew close to his fortress, and with a movement as smooth as oil pointed the gun at Guendalina's temple.

Drained as she was, she still mustered the strength to start sobbing.

Now he was deliberating his first move. Like a veteran chess player.

'Fuck, he's got a hostage,' Rizzo said to Ferrara.

The two of them were about a hundred yards from the house,

hidden in the bushes, and Rizzo had his infra-red binoculars trained on the window of the former convent.

Ferrara borrowed the binoculars and looked for himself. Lit from behind, the scene at the window left little doubt as to what was happening.

'Damn it, that must be Angelica's friend! At least she's still alive.'

'Angelica Fossi told us the truth, there's no doubt about that now. What are we going to do, Michele? He's got a gun to her head. We can't risk going in.'

'We'll wait for his next move. He must have something in mind.'

He had just finished speaking when he heard his phone ring. He looked at the display. Caller unknown. Who could it be at this hour?

'Hello?'

'Hi, Chief Superintendent. Genius here.'

The voice was clear, calm and resolute.

'We don't want to harm you. We know you've got Guendalina with you. We're concerned for her safety.'

'You know something, Gatto? I don't give a fuck, not about her, not about that dyke Angelica.'

'Give yourself up and we'll find a solution.'

'What the fuck are you talking about? Give myself up? I'm the one, the only one, who's dictating the conditions now!'

'What conditions? Let's hear them.'

Someone shone a very strong torch at the window behind which Genius was hiding. He covered his eyes with his hand. He was starting to realise just how alone he was in this situation. One against many. But that didn't scare him. In fact, it excited him. He pushed Guendalina's face against the glass so that they could see her better.

'First of all, put your weapons away, all of you, and switch that fucking torch off.'

Ferrara signalled to his colleague, who immediately shone the torch in a different direction.

'And don't try and come any closer. I've hidden bombs everywhere. Devices you dickheads don't even know exist. Any move you make, they'll explode. Understood?' Interpreting Ferrara's silence as an answer, he went on, 'There's one safe route to get to me, but only one person can use it. They'll have to walk along the path I've marked out with white poles. Can you see them? Just one person, like I said, and don't try any funny business, because I've anticipated everything, absolutely *everything*.'

'OK. Who should come?'

'You, Gatto. Only you can come.'

'I'm afraid that's out of the question. I'd rather you came out with your hands up. I guarantee that no one will harm you. I give you my word.'

Ferrara was trying not to let him see how worried he was by the situation, but it was an effort even to pretend.

At moments like these, just one false move, a single wrong word from the negotiator, was enough to tip the balance. And Guendalina was too exposed, tied up as she was, and with a gun aimed at her head, for the police to risk a mistake.

'Your word? I'm not sure what good your word is to me, Gatto! If you want this whore, you'll have to come and get her. Then you and I will be able to have a nice little chat, face to face, and that's it.'

'I won't allow—'

'Shut up! I haven't finished yet! When are you going to realise that I'm in charge here? Now, once we've had our chat, you'll ask for a car, and only the two of us and Guendalina will get in. If anyone tries to follow us, I'll kill you both. And I warn you, if anyone else even tries to come any closer, everything will be blown sky-high. Even this fucking place. *Boom*. Have I made myself clear? And you'll have a fair few deaths on your conscience.'

'What do you mean?'

'Ah, you still don't know ... I expected more of you. It's full of children in here. I can't stand them any more, always clinging to me – they remind me of all the years I spent here ... I can't wait to get rid of them, but if you do everything I say, you can have them. Whatever happens, I won't be here any longer.'

Silence.

He had hung up.

Ferrara and Rizzo looked at each other, unsure what to do next. They had still not received confirmation on who lived in the former convent, so what De Robertis said might well be true.

They had to act as if that maniac was telling the truth. Besides, was there any alternative?

For two hours that seemed like an eternity, they stayed where they were, waiting for the next move. Inside they were boiling with rage, but they could not rush things and risk screwing everything up in their haste. In any case, Genius was still inside the building, and he would have to make his move sooner or later.

Ferrara's mobile rang.

Caller unknown again. Genius.

'Yes?'

'What are you doing? Do you still need time to think it over? I'll give you a minute, just sixty seconds, not a second more, and then I'll kill her. First her, then all the others. Just imagine that! A real bloodbath! Sixty seconds, Gatto, starting now.'

And he hung up.

After a moment, Ferrara shook his head in a gesture of surrender and removed the under-arm holster holding his pistol.

'Here,' he whispered, giving it to Rizzo.

'But, Michele—'

'No buts. Unfortunately we have no alternative. He's crazy, and he really will kill her, I have no doubt about that, and then he'll do the same to those children, assuming they really are there.

354

What I want right now is to look him in the eye. He knows too many things about me, and I want to find out why. He doesn't want just any of us, it's me he's after.'

'But this is absurd, Michele! We've got NOCS ... he's surrounded ... there are the helicopters ...'

'There's no point going round in circles, Francesco. If you can see an alternative, tell me now.'

'But—'

'I'm going, Francesco, it's me he wants.'

And he set off towards the door of the building with his hands up, without looking back at all, following the suggested path marked by white wooden poles.

The sixty seconds were already almost up.

There was nothing but a tomb-like silence all around.

When he was a few yards from the door, Ferrara stopped for a moment and took a deep breath. Genius had not given him any scope for negotiation. If he had not followed his instructions to the letter, he would have put too many lives at risk – Guendalina's, his men's, perhaps even innocent children's – and he couldn't allow that.

Anyway, this wasn't the first time he had found himself in such a situation. In his days in Calabria, in high-risk operations against the 'Ndrangheta, he had always been at the head of the team. Always the first to step forward when they needed to bring in dangerous fugitives who were willing to kill. The fact remained that in the past things had always turned out all right in the end.

Now, though, he wasn't so sure. Instinct might not be much help against this madman, whose moves were impossible to anticipate. But he had no choice and, now that he was only a few steps away, he certainly couldn't go back.

He took another deep breath, filling his lungs, and continued up the small slope to the front door.

When he was just a few feet away from it, he stopped and waited. He looked around and listened carefully. There was no sound, not even from inside. He pondered whether he should knock or ring the bell, which he could just make out to the right of the door thanks to the light from his colleagues' torches. He imagined Genius standing behind the door with his gun still pointed at the woman's head. He took another step forward and found himself just an inch or two from a neat dark green doormat with the word WELCOME on it.

He turned towards his colleagues for a moment, as if for advice, then steeled himself and raised his foot to step on the mat.

As soon as his foot came to rest on the letter C, there was a huge explosion, then another immediately after it, then a third.

Soon the whole area was lit up by the explosions. They looked like fireworks.

Ferrara was blown backwards. A wave of heat seemed to envelop him. He could taste smoke and gunpowder in his mouth.

He touched his chest and found the torn remains of his shirt, reduced almost to shreds. Then he felt a burning sensation, passed his hand across his forehead and saw blood. His hair felt sticky and there was a slight pain in his right ankle.

He heard shouting behind him. He could clearly distinguish Rizzo's voice calling him from among a lot of other voices.

He spotted Rizzo lying on the ground. With some difficulty, he managed to get up and run to him. There was a cut on his left cheek, although it did not look especially deep.

He helped him up.

'Fuck, Michele, I really thought I was going to die this time . . . That bastard . . . '

'I thought the worst too. But we're both alive, thank God.' He ran his fingers through the shredded remains of his shirt. 'A good thing I was wearing a bulletproof vest.'

Ferrara slung Rizzo's arm over his shoulder and walked him to a car.

He looked around and saw that other officers had been injured too.

Genius had mined the whole area around the house with remote control devices. But there was no trace of him.

Was he still shut up in the former convent or had he taken advantage of the opportunity to escape?

He looked up towards the house and noticed that one of the explosions had blown the door off its hinges, leaving a rectangle of light through which smoke continued to billow out.

Or had he been injured too?

Ferrara was pondering his next move, whether to rush in through the door or not, when the silence of the valley was shattered by the loud roar of an engine. It came from the back of the house.

In the blink of an eye, a large four-by-four stopped right in front of them.

'Don't shoot!' he ordered his men. He was in their line of fire. He let go of Rizzo's arm, and walked slowly towards the four-by-four with his hands up. In the light of the dashboard, which was still on even though the first glimmer of dawn was starting to appear, he saw Guendalina sitting terrified in the passenger seat with the gun still aimed at her head.

Genius lowered the window and, with a wild laugh, cried, 'Go to hell, Chief Superintendent!'

He had laid the perfect trap, and they had walked straight into it. Ferrara looked at him and was immediately struck by the expression in his eyes. They really were a madman's eyes. He held that depraved gaze for a few moments and felt a shiver run down his spine.

Was it really him? No, it wasn't possible . . .

Just then, the tyres spun on the gravel and the four-by-four set off at top speed down a dirt road that led to the M67.

Ferrara used his radio to request some ambulances to be sent immediately. Then he ordered the helicopters to follow the four-by-four.

It wouldn't be easy to follow him for a few minutes yet. But then the daylight would help them.

86

Where was that bastard hiding?

After half an hour of solid searching, helped now by the
dawn light, one of the helicopters located the four-by-four in
the Cavallino area. But there was no one on board. He had
abandoned it with the passenger door open, and must now be on
foot.

Was Guendalina still with him? Or had he killed her and
thrown her body somewhere?

In the meantime, the injured had been taken to the hospital in
Vicchio, although nobody seemed to be seriously hurt. After
having his forehead treated by the paramedics from one of the
ambulances, Ferrara had started to coordinate the search. Soon
the patrol cars from the Mugello Carabinieri, who had been
alerted over the emergency radio frequency, would be arriving
too. They needed to bring in the fugitive, but above all they
needed to save the hostage. If it was not too late.

The manhunt was under way. The whole area would be
combed thoroughly.

Teresa and Angelica had heard the explosions and seen the clouds
of black smoke rising up into the sky.

Angelica would have liked to run straight there and rescue
Guendalina. She had heard, via the portable radios, that a woman

had been taken hostage. It could only be her: she had understood everything now.

'I beg you, let's go over there with the others!' Angelica implored.

'I'm afraid that's not possible. We have to stay here and wait. You must stay calm – the Chief Superintendent knows what he's doing. I promise you.'

'But that man's crazy, he's violent, he's unpredictable. Have you seen what he did?'

'Trust us,' Teresa said. Her hands were tied, and there were too many thoughts going through her mind to keep listening to Angelica.

She put a hand on her shoulder, then put her radio earpiece back in to follow the progress of the manhunt.

But the radio was a jumble of voices. None of the tactics seemed to be working.

'That way ... with a woman ... he was armed ... hurry hurry! He threatened us, he wanted the motorbike ... he shot my friend in the leg ... '

The two young leather-clad bikers were at Passo del Mugalione, the pass over the Apennines, near San Godenzo. One lay on the ground on a traffic island beside a road sign reading FORLÌ 53. The other had seen the police car approaching with its lights flashing and had waved it down.

On board were Venturi and Rossi. They immediately got out of the car.

'Go ... he went into that wood!' shouted the same young man, pointing in the direction in which he had seen the two running away.

'How long ago did they go into the woods?' Rossi asked, checking the condition of the wounded boy.

'Not long ago, no more than a couple of minutes ... Don't waste any more time, I've already called an ambulance for my friend. It should be here any moment now.'

Venturi sent out the alarm over the radio to the other cars, giving their position, then he and Rossi ran towards the area the young man had pointed out, guns at the ready. They were not used to this kind of chase, but there was no time to think right now. All they could do was go.

After running along the main road for about a hundred yards, they moved onto a kind of mule track. On either side were tall beech trees, which became more tightly packed as they moved through them. Then they spotted a shadowy figure moving among the trees. They stopped, exchanged glances, and went on, more cautiously. They heard the sound of a helicopter, distant at first, but then, within a few seconds, it was right above their heads, although they could not see it due to the very thick vegetation. They immediately felt safer, but their hopes vanished as quickly as they had sprung up: the helicopter was not going to be of any use in this terrain.

'Stop! . . . I said stop . . . you're surrounded!' Venturi yelled in the direction of where he had seen the figure. Immediately, the man appeared again.

'Get away or I'll kill her!'

The gun was pressed right up against Guendalina's head. By now, the girl was too terrified even to cry.

'Put the gun down. There's no way out.'

'If you try and follow me, there'll be trouble, for her, for you, for all of you! You've seen who you're dealing with. Don't play games with me.'

In the meantime, the whole area had been transformed into a war zone. Other officers had arrived, lots of them. And a second helicopter had joined the first. All the possible escape routes were now blocked off.

But Daniele De Robertis was still roaring like a lion.

A lion who no longer had anything to lose, and would go down fighting.

'Send those helicopters away or I'll kill her now,' he shouted as loudly as he could.

They saw him move behind a tree, one arm tight around Guendalina's neck, pulling her along behind him.

I can't take it any more, I'd rather die, she was thinking as she let herself be dragged along. She had stopped resisting, convinced now that there was no way she could get out of this alive. There was going to be a shootout and he would probably use her as a shield. That was the only reason he hadn't killed her before now. But she would end up dead anyway, killed by him or by friendly fire.

'Let her go now and we'll spare you.'

Genius recognised that voice immediately. 'Ah, you're finally here too ... Did you think you could actually win, eh, Gatto? That you were more cunning than me? You're just a *policeman*! You have to pay!'

'It's me you want, let her go!' Ferrara replied, moving closer, as some of the NOCS officers took up positions around him.

'Come on then, come on. And you, you whore, keep still or I'll blow your head off.'

But Guendalina did not obey.

She suddenly assumed a determined expression, full of rage, even hatred. The terror with which she had lived for the past few days had gone from her eyes. Whether out of desperation or out of hope reawakened by the presence of all the police officers, she gathered all her remaining strength, spun round and threw herself at him.

She kneed him in the groin with remarkable precision and speed. He groaned and twisted his head to the side. It was only a brief movement, but long enough for the bullet fired from a precision rifle by one of the NOCS officers to hit the wrist of the hand with which he was holding the gun.

He fell to the ground and tried to get up again, but gave up all such foolish ambitions when three men tackled him and pinned him down.

Genius had been defeated.

As Venturi handcuffed him, Genius gave Ferrara a malevolent sneer. It was as if even at the moment of surrender, he was laughing at Il Gatto for daring to challenge him.

First stop: the hospital.

Then, obviously, the prison.

Ferrara ran over to Guendalina, pulled her to him and held her in his arms until she had stopped sobbing.

By the time they moved apart, the sun was already high in the sky.

The nightmare was finally over.

87

'Darling!'

With bright eyes and trembling hands, the two women ran to each other and embraced.

At her request, Guendalina had been brought straight to Angelica's house. And now, in front of the door, they were clinging to each other, their mouths pressed together, their kisses becoming ever deeper and more desperate.

For many hours, hours that had seemed endless, they had been afraid they would never see each other again.

Teresa was moved as she watched them. She wished she had someone who cared about her that much.

Having made sure that Genius was in good hands, Ferrara had gathered all his available men together. The maniac was under arrest, but that was not the end of it.

Taking great care to avoid any other possible unexploded devices, they entered the former convent and searched it from top to bottom.

They did not find anything unusual in the hall, but there were plenty of surprises elsewhere.

First and foremost, the children: there wasn't a single one. That madman had made them up in order to have the police by the balls.

But there were many surprises in the vast, dusty underground room.

One in particular: Daniele De Robertis' diary, with its worn black leather cover into which the words EVIL GENIUS had been carved with a knife or something similar.

Its pages, which Ferrara immediately began to leaf through and which would keep him occupied for several hours, included references to Enrico Costanza, to the statue of Perseus in the Loggia dei Lanzi, to the Cuban girl, Florinda, and to a certain Sir George Holley, an Englishman dubbed 'the Great Beast', a plan of whose villa was attached.

It was like a collage of the events of the past few months, with dates, names, places and descriptions.

This diary was extremely valuable.

There was no mention in it, though, of Serpico, Fabio Biondi or Beatrice Filangeri. As if he had played no part in their deaths.

And, as Ferrara was wondering who this Sir George Holley could be – he had never heard the name before – Officer Belli came up to him. She had found the photo album stolen from Teresa in an old cabinet.

'Well done! It's only right that you should be the one to return it to your commanding officer.'

In spite of her fatigue, a huge smile spread across Alessandra's face. Maybe the door to the *Squadra Mobile* would remain open to her for longer than the planned month.

Ferrara settled into an armchair, the fatigue of the night making itself felt in spite of his curiosity, and plunged once more into the pages of the diary. He leafed through it again and, on a page dated 6 July 2004, he found these lines, set out like a poem:

To Leonardo, my twin,
united at birth, but in life separated by destiny
which did not want us together,
different from the others,

two distinct people,
but with one soul,
I could not hold your hand as you lay dying
could not feel your grasp,
could not close your eyes after the final moments
no, all this was denied me,
you died alone,
in a distant land,
murdered,
and I was unable to do anything to prevent it,
but I will avenge you,
I swear it,
I will live for that alone.
From your Daniele.

EPILOGUE

Monday 13 September

'We are now coming in to land. Please close your tray tables and fasten your seatbelts.'

It was the voice of the air hostess on the 10 a.m. Florence–Paris flight.

Teresa and Officer Belli both looked out of the window. In the space of a few minutes, the clouds thinned enough for them to recognise the city below them.

Their appointment was for five in the afternoon.

Ferrara had called the previous day. One ring, two, three, no answer. At last a woman had said, *'Allô?'* in an unsteady voice. He had introduced himself. Fortunately, they had been able to talk in Italian.

Ferrara had told her that Daniele De Robertis had been arrested and that he needed to clarify a few things with her. At first the woman had seemed distraught, then, after listening to the story Ferrara told her over the many miles of telephone wire, she had said in a calm voice that she did not believe a word of it. Unperturbed, he had asked her to come to Florence to meet him, but she had replied that it was impossible as she was confined to a wheelchair.

That was when he had decided to send the two women police officers to her.

Now they were waiting in the drawing room of an elegant apartment in the Rue Clément Marot in the eighth arrondissement, a stone's throw from the Champs-Elysées and the Seine.

They heard the door open and turned to see an elegant woman in her seventies, dripping with jewellery, approaching in an electric wheelchair. They had learned from the French police that she was a rich heiress, descended from a family of bankers, who over the years had invested her inheritance in several estates and properties in both France and Italy.

'I'm Superintendent Micalizi,' Teresa said, 'and this is my colleague, Officer Belli.'

'Pleased to meet you. I'm Madame Chantal Perrin. I speak and understand Italian very well.'

'Yes, Chief Superintendent Ferrara told us that. We've been sent here because we have some questions to ask you, if that's convenient.'

They sat down on a sofa but, just as Teresa was about to speak, the old woman told her that she had something to say.

'You know, Daniel, mon petit enfant, has been more than a son to me. I adopted him – I was living in Italy at the time – when I bought at auction that former convent that had been used as a home for orphans and abandoned children to help reintegrate them into society. I was immediately struck by his eyes, and by his reserve and generosity . . . Daniel's no killer, he's the son that every mother would love to have. And then when he grew up, he became a great IT expert, in demand all over the world. He's a phenomenon. He can do things for the common good and human progress that are only possible for a true genius. If you hope to learn anything from me that might incriminate him, you're very much mistaken and have merely wasted your time in coming here. He didn't kill anyone, and he isn't the Evil Genius your Italian newspapers are talking about today.'

They tried approaching the subject from a different angle, but without insisting: it was only too obvious that they would not learn anything.

So they said goodbye and went on their way.

The woman would never reveal anything about that genius, either about his humanity or his evil. In her eyes he was nothing but a force for good.

In the two police officers' eyes, on the other hand, there was nothing but sadness at the disappointment the woman would soon experience.

San Gimignano

As soon as he had finished reading Genius's diary yet again, Ferrara set off with his team. There could only be one destination: the villa of that unknown Englishman.

It was a beautiful old villa, almost a castle.

When they rang at the dark wooden front door, the caretaker came out from his lodge, which was to the side of the main house, and let them in without protest.

But *he* was not there. Or, rather, he was no longer there.

The caretaker told them that his lordship, Sir George Holley, had left that very morning at about eight on a private flight from Pisa airport.

The team got back in their cars, turned round and drove out of the vast courtyard. On the black wrought iron gate was a frieze of three entwined roses which Ferrara was convinced he had seen before, although he could not remember where.

On the long drive back, Ferrara continued reflecting on what had happened, on the links between the various protagonists in this case, and on the mystery man known as the 'Great Beast'. He suddenly remembered his telephone conversation with Markus Glock two nights earlier. He had found a note from Fanti on his desk saying that Glock had called, and had called him back immediately from his mobile. That was how he had discovered that Marshal Gori was in Munich.

He now told Gori about the capture of Daniele De Robertis the previous day and about the incredible discovery that Daniele had been Leonardo Berghoff's twin brother.

He waited for some expression of surprise at the other end of the line, instead of which Glock burst into loud laughter.

He already knew everything.

The Carabinieri and the Prosecutor's Department had slipped up massively: monozygotic twins were the only people to have the same genetic profile!

'I'll come and see you in Florence soon, Michele,' Glock said cheerfully.

'I look forward to it, you'll be my guest. I know what you'll really like: a Florentine steak and the last word in red wine.'

For the rest of the journey all he could think about was the 'Great Beast'.

Was he, Sir George Holley, behind the deaths of Antonio Sergi and Fabio Biondi – and even the 'suicide' of Beatrice Filangeri?

Was he the driving force operating behind the scenes?

Was he the head of the Black Rose?

The fact of the matter was, the man knew exactly what he was doing, when to make his moves, and must surely have contacts who were protecting him. For example, someone who had made it possible for him to flee before the police came knocking on his door.

There were too many doubts filling Ferrara's head during that car journey for him to think he could let all this go and start a clean page.

When he closed his eyes he could still see Daniele's demonic smile and, even more clearly, that frieze on the villa's black gate. His obsession with Sir George, the 'Great Beast', would haunt his dreams until he threw light on these mysteries.

It was time to get to the source of this long trail of blood.

It was time to uproot the Black Rose.

Acknowledgements

My thanks go to my publishers, both Italian and foreign; to my editors Paola and Gianluca; and to my agents, Luigi and Daniela Bernabò. Daniela recently passed away, leaving a void behind her.

And most of all, to my wife, Christa, for her enthusiasm and patience, and to my sister, Rosa, for her invaluable advice.